WINTERMAN'S
COMPANY

WINTERMAN'S
COMPANY

*David
Lightfoot*

SUNK ISLAND

PUBLISHING

Lincoln

WINTERMAN'S COMPANY
first published 1995 by
Sunk Island Publishing
P.O. Box 74, Lincoln LN1 1QG, England

Typography by John Wardle
Cover design by Geoffrey Mark Matthews
Illustration © J Salmon Ltd, Sevenoaks

ISBN 1 874778 01 9

Printed by Intype, London

When bad men combine, the good must associate;
else they will fall, one by one, an unpitied
sacrifice in a contemptible struggle.

EDMUND BURKE
Thoughts on the Course
of the Present Discontents
                              (1770)

CHAPTER ONE

THROUGH THE DOOR FROM THE CLOISTERS CREAKED FOUR CRASH-HELMETED MEN IN LEATHER SUITS AS BLACK AS THE CATHEDRAL TRANSEPT. THEIR SMOKED plastic visors were up and they paused for a few moments, as planned, to accustom their eyes to the gloom. At a signal from their leader they strode on along the east transept and turned sharply left, their rubber-soled boots squeaking on the flagstones. A right turn brought them into the Angel Choir. They halted at the foot of some scaffolding that climbed to the ceiling. The loom of the city lights through the great windows enabled them to make out each other's faces.

'Anyone uncertain of the procedure?' asked the tallest of the four in a whisper.

Receiving no reply and hardly waiting for one, he began to climb a ladder up to the first level of planking. Two others followed at precisely spaced intervals while the fourth remained at the foot of the ladder, peering about into the darkness. The three men climbed on up the scaffolding until they were level with where a pillar began to curve outwards into two arches. An electric torch flashed on and its beam oscillated over the carved stonework.

'There!' sighed the one who had spoken before.

In the narrow beam they saw staring back at them a face which none of them could look at for very long. The hundreds of tourists who daily gazed up at it from the floor below could have no idea how unnerving it was at such close quarters and so highlighted. In the popular imagination the features of the thing, known almost affectionately as the Lincoln Imp, were virtually comic – a Pekingese furious at having its ears pulled flat sideways. Up there, within touching distance of what felt like a rickety shelf on the side of a cliff in a monstrous pot-hole, all humour seemed inappropriate.

The second man began to untie the strings at the neck of an old duffel bag. His fingertips were clumsy with anxiety and grew clumsier as his anxiety grew. Eventually, with another sigh from his leader, he pulled out something wrapped in linen. Unwinding cautiously, as though what he held were alive and might spring from his grasp, he at last set down on the wooden planks in the torchlight a stone replica of the demon on the pillar.

The only difference between the two images was the fact that the Lincoln Imp itself was attached to the stonework, being part of it. The now unwrapped image stood freely on its own broad base, balancing like its twin on its left leg, the right held across its thigh by both three-fingered hands. The grotesque pair faced each other in the beam of the torch which was now shining over the shoulder of the replica.

The leader of the group addressed the man who had so far done nothing except remove his leather gloves. The torch beam under his double chin revealed some of his fiery, sweating face. The only sound in the vast emptiness was of his breathing with difficulty, until the leader's voice hissed at him: 'Are you ready to begin?'

CHAPTER TWO

GARETH BURDEN FLINCHED. WITH A SNORT HE HURLED HIS BALLPOINT PEN THE SHORT LENGTH OF THE CARAVAN. THEY HAD DARED TO COME AGAIN, after his warning that morning at the end of Assembly. The scream that had rent the peace of the autumn night had been ridiculous – a parody of a noise from one of the horror movies which they spent so much time watching, to judge from what they wrote in his English lessons. For a second or two before he had realised what it must be, the nape of his neck had contracted partly from the shock of the scream's suddenness and partly from the chilling inhumanity of the way it continued on one note.

He suddenly wished he had taken up Thompson on that offer of a Staffordshire bull-terrier and resolved to ask him on Monday if the dog was still for sale. He resisted an impulse to rush out and confront them: that was what they wanted him to do. They would probably enjoy watching him from the edge of the wood. He slumped against the upholstered bench seat that ran along the caravan wall. When the scream came again, nearer, truncated as if a radio had been switched off, he shuddered with anger and frustration. This could go on all weekend; he had to do something about it, late though it was.

How was he to assemble the second issue of the magazine in time for the printer's deadline when he was distracted by these cretins? How could he even read, or listen to his transistor? He surveyed the small formica-topped table heaped with sheets of A4 paper. It was all there; only the final arrangement of the poems and articles into some balanced order was required.

That, however, demanded his total attention. The first issue of *Jejune Incest* had been so successful precisely because of the care he, as editor, had taken over the last stages of polishing. He was proud of his work. He only wished he could earn a living by it. It beat teaching these chimps. In an effort to calm himself, prove his indifference to the adolescent morons outside, he picked up a piece that Sidney Winterman had written and mentally rehearsed its contents: *The Place of the Magical in Poetry* . . .

From near the curtained window came a wolf-howl. Gareth suddenly knew it was Darren Eames. It was not even a very good wolf-howl. The boy read aloud in class with maddening slowness and this bungled imitation of an animal noise virtually identified him. Dean Frost and Wayne Platt would be out there too, of course. They were arrogantly close. He calculated again that a dash through the door might enable him to collar one of them, but he concluded that all he would do, if he caught one, would be to bluster. They no longer paid him any heed in the classroom, so why should they respond to his anger outside school? If he made a great fuss, they would trouble him all the more. His only hope of escaping their attentions was to pretend, to demonstrate, that

11

they did not bother him. Cajole. Appease. Something in him recoiled at his cowardice. He flinched again as a pebble, possibly even a stone as big as a fist, clanged off the caravan roof.

He needed advice on the best way to handle this. Sidney Winterman had been the only member of staff at St. Cuthbert's to offer him hospitality since his arrival in September. He recalled with a glow of sudden pleasure the excellent dinner that his very attractive young wife had cooked. He recalled too the pressure of her knee against his under the table in the cosy kitchen where they had eaten that Italian food so informally . . .

A glance at his wristwatch showed it was just after nine. Sidney seemed not to have any problems at all with discipline. He would go to him now. He could not stomach cowering in his own home, however humble and temporary it was, for the rest of the night until they decided they were bored and slouched off home to bed. There was no point in going on with issue two of *Jejune Incest*. He stood up and tugged on his waxed-cotton jacket. The propane gas-lamp's subdued roar melted into complete silence. In the after-image behind his eyelids he was surprised to see Mrs. Winterman's face smiling at him.

When his eyes had become accustomed to the total darkness and his mind to the knowledge that he very much hoped he would soon see Winterman's wife again, he stepped out into the night. He did not look around the field in which his caravan was parked but locked the door as casually as he could and strolled over to his green Citroen 2cv. The loom of Lincoln silhouetted the wood behind the caravan. He felt suddenly sick with mingled apprehension and anger. He was ashamed at the relief he felt at the thought that he was, at

12

least temporarily, going to escape from the scene of his humiliation.

The engine started with the familiar and reassuring noise of a washing-machine about to self-destruct. He set the car in ungainly motion across the meadow, aware of dark shapes running alongside just out of range of the headlights, whooping in derision above the clatter of the engine. He turned right after lurching over the depression at the open gate and headed for Lincoln. As he came to the edge of the ridge where the road dropped down to the valley of the Witham he noticed that the cathedral was not floodlit as it usually was.

CHAPTER THREE

THE MAN WHO HAD REMOVED HIS GLOVES NODDED AND KNELT ON THE BOARDS. HE REACHED OUT HIS LEFT ARM TENTATIVELY LIKE A LITTLE BOY BEING DARED to touch an electric fence and allowed his fingertips to rest on the Imp's forehead. Withdrawing his hand a fraction, he replaced it again quickly, this time cupping his hand over the face and pressing little finger and thumb over the ears. His other hand he stretched out to hold the replica in the same way. His leader switched off his torch and at once the chanting began.

It was so quiet at first that anyone passing below would not have heard it. It grew in volume, however, until somebody directly outside on the cathedral lawns would have turned his head in surprise. The noise he was producing had a nasal quality to it, with variety provided by flexing the Adam's apple. It was nearer to a Tibetan mantra than anything ever heard before in Lincoln cathedral. It did not go on for very long because the man making it suddenly gasped involuntarily as though someone had very deliberately and very accurately hit him with the tip of a pickaxe just below the last bone of his spine.

He stiffened where he knelt after arching forward. Whether he could see the torch beam that came on and played over his face the other two could not tell for his eyes were staring as though at some object a very great distance away out in the night sky beyond the great east window. That was before they snapped shut and what looked to them like blood, but blood with a lot of grey sludge in it, began to seep from under his eyelashes. It was when the same slime flushed out of his nostrils and mouth as well that they realised he was not going to make any more noise.

They were wrong about that.

For the remainder of their lives they would never be able to listen to someone pouring a first drink from a newly opened whisky bottle without the glugging that it makes reminding them of the sound that his skull made as it imploded.

CHAPTER FOUR

'How do you do it?' asked Gareth. He smiled
in anticipation at the plosive gurgle the
whisky made as it pulsed from the bottle.
He nodded acknowledgement and approval as Winterman
stopped pouring him a prodigal measure. 'How do you assert
yourself over them so effortlessly?'

Winterman did not reply at once but smiled to himself
and gazed around the small bedroom which served as his
study. Three of its walls were shelved to the ceiling in pine.
The shelves were filled as much with small curios and objets
d'art as with books. Statuettes of Apollo and busts of Brahms
and Socrates nestled against bookends shaped into impala and
wildebeest.

' "I'd like you to read this," said Winterman thoughtfully,' said Winterman. He pulled down from a high shelf a
slim book that had been lying spine down, its title hidden,
and handed it to Gareth with a slight arching of his eyebrows
as though inviting some comment. 'I'd prefer not to prejudice
you either for or against by any introductory remarks,' he
continued. 'Except to say that my life hasn't been the same
since I,' he hesitated fractionally, 'discovered it.'

16

Gareth looked at the title and author. He could not avoid his own eyebrows lifting as he looked back up sharply at Winterman as though trying to assess whether he was playing on him one of the hoaxes for which he had acquired notoriety in the staffroom.

'And don't be put off by the title!' added Winterman, sitting down and sipping his whisky before he had settled in his armchair with the eagerness of a practised drinker of spirits.

'*Dark of the Moon*,' read Gareth aloud, ' - *a Practical Manual for Wizards*. Do you seriously want me to spend time reading this, with *Jejune Incest 2* still not at the printer's?'

'It won't take you long, partly because once you start you'll either put it down very soon and never take it up again, or you'll devour it at a sitting. I suppose it depends on the sort of person you are. I think you'll be up until the small hours with it.'

Gareth sipped his whisky and scowled humorously at Winterman who sat opposite him kneading the skin of his cheek through his grey-red beard. 'By H I Emsvir,' he read out. 'Can't say I've heard of him.'

'You asked me how I control my classes with such apparent ease. By tomorrow you'll know. Within a week or so you'll be able to do the same.'

'Thanks,' said Gareth, slipping the little book into the poacher's pocket of his jacket where it hung from the corner of a chair near Winterman's desk. He felt a sudden flush of confidence in the man, gratitude for his help and a desperate envy of his circumstances. 'Sorry to bother you so late, Sidney,' he said. 'But I really didn't know where to turn. God, I covet this study of yours! It's so peaceful in here.'

They both listened to the sound of footsteps approaching the door. Gareth stood up as Winterman's wife came in with a tray on which she had arranged coffee things, plates of cheese, slices of apple, pickles and what looked like home-made chocolates. As she set it on the edge of the desk he surreptitiously reminded himself of the extreme voluptuousness of her small figure. Without appearing vulgar she gave the impression that her blouse and skirt were a size too small for her. The pale green of the outfit set off her thick auburn hair, which she swept back over one small ear as she opened her slightly large mouth at him in a lazy smile.

Winterman, who had not risen, was nodding in agreement and now closed his green eyes briefly in what seemed to Gareth unashamed contentment. 'Don't worry, my lad,' he murmured, opening them to grin briefly at his wife, 'you have it in your power to possess the same and much more.'

CHAPTER FIVE

═══════

TEMPLE TRIED TO SMILE BUT HIS TONGUE AND THE INSIDE OF HIS CHEEKS WERE STICKY DRY. HE LOOKED AGAIN AT THE FACES AROUND THE OAK TABLE. HE knew that any moment now the Prior would call on him to speak and he was far more nervous than he had anticipated. The atmosphere in the low-ceilinged room was fuggy and he already had a headache. He could see above the glare of the recessed lights that the real ceiling was in fact much higher than the perforated pasteboard false one that seemed only a few feet above their heads. The smoke from the cigars of several esquires was vanishing up into the space above. From somewhere he could hear the humming of an extractor fan. Or was it his own pulse throbbing in his temples? He wondered why they had gone to the expense of lowering this ceiling in the conference chamber but there were many aspects of commandery policy that he did not yet pretend to understand. It was obedience, not understanding, that was required.

'Esquire Temple,' he heard the Prior say, 'will now give us his report.'

He looked down from the ceiling and saw the eyes of the

other twelve all intent on him. It was to the Prior, however, that he addressed his remarks every time he looked up from the single sheet of paper on the table in front of him. The old man's blue-grey eyes fixed him through the thinning fug of tobacco smoke.

'Entry to the cathedral was simple,' he began abruptly. He had at least learned that the Prior loathed unnecessary preamble and was aware that everyone present knew the vital importance of the mission from which he had not long returned. 'This is almost entirely due to the thorough preparatory work of Esquire Springfellow, who is to be commended for his efficiency. I reduced the party to four. The spiritualist medium selected for the actual transference never, I believe, at any time knew what was going to happen to him.' He looked swiftly around their solemn faces, challenging them to demur. 'The disposal of his body in the heavy-duty plastic bag did pose a minor problem. He was heavier than we had calculated, even allowing for the fact that – ' He coughed and took a sip of water from a tumbler in front of him. ' – the fact that his head . . . '

His voice trailed away in the murmur of comment that arose around the table. He stared into the tumbler as though scrying terrible events within its Jacobean cut-glass sides.

'I understand, Esquire Temple,' he heard the Prior droning, 'that witnessing the disintegration cannot have been pleasant. You were, however, thoroughly prepared for this, er, this effect during your extensive and, I may say, expensive – '

'It's not that!' said Temple, staring up the table at the Prior. He could see from his sour expression that he was not taking kindly to the interruption. Temple paused and looked around, swallowing with difficulty.

'Yes?' prompted the Prior in a tone that frightened all the men watching Temple with that instinctive distaste that the ambitious feel for someone they sense is about to admit to failure.

'When his head . . . went,' continued Temple, shutting his eyes and keeping them closed for the remaining words of his sentence, 'his crash-helmet rolled onto the planking and fell off.'

The silence in the conference chamber reminded him of the dark vault of the cathedral.

'I'm afraid,' he added – and he knew he was – 'that, in the dark, in the rush – given the strict schedule to which we had to operate . . . Well, we had no time to retrieve it.'

CHAPTER SIX

'**M**UCH MORE!' HISSED WINTERMAN, HIS SNARL MODULATING TO A LAUGH AS HIS HANDS SLID UP OVER HER RIBS TO CLUTCH HER BREASTS.

Angharad was straddling him as he lay on his back on the rug in front of the dying coal fire, meticulously spiralling herself towards climax at her own pace. Her auburn hair which some five minutes before had hung in a teasing tent around his face was now flung down her back. Her chin whose pertness he never tired of mentioning strained up at the flickering shadows on the ceiling. Her fists beat against his thighs in time with the roll of her hips whose breadth she knew pleased him more than almost anything else about her body. She recalled how Gareth Burden's eyes too had kept flickering appreciatively over her hips and wondered whether Sidney had noticed the look of almost helpless lust the young man had given her as she had left the study with the empty tray. She interlocked her fingers with his as she felt herself slowly coming.

'Much!' she heard him sigh as she recovered from her crumpling onto his chest to feel him patting her plump flanks with both hands.

With the unhurried ease of frequent practice she rolled at his familiar signal onto her side and then languidly under him as he mounted her, still yoked. She slid the soles of her small feet to the precise spot at the base of his spine where she could best feel his powerful body flexing. She knew how much he loved this final, relentlessly urgent last lap of his love-making – almost always the same, unvaried strenuous crescendo up to the final three (rising, short, falling) grunts. But this time his rhythm was different: wilder and more deliberate.

She eased her face away from his beard as he tongued the hollow where her neck joined her shoulder. To her slight surprise she saw that his eyes were closed tight and a frown was creasing his brow. He seemed to be trying to recall a name that eluded him. He was somehow . . . absent. For an uneasy moment the uncanny thought crossed her mind that he was pretending to be making love to someone else. It was only during her astonishment at the ferocity of his final flurry of thrusts that she sensed beyond doubt that he was pretending to be someone else making love to her.

CHAPTER SEVEN

GARETH LOCKED HIS CARAVAN DOOR BEHIND HIM AND PULLED OFF HIS JACKET. HE STOOD STILL BEFORE STRIKING A MATCH TO LIGHT THE LAMP, LISTENING to the night sounds. The boys had gone. It was too late by now even for them. Relaxing at last, he took Winterman's book from the poacher's pocket and from another the half bottle of whisky that he had bought over the bar at the village pub he had found open after hours. It was a luxury he could not really afford but he had felt miserable enough to treat himself.

He lit the lamp and, reassured by its homely hissing, reached up into a cupboard for a glass. In the rhythmic drone of the lamp the caravan shrank around him as he settled onto the window seat. He opened Dark of the Moon and scanned the contents page. After reading a few chapter headings he poured himself a very large whisky. He took a pull deep enough to provide enough liquid to wash around his mouth as though cleaning his teeth. The liquor stung his gums and probed a vaguely sore tooth. Its fumes tickled his sinuses deliciously before he swallowed slowly.

'*One: the Nature of Mind Power*,' he read aloud, murmuring to himself. *'Two: the Acquisition of Mind Power. Three: the Application of Mind Power.'*

He poured himself another glass, larger even than the first, and began to read the first chapter. When he stopped reading he was surprised to find, after stretching himself and drawing back the curtain, that it was almost first light. He turned off the lamp, mumbled sleepily to himself a reminder to buy a new cylinder and stumbled through into his small bedroom. He removed his shoes and fell fully clothed prone onto the bed. His last waking thought was that he should have drunk a pint of water to forestall the hangover which his parched throat was heralding. His first thought as he started dreaming was of Angharad Winterman.

CHAPTER EIGHT

'IN CONCLUSION,' SAID TEMPLE, PULLING FORWARD ON THE KNOT OF HIS TIE TO EASE THE TIGHTNESS IN HIS THROAT, 'I SHOULD MENTION THAT THE USE OF motorbikes in such an operation may not be as advantageous as first thought. Their speed and ability to bypass traffic-jams can be the very things that draw unwelcome attention from those elements of the Police that are not under our influence. And in this particular operation the panniers were unsuitable.'

He picked up his sheet of paper and folded it conclusively. To his continuing surprise the Prior had not seemed too concerned about the loss of the crash-helmet. Nor had he bridled at his daring criticism of the planning of the transference operation. He was nodding now as if encouraging him to stop.

'There was one other point, sir,' continued Temple, feeling bold enough to speak a fraction before he sensed that the Prior was going to comment upon his report.

'Yes?' The Prior was looking at him strangely as if noting details of his features for future reference.

'The replica is now heavier than it was before the transference.'

'Significantly so?' It was Springfellow who interjected.

The Prior's face tightened dangerously.

'Considerably so. It actually affected the handling of the motorbike on corners.'

A ripple of comment flowed around the table. The Prior slapped its edge with the tips of his long fingers. 'Order!' he barked. 'Was this anticipated?' The question was addressed at, rather than to, Springfellow who shook his head thoughtfully and then gestured with a combination of raised forefinger and eyebrow to the youngest member of the company – a man of about thirty-five. He rose at once and crossed to an oak sideboard. From it he brought an object wrapped in linen. The manner in which he carried it and the noise it made as he set it down on the table in front of the Prior suggested that it was weighty.

The Prior stood up and they all did the same. He began to unwind the linen in a series of flourishes that Temple found surprisingly distasteful.

'Knights and Esquires,' said the Prior in the tone of voice men normally reserve for proposing toasts at weddings, 'prepare to do homage!'

CHAPTER NINE

GARETH WOKE LATE ON THE SATURDAY MORNING. HIS FIRST ACTION WAS TO LEAN OVER AND OPEN THE WINDOW. THIS INVOLVED FIRST TUGGING AT AND then shoving away from himself an awkward double-hinged contraption that let in sufficient air to clear the fuggy atmosphere of the small room. He sank back onto his pillows sighing and aware at once that he had drunk too much whisky. He needed a long drink of lukewarm, weak, milky tea but he was too sluggish yet to rise and brew it. His eyes tracked grittily around the room. The only decoration was a poster of Botticelli's *Primavera* stuck up with bluetack to the wall at the foot of the bed. As he squinted at it the contents of *Dark of the Moon* filtered back to him and he closed his eyes.

A wild excitement seized him: if what he had read were even partly true ... But how could it be? And yet Winterman ... The basic message of the book, as of most of its type – he had read some similar though none quite so direct as this – was that the faculty of visualisation was infinitely more powerful than most people imagine. Properly controlled, it could achieve astonishing effects, alter the course of events, attract wealth, health, love ...

28

He recalled snatches of his conversation with Winterman in his study and his mounting unease as it began to break in on his awareness that the possibility of changing the conditions of his very unsatisfactory life was within his own power. He remembered too how his excitement had altered in character when Winterman's young wife had entered the study with a supper tray.

He stretched his limbs towards the four corners of his cramped bed. He smiled to himself; he would put *Dark of the Moon* to the test. Closing his eyes more tightly, he summoned up from his memory a mental picture of Angharad Winterman.

He pictured her standing in the doorway of his bedroom as she had stood in the doorway of her husband's study the night before. Instead of a tray she was holding a pile of the clothes she had just stripped off her small but buxom body. She moved towards him, dropped the clothes onto the linoleum – he heard the buttons of her blouse tick – and tugged back the blankets. He performed the same action with his own stiff arm. He felt the edge of the mattress dip beside him as it yielded to the pressure of her knee.

A dog's barking broke his train of thought. He opened his eyes, cursing. When the barking drifted away deeper into the wood he relaxed into a doze again and recommenced his fantasy from the beginning. This time her summoned image formed with even greater clarity. He could hear the slightly sticky pluck of her small bare feet on the floor. Without the stimulus of touch, he felt himself respond.

He sat up abruptly, feeling absurd. There was nothing magical about this! But his arousal would not subside. It throbbed against the hard muscle of his belly. Lying back, he repeated the process until the mattress sagged again and a scent – of lilac? – choked his nostrils. Fingers – hers? his? – curled around his shaft. Fragrant hair brushed his cheek and throat.

As the desire to rub himself over the edge into relief grew almost irresistible, he resisted, opened his eyes and steadily regained control of his heartbeat. For the fourth time he brought her, hips swaying, from the door to his bed. And for the fifth and sixth, until he felt he would be able to rerun the whole scene on the inside of his forehead as effortlessly as replaying a video-cassette.

When he had subsided, mentally and physically, he got up, taking deep breaths of the now chilly morning air. He dressed carefully and cooked himself an elaborate breakfast of bacon, eggs, fried bread, crumpets, toast and a large pot of tea. At intervals he closed his eyes with his mouth full of the food at its most flavourful and recalled what he thought of as his Angharad-construct, visualising it all at breakneck speed, so that it lasted only a few seconds. As he made himself a second pot of tea he amused, and delighted, himself by running his mental film in reverse. Satisfied with his strengthening control, he consulted *Dark of the Moon* for the next step.

CHAPTER TEN

LL EYES WERE ON THE STONE FIGURE WHICH THE PRIOR WAS SETTING BEFORE THEM ON THE TABLE. OWING TO A SLIGHT UNEVENESS IN ITS BASE IT rocked from side to side barely noticeably for a few seconds after the Prior's hands released it. The total silence in the room allowed the sound of the oscillation to reach even Temple at the end of the table. He had difficulty in raising his eyes to look at it but knew he would be unable to resist. He looked up and felt the old mixture of fear, excitement, fascination and achievement. He was involved in a mighty enterprise; there was no turning back now.

'Commit yourselves!' intoned the Prior, as if echoing his thoughts. 'Know that he will recognise and punish anyone who fails him.'

Silence fell again. Temple's mind raced. There was no question of his loyalty, was there? Had he not been one of the first to be selected? Was it not for his knowledge that they had chosen him? Yet he did not like the way Springfellow was squinting at him across the table. He looked away in confusion and tried to gather his thoughts. These spells of disorientation bordering on panic were becoming too frequent. He became aware that the Prior was speaking again. The replica of the Imp – if indeed it could any longer be thought of as simply a replica – was being wound up again in its linen shroud and placed in a wooden case that seemed to have been designed to accommodate it, so snug was the fit. An Esquire was placing the case on the sideboard.

'The transference, then,' continued the Prior, as though his previous remarks had been in a normal conversational tone, 'may now be considered complete. We can release at will. The next step is to contact the Albion Front and inform them that we are ready. As soon as I have done that, I shall summon you to a full commandery meeting. There remains for the present only the question of the safe disposal of the transferent's corpse. Esquire Temple?'

'In hand, sir,' he murmured.

'There must in this case be no deviation from the plan. Any hint of an unexplained death . . . ' The Prior shrugged and shook his head with a fastidious little shudder.

He turned to nod to the man standing at the sideboard, who produced a key and unlocked a cupboard. The case containing the Imp was eased slowly inside, the cupboard locked and the key given to the Prior. He rose to his feet swiftly for a man of his years and declared the meeting closed.

Temple rose with all the others and remained standing until the Prior had left the room conversing in confidential tones with Springfellow. The meeting relaxed at once into that buzz of banal small talk that often follows an intense gathering. Temple sat down again on the edge of his chair. He felt both hot and chilly in swift succession. It reminded him of the occasional malarial attacks from which he had suffered in East Africa. Someone's hand rested on his shoulder and he heard a few words of congratulation on the success of his mission. He smiled up perfunctorily at whoever it was, repressing the thought that he wished he had failed.

CHAPTER ELEVEN

WINTERMAN'S HAND RESTED LIGHTLY ON HIS WIFE'S SHOULDER AS HE ROSE FROM THE BREAKFAST TABLE. 'DO YOU THINK YOU COULD help me out with a little staffing problem, my dear?' he asked.

She tilted back her face to be kissed and asked what he had in mind.

'The young man who came round last night – Gareth Burden – the one we had round for dinner earlier, remember?'

'Of course I remember! I cooked something Italian. He's rather handsome, isn't he? Reminds me, a bit, of Al Pacino.' She grinned playfully. 'What about him?'

'Aren't you driving out to Sleaford this afternoon to see your painting friends?'

'You know I am. As you know I'm not friendly with Toby and Jocelyn just because they paint. Why do you ask?'

'I'm going to be busy this afternoon on the book but I thought you could call in on him at his caravan on your way. He's not far off the main road, near Temple Bruer. Just say hello. Show an interest. And take him something I forgot to give him last night.'

'I was hoping there'd be some concrete reason for my dropping in alone on a bachelor!'

'Who said he was a bachelor?'

'He did. The night he came for dinner.'

' "Yes!" drawled Winterman thoughtfully," drawled Winterman thoughtfully. 'I suppose he did announce the fact as if it were a declaration of a permanent state of affairs.'

'What's his problem, then?'

'Discipline. He hasn't got any. With one Year Eleven class in particular. They're difficult with most staff but seem to be reserving their best performances for him. Pestering him at his caravan too.'

'And you want me to go there?'

'Oh, they only seem to be a nuisance when it's dark. So far, anyway. Trouble is, they'll get bolder, that lot. Unless we do something.'

'Do you have anything in mind?'

'Oh yes!' He smiled at her strangely as he removed the marmalade from the table. ' "In mind is the operative phrase," said Winterman, smiling strangely.'

CHAPTER TWELVE

J ASON EAMES LOOKED QUICKLY OVER HIS SHOULDER TO CHECK AGAIN WHETHER ANYONE WAS WATCHING. HE HAD VERY NEARLY NOT BOTHERED WITH THE SATURDAY overtime but this might make it worth the trouble of getting up early. He bent down and picked up the helmet. From a swift examination it seemed, apart from a scuffmark on the crown, almost new. The lining was slightly stained but that could be cleaned up. He tried it on and realised at once that it was too big for him. It could be sold, though, or he could even give it to his brother Darren. He would be old enough to ride a moped legally soon.

He took less time to wonder what such an object was doing lying on the floor of the Cathedral than he did to decide he would appropriate it. Holding it by the chin-strap, he walked back to where his firm had been given a small room to make tea and eat their pack-ups. He hooked the helmet over a coat-peg and draped his parka over it.

Forbes, the foreman, came in and hung up his donkey jacket. 'You're bloody early!' he remarked with amicable grumpiness. 'What's up wi' you?'

'Nothin'!' grunted Jason, aware suddenly of the onset of

the sort of headache that usually made him quarrelsome. 'What're we doin' today? Taking down that scaffoldin' at top end?'

'Aye, and not before time. I thought we'd have had it down days ago. It was scheduled for last Thursday but at the last minute the gaffer came in all of a fluster and tells us to leave it up till today. Can't think why. The stonemasons have been finished up there for some time. Hey,' he added with a jerk of his grey head, 'who's been wearing this parka of yours? Hunchback of Notre Dame?' He brayed at his own joke and, not expecting a reply, turned away, gesturing to the lad to follow.

'What's up wi' you?' asked the foreman as they walked out into the East transept. 'Get up wi' a sore head? Can't you even try to laugh when someone cracks a joke?'

Jason mumbled, rubbing both ears in cupped hands. 'I was fine coming to work. It came on – '

Forbes waited for him to catch up and looked at him sharply. 'Came on when?'

'Soon after I got here,' he said, suddenly hesitating as if he were remembering something the importance of which had escaped him at the time but was now acquiring significance.

'Well,' laughed Forbes again, 'if it gets worse, you shall have to go home, won't you? And lose time and a half!'

The youth's response was to crouch down on the flag-stones, curl into a squat and then fall forward onto his knees, one hand on the ground, the other shielding his eyes.

'What's the matter with you, lad?' His tone, as he crouched over him, was suddenly one of anxiety.

'Mr Forbes!' Jason's voice was a schoolboy's again. 'God, Mr Forbes! I can't see!'

'Stay just as you are, lad,' ordered Forbes, starting to run back towards the Cathedral entrance where there must be someone who could help, 'and don't move.'

'No!' screamed Jason.

The ferocity of his cry stopped Forbes in mid stride.

'But, Jason,' began Forbes, coaxing.

The youth had removed his hand from his eyes and was trying to stand up. Forbes realised that the boy's last remark had not been addressed to him at about the same as Jason arched backwards in a convulsion as though he had been struck a vicious blow near the base of his spine. He managed to gather him into his arms as he collapsed and lower him to the floor as gently as he could, relieved to hear someone running up behind him, drawn by the screams. He turned to see an elderly clergyman in a blue cassock bending over them.

CHAPTER THIRTEEN

─────

GARETH ALMOST DECIDED TO IGNORE THE FIRST KNOCK ON THE DOOR. IT MADE HIM JOLT HALF OUT OF HIS CHAIR AND REALISE HOW TENSE HE STILL was. If they were now cheeky enough to walk up to his door in broad daylight, the best thing he could do would be to show his utter indifference. When the knock came again, equally confident, he strode across the caravan and yanked the door open, glaring and ready for violence. He felt himself blush as she started to laugh at him.

'Why, Mrs Winterman!' he muttered, trying to laugh back. He wanted to scan the field to see if anyone was watching them but was unable to take his eyes off her face and figure. She too seemed to be having difficulty preventing a blush rising above the line of her chin.

'Aren't you going to ask me why I've called?' she asked.

'I will,' he mumbled. 'Come in, come on up, mind the step.' He backed away, noticing that over the shape of her body she was wearing some pale green overall with straps that crossed over at the back. He shut the door behind her at once and invited her to sit at the table. The dress material was so tight against her body that any stain, he thought, would mark her flesh at once.

'Sidney asked me to give you this,' she said, sitting down and then rising briefly to reach into a pocket. After some fumbling near her groin she pulled out a pebble the size of a plum and the colour of a gooseberry which she held out for him to take off her palm. The stone was warm in his fingertips.

He remembered that *Dark of the Moon* had mentioned the use of a pebble for certain rituals. Thanking her, he stood looking hard at it as though he was expected to identify it before being allowed to change the subject.

'I parked the car further down the lane,' she said, 'and walked across the field from the stile.'

'That's why you startled me.'

She undid her paisley silk scarf that was loosely knotted at her throat. Removing it, she spread it out on her rather plump thigh and began slowly folding it into a series of smaller and smaller triangles.

'It's warmer than I expected.'

'These vans,' he said, slithering his eyes up at the ceiling, 'are either hot or cold. Can I get you a drink?'

'Do you by any chance have any cold milk?'

He moved to the refrigerator. 'Everything's gas here,' he explained, placing the pebble on top of the refrigerator. He noticed from the loud click it made on the metal that his hand was shaking.

'Are you going to buy a house?'

'If I decide to stay in Lincoln.'

'And what would make you do that?'

He came back to the table with a jug of milk and a glass.

'The friendliness of the natives.'

'I understand you're having problems with some of them.'

'Sidney's helping me.'

'Do you believe,' she asked as she poured the milk, 'in the power of the mind?'

He thought of what his mind had been concentrating on earlier and of her all too physical presence at that moment. 'Increasingly. Do you?'

She pouted. 'After a year or so married to Sidney I no longer know what to believe.' She drank deeply from the glass of milk, not pausing until she had drained it with an upward tilt of her jaw.

He watched the muscles moving in her throat and sat down opposite her, partly because he suddenly felt slack at the backs of his knees but mainly because he was concerned that she would notice the erection he could feel building up along the side of his right thigh. The idea of her probably frequently becoming one flesh with Winterman on an official basis disturbed him to the point of wanting to point his head and the roof and howl. She was so like the mental picture of his ideal woman – the petite but buxom redhead who had in turns tormented and brought relief to his adolescence – that he had difficulty convincing himself that he was not actually imagining her sitting at his table as he had earlier that day imagined her coming into his bedroom.

She slowly wiped a thin moustache of milk off her top lip with the tip of her index finger. Sucking it dry, she leant forward closer towards him until whatever perfume she had splashed between her breasts chased up his nostrils. *'Jejune*

Incest,' she read aloud. 'Why have you called your magazine that?'

'You know that I edit one?'

'Sidney tells me a lot about you.'

He nodded slowly, adjusting his position on the seat carefully. 'I've called it that as a sort of *lucus a non lucendo*.'

'I'm sorry?'

'A light from not shining. It's an ironic hope that it'll be the opposite of what it seems.'

'You mean like calling a bald man Curly?'

'Precisely!' He experienced a flush of pleasure at the realisation that she was as intelligent as she was beautiful. 'Poetry can be a very incestuous affair. By which I mean, of course, that lots of editors simply publish the work of friends, cronies, fellow-travellers or other editors. And a lot of what they publish is – to quote the *Oxford English Dictionary* definition of jejune – meagre and unsatisfying to the mind.'

'Ah!' she said, widening her green eyes. 'The mind again!'

CHAPTER FOURTEEN

'FINGERWIGHT WILL BE YOUR CONTACT. YOU ARE TO RELEASE ONLY ON HIS ORDERS. THOSE WILL BE DELIVERED IN PERSON — NO LETTERS OR telephones. Does that answer your question?'

The Prior nodded, eyeing with distaste the woman in the armchair opposite. He realised that what he resented most about Ms Millington was the surprise she generated by looking such an apparent nobody while being an obviously important person. Her assistants seemed to be in awe of her, coming and going at her bidding like eunuchs. Yet, to look at, she was worse than unremarkable. She was actually ugly – slightly above middle height for a woman, so slender she could have passed from behind as a gangly teenage boy, an illusion fostered by her cropped blonde hair and trouser suit. Her face was so androgynous that it demanded, at first sight, a double-take to decide on her sex. The horsy teeth were moist with saliva and smeared with – he looked away. Her voice was throaty but with no hint of passion. Indeed the thought of her engaging in any form of sexual activity almost provoked him into a snort of laughter. When he looked back at her, pale blue eyes mooned at him through enormous butterfly glasses in a shade of pink that clashed with that scarlet lipstick. She was evidently used to men looking away from her.

'Now, perhaps you could tell me the precise effect that this particular,' she hesitated, her voice rising a semi-tone, 'entity will have. Compared, you understand, with that used in the New Year riot back in 86/87.'

The Prior tilted his jaw upwards, considering. He wanted to be careful how he phrased his reply. The Albion Front had expressed itself to be more than pleased with the results of their first joint experiment in crowd stimulation, and in the others since then. That New Year riot in Lincoln had been spectacularly successful, all the more so for being totally unexpected. What had so taken the Police by surprise had been the sheer ferocity of the violence directed against them over such a relatively prolonged period.

'The first Lincoln experiment,' he said, 'was, of course, produced by the release merely of a gargoyle-sprite of no great importance in the infernal hierarchy. Nevertheless, the effect is well documented. The release of a demon of the rank of the so-called Imp would be – how can I compare the two?' He rolled his hand around from a loose wrist, searching for a simile. 'Well, let me say that, if the gargoyle-sprite were a howitzer shell, then the Imp would be a one megaton thermo-nuclear bomb.'

'Is it appropriate, in this context, to talk about range?'

The Prior nodded, enjoying her need to defer to his superior knowledge. 'The destructive urge spreads, of course, from mind to mind and is therefore dependent to a certain extent upon the physical proximity to each other of the members of the crowd. It will dissipate if it is not continuously generated but, with the Imp, there is no problem with generation. There is also the *totum-partibus* effect to consider.'

He paused to watch her bleached eyebrows lift fractionally. 'That is the fairly well known phenomenon of group psychology popularly described in the observation that "the whole is greater than the sum of the parts". The destructive impulse draws nourishment from its own increase. What you might call,' he permitted himself a slight chuckle, 'a vicious spiral.'

'The size of the crowd will be our concern,' she said.

'But of course! The range, therefore, as I have said, is rather limited by the extent of the crowd. But the actual intensity of the violence is unfortunately – since we have little previous experience ourselves and very few reliable records of attempts in earlier centuries – almost incalculable.'

'But, as you said, vastly greater.'

The Prior pouted. 'In fact, I did not actually say that. I said the Imp has infinitely more destructive potential than the gargoyle-sprite. But there is a possible problem in its application.'

'Why was this possibility not mentioned at the very outset of our negotiations?' The woman had visibly stiffened in her chair.

'Our research into earlier experiments was not complete – and that raises another problem that I must mention – but, to move on, Ms Millington, we must face the possibility that the force of the hatred generated in the members of the crowd will be lessened by reciprocal destruction.'

Again the arching of the thin eyebrows. The Prior felt once more resentful at having to deal with a woman whose intelligence was clearly limited. Whatever her real position in the hierarchy of the Albion Front, she had achieved it by some mysterious quality that originated somewhere other than in her brain or in her face.

'The members of the crowd,' he said, 'may simply turn on each other.' He paused while he watched her face react to the implications of what he had just said. 'There would be considerable carnage but, as it were, misdirected. Unless, of course . . .'

'Yes?' She leant forward in her chair until he could smell her acid breath over the coffee-table.

'Unless,' he went on, leaning back, 'the crowd could be given something, or preferably someone, that it could hate more than its members would find themselves hating each other.'

'I think our Media Department could manage that. You realise, of course, that our aim is public disturbance on such a scale that a State of Emergency will have to be declared, followed by a vote of no confidence in the Government and a General Election?'

'With further disturbances on Polling Day and an intervention by the Armed Forces, yes.'

For the first time during their meeting her dry-skinned face rumpled into what could pass for a smile. It vanished at once as she asked: 'What was the other problem?'

'Some of our clairvoyants,' he said, stifling a spasm of coughing, 'have reported that there is a third party – with no connections with either your organisation or ours – who seems aware of the identity and purpose of the Imp.'

Ms Millington became very still.

'Do you have a name?'

'Not yet, but we're very close.'

'Or a location?'

'Oh, very near to us. In Lincoln.'

'I must consult with my superiors about this.'

'Perhaps at our next meeting you could indicate how you, on your side, propose to deal with the problem. Your reaction rather affects how we proceed. This interloper, you see, may become aware that we are aware of him. Or of her. Do you want us to risk trying to identify him in the mean time?'

She pursed her lips and then nodded slowly as though she had sprained her wiry neck. Before he rose to leave, she gestured to him to wait. 'You mentioned earlier experiments. Which were they?'

He shrugged. 'We have no proof, though plenty of evidence, as is the case with most things occult. We are virtually certain that the pogroms against the Jews in York and Lincoln during the thirteenth century were similarly inspired – quite possibly by the very same agency. Then there's Russia and, of course, Nazi Germany. You will also realise that these were successful precisely because the members of the rioting crowds were given specific human targets at which to direct the hatred that was generated. The mobs all hated the Jews significantly more than they hated anyone in the crowd. And I need hardly mention the most obvious example.'

He stood up and watched her eyebrows but she surprised him by smiling in swift comprehension.

'The crowd before Pontius Pilate,' she drawled, a smile of immense satisfaction bringing her face as near, he thought, as it would ever come to beauty, 'baying for the crucifixion of Jesus Christ . . . '

CHAPTER FIFTEEN

═══════

'IT MUST BE REMEMBERED,' TYPED WINTERMAN, 'THAT THE JEW COPIN TESTIFIED, UNDER THREAT OF TORTURE AND DEATH, THAT THE BOY HAD BEEN crucified by his fellow Jews in mockery of Christ's death.'

He raised his hands from the keyboard and massaged his face, grunting pleasurably to himself. Sitting back in his chair, he twisted towards a side-table and riffled through some papers on it. He began singing tunelessly as he selected a sheet and set it alongside his word-processor.

'It would seem,' he continued typing, 'that Little Saint Hugh, as he came to be called, an eight year old Lincoln boy, was last seen alive playing football with Jewish children in the district of Dernstall at the bottom of Steep Hill near the house in which Copin lived.

'A later ballad embellished the facts by saying that Copin's daughter enticed the boy inside with a red and white apple and that it was she who murdered him. The songwriter even records the dialogue between the murderer and her victim.'

Winterman began humming aloud the tune of *God Rest*

ye Merry, Gentlemen and then, reading from the paper, broke into song:

He kept the ball there with his feet
And catched it with his knee
Till in at the cruel Jew's window
With speed he garred it flee.
'Cast out the ball to me, fair maid,
Cast out the ball to me!'
'You ne'er shall have it, my bonny Sir Hugh,
Till ye come up to me!'

He typed out the song and was about to sing it again when the telephone on the wall of his study rang. It was his wife. He listened in silence apart from humming occasionally, his eyes flickering over the monitor screen.

'Of course I don't mind your staying to dinner!' he chuckled eventually. 'Never turn down an invitation to a free meal . . . Right, then, I'll expect you about eleven.' He sat back in his chair to listen to some more. 'No . . . It's a good chance for me to get on and finish this chapter . . . Of course I'll be able to fix myself up with something! . . . You called in on young Gareth? . . . Was he? . . . Take care driving home.'

He hung up, smiling and poised his hands at once over the keyboard. 'After a ten day search,' he typed, 'Hugh's mother found his body in a well. It had been put there, according to Copin, who had been promised his life if he confessed, because the Jews had tried but failed to bury the body. "The earth," they had claimed. "had vomited it forth." '

'This was the start of the process by which Hugh came to be regarded as a martyr. The Cathedral Canons took charge

49

of his body; there were expositions to crowds of sightseers; and finally burial with great solemnity. Copin himself, notwithstanding the promises made to him, was lashed to a horse's tail and dragged to Canwick Hill gallows where he was hanged. About ninety other Jews were arrested and sent to London. Eighteen of these were hanged without trial. The rest were eventually granted a trial by jury (of twenty-Four knights and twenty-Four London citizens) and all found guilty and sentenced to death, except two. It was thanks to the pleas of the Earl of Cornwall that they were spared.

'It is interesting to note, however, that prior to Cornwall's intervention a number of friars appealed to the King to show clemency. It is the intention of this book to demonstrate that the motive behind this appeal was not so much ordinary Christian charity as an attempt to avert a curse. The friars not only knew that the Jews were innocent, they knew who was guilty of the murder.'

CHAPTER SIXTEEN

———

DARREN EAMES HOPPED AND SKIPPED ACROSS THE HOSPITAL CAR-PARK. A CRASH-HELMET SWUNG FROM THE END OF HIS REVOLVING ARM. HE whooped once in simple pleasure. The depression he had felt having to sit at his brother's bedside in the stuffy ward had lifted, replaced by the delight at having been given the helmet. It was the first thing that Jason had ever given him apart from Christmas presents and it was their mother who always provided the money for those. He had not quite understood what his brother had been mumbling but the gesture with which he had pushed the helmet towards him had been clear enough. After that he had dropped back into unconsciousness.

He stopped at the first fish-and-chip shop that he came to and ate the large portion as he walked along the street, the helmet swinging by its strap from one wrist. After wiping his hands on the wrapping-paper, he dropped it into the gutter near Wayne Platt's house. The front door was open. He jumped from the pavement to the doorstep in one hop and leant in, calling out his friend's name.

Wayne appeared in the narrow hallway, wiping tomato

sauce from the corner of his mouth with the back of his hand. Darren grinned a greeting and threw a set of ignition keys into the air, catching them with a snatch of his fist and repeating the action wordlessly.

'Whose are those? Have you nicked a bike?'

In reply Darren tossed the crash-helmet at his friend's testicles. Wayne caught it with a grunt of protest.

'Have you nicked this as well?'

'Our Jase gave it us. Didn't say where he got it. He's not say anything at the minute – he's in hospital.'

'Did he give you the keys to his bike as well?'

Darren nodded. 'He's gone all funny. Usually carries them around with him everywhere, even when the bike's locked up at home. Fancy going somewhere when it gets dark?'

Wayne started to grin. He licked more tomato sauce off his upper teeth with the tip of his tongue and swallowed thoughtfully. 'Burden's caravan again?'

Darren put the crash-helmet on his head and rapped it with his knuckles. 'Be ready when I call for you.' He tugged the helmet off and looked at it as though seeing it for the first time. 'I think I'll try this out. Bit of all right – for nothing!'

'You always were a lucky bugger,' said Wayne.

CHAPTER SEVENTEEN

ARETH SUDDENLY FELT PRETERNATURALLY
FORTUNATE. HE SHUT DARK OF THE MOON AND
PLACED IT ON THE TABLE BEFORE HIM. HE ALLOWED
the spasm of excitement to flush down to his feet and crossed
his legs rapidly. He had almost convinced himself that Angharad's arrival so soon after his visualisation exercises could not
have been a coincidence. As soon as she had gone he had
returned to his bedroom and mentally summoned her
another three times. The process had excited him to such an
extent that his deliberately unrelieved arousal was still, hours
later, a dull ache. He had worked hard on the magazine,
breaking off only for a rushed sandwich of cheese and rather
stale brown bread but the physical reminder between his
legs of her continuing presence in his mind weakened his
concentration at regular intervals.

He leaned back against the cushioned wall-panel of the
caravan and closed his eyes. This time he formed a picture, as
instructed by *Dark of the Moon*, on the inside of his forehead.
At first the image of Darren Eames was vague and refused to
form. He could shape the face and shoulders but when he
tried to visualise the slender body, the head blurred. He per-

sisted, breathing rhythmically and deeply, until he gradually constructed a more detailed image of the youth. He pictured him standing, dressed in a black leather jacket and blue jeans, a hand in his pocket, the other cradling a red crash-helmet. His weight was on one foot, one dirty trainer pressing on the instep of the other. His face was slack, the thick lips parted in a vacant and puzzled expression, the forehead creased as though straining to understand some instruction that he had just been given. He kept him standing there until he was satisfied that he could open his eyes, close them again and reconstruct the image instantly. This he then did three times.

Opening his eyes again, he rested and rolled his stiffening neck about. He sat up, listening intently. He thought he had heard a car change down a gear on the road beyond the hedge. He settled to his visualising again. When he had Darren standing motionless with his helmet, he made him put it on and tighten the chin-strap under his acne-red jaw. The helmet altered his features. It accentuated the narrowness of his face and the short distance between his eyes. But there was some other difference that Gareth could not understand at once. There was a change in the image's expression that made Gareth stiffen where he sat. He was intending to make the youth afraid – but not yet and not that much.

Without Gareth's willing it, Darren's imagined face had collapsed into a plastic caricature of terror. His hands clawed up at the shiny sides of the helmet and his mouth gaped in a noiseless yell. Gareth felt the strong urge to open his eyes but he also wanted to keep them closed in order to go on observing the lad's agony. His heartbeat quickened but when the knock came on the door he lurched to his feet as though surfacing from a nightmare, sucking in air through his mouth and pressing a splayed hand to his ribs.

He opened the door and saw firstly that it was night and then that Angharad was standing on the top step. Without a word he stood back to let her in and without a word she entered while he closed and locked the door.

CHAPTER EIGHTEEN

THE VOLVO ESTATE WHINED BRIEFLY IN REVERSE GEAR ACROSS THE UNLIT FARMYARD. IT CROSSED TEMPLE'S MIND AS HE LOOKED OVER HIS LEFT FOREARM stretched along the back of the seat at Springfellow's beckoning hand bringing him closer to the outhouse door that a stab on the accelerator would do it. He was far enough away to gather sufficient momentum to crush him yet not so far that he would have time to react and leap aside. But not enough was to be gained yet by disposing of his rival. The Prior's telephone call had made it clear that they must as a matter of urgency discover who was the external source of interference, the man or woman who seemed to have independently realised the significance of the Imp and the true cause of the various apparently spontaneous riots up and down the country. Springfellow was one of their best clairvoyants. As if to prove it, he skipped aside before the Volvo braked, rapping on its roof. Temple wound down his window and peered out into the night air.

'Lights and engine off!' said Springfellow, coming to stand beside the driver's door. The darkness in the farmyard, surrounded on three sides by buildings, was almost total as he complied with what to him had sounded a little too much like an order. Through the gap between the corner of the three-storied Georgian farmhouse and the stables he saw the faint orange loom of Lincoln behind a stand of chestnut trees on the horizon.

He stepped out of the car, feeling the cobblestones of the yard slippery under his biker's boots in the moist evening air. They walked together in silence to the back of the Volvo. Temple unlocked the tailgate and swung it up. Almost before Temple could bring his arms down to his sides Springfellow had started tugging at the heavy-duty plastic bag. They slid it towards them, grunting a little. Temple had wanted to leave a job like this to some of the other junior esquires but Spring-fellow had insisted on their taking no risks at all.

'I'll take the legs,' panted Springfellow, starting to bend his own.

As he hooked his arms under the bulk of the torso, Temple remembered that the corpse in the bag had no head. The feeling of panic seeped over him again and the yearning to be suddenly far away, doing normal boring things. They carried the bundle into an outhouse and dumped it on the straw-covered floor. Pausing to draw breath, Temple smelt the pigs before he heard them.

Springfellow lit an oil-lamp with a match and turned up the wick. Temple could see the dozen or so pigs in their sties along the far wall. Some of them were standing up with their trotters slipping on the tubular steel of the gate, their snouts sniffing the air.

'Always hungry!' said Springfellow. 'You unzip the bag,' he continued in the tome of command that was beginning to annoy Temple, 'while I fetch the chain-saw.'

CHAPTER NINETEEN

'IN 1290,' TYPED WINTERMAN, 'ABOUT SIXTEEN THOUSAND JEWS LEFT ENGLAND NEVER TO RETURN. THE PENALTY FOR ANY WHO DELAYED AFTER ALL Saints' Day of that year was to be hanged, drawn and quartered. All their property was seized by the Crown. It was four hundred years before the Jews were to return.'

He stood up and paced the room, muttering to himself. It was important to make the next paragraph, the last in the chapter, telling enough to make his readers impatient for the next but yet not tell them so much that there would be no surprises left. He sat down and waggled his fingers over the keys.

'By any standards,' he continued, 'the treatment that the Jews in England received was unpardonable. Yet some years ago the Fathers of the City of York held a public ceremony in which they formally apologised to the Jews for what their ancestors had suffered there and sought the pardon of the Chosen People. Since then York has prospered, becoming a popular centre of a developing tourist trade. At the time of writing, the City of Lincoln has taken no such action and has rather stagnated, falling gradually deeper in economic decline and developing only the sort of social problems not normally associated with a cathedral city. Indeed the cathedral itself has in recent years been more famous as a source of ecclesiastical scandal than of spiritual leadership.

'There is a reason for this failure and folly, which goes beyond simple moral deficiency or commercial inefficiency: the City of Lincoln is still cursed and will never prosper until the source of the curse is removed. That source, as I shall show, is familiar to almost everyone in the county as it is the official emblem of the County Council, though few recognise it for what it really is. The group of evangelists, however, who once earnestly requested the County Council to stop emblazoning it on their letterheads, noticeboards and vehicles, did recognise its true nature. They were ignored as cranks, for what would Lincoln be without its Imp?'

Winterman sat back with a sigh of satisfaction and massaged his cheeks. Rising again from his chair, he went to lie on a studio-couch against the wall under the window. He made himself comfortable and closed his eyes. He slowly emptied his mind of the many ideas still swarming around in it and imagined himself toiling steadily up the familiar mountain track . . .

. . . The sun was shining and relaxing the muscles of his shoulders in a pleasant burning glow. Gradually the path steepened and the land began to slope away on both sides. He could see the path far ahead winding and dipping up the ridge which swung on towards the cloud-covered mountain-top. He came to a section of the path that levelled out. A cairn had been built beside it and he sat down in its lee, looking out over the foothills swooping below him to the fields and hedges of the plain on either bank of the broad river that

glinted in the valley. He scanned the view below, his breathing becoming more and more regular, the muscles of his face
and body more relaxed, until the sun had set and the land
grew swiftly dark. Only one light shone, far below down on
the plain. He concentrated on it and seemed to be floating
towards it like a great owl on silent wings. The light, he saw,
was coming from a window. It was the window of a small
caravan in a meadow beside a wood. In the caravan were a
young man and a young woman. He could see them now as
distinctly as if he were in the room with them. The young
man was Gareth Burden and the young woman was his wife
Angharad. Gareth was locking the door and turning to face
her . . .

CHAPTER TWENTY

D ARREN EAMES KILLED THE ENGINE OF HIS BROTHER'S MOTORBIKE AND COASTED THE LAST FIFTY YARDS. WITHOUT TRACTION THE MACHINE HANDLED awkwardly as Wayne Platt leaned out from his pillion seat to look over Darren's shoulder. They wobbled to a stop under some horse-chestnuts that overhung the road and climbed off, slapping their arms around their chests to warm up. Darren wheeled the bike through the open gateway and leant it against the hawthorn hedge.

They looked at the lights from the caravan in the middle of the field and grinned at each other in the mottled moon-light. An owl hooted from one of the trees and Wayne gig-gled nervously. Wayne started towards the caravan but hesitated when he noticed his friend fumbling furiously with the strap of his crash-helmet.

'What's up?' he grunt-whispered. 'Different fastening?'

'Nah,' yawned Darren, finally removing it. 'I thought it was going to be slack on me but it seems tight now.'

'Perhaps yer head's got bigger.'

Darren did not respond with the sort of comment that Wayne expected but slowly placed the helmet on the seat of the bike and knelt down, rubbing his temples with gloved fingers. The night air was cool but still.

'Did you notice that car parked back there just off the road?' asked Wayne.

Darren sniffed. 'Yeah. Reckon it's old Winterman's old Peugeot.'

'What the hell's he doing here?'

'Visiting Burden, I suppose.'

'That means we'd better be careful tonight. I don't want that bastard after us!'

'He might be soon anyway, if Burden's been complaining.'

'About what? He can't prove it's us.'

'He knows it's us!'

'Knowing's not proving. Let's get closer and just listen to start with.'

They moved forward together over the field, slowing to a tip-toed prance as they approached within twenty yards of the caravan, suppressing their giggles with increasing success. Two dim pools of light made yellow oblongs on the grass, one from beside the door, the other from a window across the rear wall. Failing to hear voices from what they knew from their earlier visits to be the living-room, they moved on. As they turned the corner of the caravan both boys stiffened and stood still, simultaneously making the same fascinating observation: the caravan was rocking to and fro, not violently but rhythmically, as if being buffeted by a strong wind.

The frown on Wayne's forehead faded fractionally before that on Darren's. Their grins began together and widened in the now suddenly brighter moonlight. They slid as one up against the caravan wall, their eyes level with the lower edge of the window that was braced open by two metal struts. The first noise he heard coming through the curtains confirmed Wayne's first delighted guess: it was the grunting of a man steadily approaching but still confidently remote from orgasm. Then, blending with it, began an unmistakably feminine sound, halfway between laughter and sobbing, a noise produced, he imagined, through flared nostrils and clenched teeth.

Wayne pressed a finger to his lips and moved his head nearer to the bottom edge of the window. Using both his forefingers, he slowly parted the curtains and peeped in. Though he had some idea of what he was about to see he was not expecting quite what met his eyes in the foxed glow of a roaring pressure lamp.

On, rather than in, a narrow bed he saw his English teacher, wearing only a vest, mounted on what at first from her size appeared to be a girl but almost at once was revealed as a small but shapely woman. His hands were clutching her haunches as tightly as her legs were wrapped around him, her ankles crossing on the backs of his thighs. She was naked apart from a sort of flimsy scarf around her neck. Her head was thrust back into a pile of pillows and her pale chubby arms were stretched along the headboard, her hands cupped behind both short knob-shaped wooden bedposts. Most of her hair, an oily black shot with copper in the lamplight, was flowing over one shoulder. And every other part of her was rippling too. It crossed his mind that he would have difficulty staying on top of a woman who moved as much as that, though Burden was riding her with obvious determination and enjoyment.

'Oh-come-and-have a look at this,' Wayne moaned in a

whisper, turning to Darren, adding after a moment's thought, 'He's shagging old Winterman's wife!' To his surprise and annoyance his friend had moved further off and was squatting on the grass, holding his head in his hands. Wayne turned back to the window, torn between the desire to have Darren also witness their English teacher deriving such energetic satisfaction between the legs of their Deputy Head's wife and the pleasure he himself was feeling between his own as he watched them.

He flickered his eyes away again and saw Darren rolling on the ground, his legs jerking in a parody of the woman's. At first Wayne thought that the slow rising yell, which must have been audible from the road, was coming from the coming Mrs Winterman but realised that it was not at about the same time as, looking back through the window, he saw that Burden had realised it too.

When Wayne reached Darren he was trying to stand up but his apparent need to keep both hands pressed to his ears prevented him. He squirmed backwards over the grass, alternately kicking and attempting to rise. Failing, he screamed again. Wayne could not understand why Darren kept telling him to keep away from him. He stepped back, glancing anxiously over his shoulder at the caravan. When he looked back the moon slid completely clear of cloud and he saw Darren's face twisted by some dread beyond its previous experience. He wanted to help but knew there was nothing he could do for him. When he heard heavy footsteps from the caravan and its door being flung open, he did something for himself and started to run.

CHAPTER TWENTY-ONE

———

HURRYING BACK FROM MATINS, THE PRIOR WAS SURPRISED TO OPEN HIS CONSERVATORY DOOR AND FIND A SANDY-BEARDED MAN IN HIS EARLY FORTIES lounging in one of the cane chairs brushing the lapels of his pale grey suit. He was even more astonished to see his dog – a Dobermann-Boxer crossbreed – lying asleep beside him. Before he could speak, the man rose and introduced himself.

'Forgive what must seem a gross invasion of your privacy, sir. You will understand when I tell you that my name is James Fingerwight that it was not advisable for me to be seen at your front door.' He extended a hairy hand which the Prior shook warily. 'And please do not think that your dog has failed in his duty. I took the precaution a using one of the aniseed-flavoured sedative pellets that the Front has issued to people of my rank. We now have – I'm sorry to disappoint you – biochemical means of invalidating almost all the virtues, loyalty included.'

The Prior removed his raincoat and blinked up through the roof of his conservatory at the fitful autumn sunshine before choosing a chair. 'It can be cold in church,' he said.

'I am rather surprised – but not for that reason – that you

attend one,' said Fingerwight, sitting down again as though the house were his and the Prior his guest.

'What the Front would call Deep Cover.'

Fingerwight smiled. 'That I understand. I work as an adviser for the Local Education Authority.'

'But you did not come here to tell me that.'

'No, though the fact is germane to what I have been instructed to tell you. Tomorrow I'm visiting a Lincoln secondary school. St Cuthbert's, to be precise.' He paused but the Prior waited for him to continue. 'We now have reason to suspect that the Deputy Head there – a man called Sidney Winterman – is aware of the true cause of the Riots and may therefore be potentially dangerous to us.'

'Can you have been witholding information from your admirable Ms Millington? When I spoke to her yesterday she seemed unaware of the existence of this interloper.'

'She would have been.' Fingerwight smiled again. 'Since then I've been telephoned by acquaintances of Winterman's wife. She had dinner with them last night. During the meal she told them even more about the book that her husband's writing than she had on previous occasions – they all have painting as a common interest. She didn't say much but once she started on his theories about the Riots . . . They're loyal Party members. Rang me as soon as she left. And I rang Ms Millington. Which is why I'm here now; she wants some action sooner rather than later.'

'But you said it was you that are going to his school tomorrow. What do you want me to do?'

'Provide me with the means to test the power of the Imp. And test the full extent of Winterman's knowledge and involvement.'

The Prior raised his head in the stiffnecked manner that could bring a commandery meeting to total silence. It had no effect on Fingerwight who squinted at his wristwatch as he went on talking.

'To be specific: we want you to let me have the Imp replica and the words of the releasing and, of course, revocation rituals.' He looked carefully at the Prior as though concerned that he might be feeling suddenly unwell. 'Until tomorrow evening only.' He paused. 'I have that, er, instruction in writing, if you require confirmation.' He reached into the inside pocket of his suit.

'Have you the slightest idea what you are proposing?' The Prior's voice was taut with a disbelief that verged on contempt.

Fingerwight's smile tightened into an unpleasant rictus.

'Excuse me, sir. This is not a proposal. It is an, er, . . . a directive. This potential source of interference must be confirmed and, if necessary, eliminated. And a riot in a school would be an invaluable experiment. Surely you see that?'

CHAPTER TWENTY-TWO

GARETH WOKE UP LATE ON THE SUNDAY MORNING. HE HAD TAKEN A LONG TIME TO FALL ASLEEP AFTER THE EVENTS OF THE PREVIOUS NIGHT BUT ONCE tiredness had finally overwhelmed him he had slept deeply. His dreams had been vivid and simple. He woke to a fading memory of the weight and warmth of Angharad's legs around his waist. His groin was still redolent of her excitement as he twisted under the cotton sheet to hide from the weak but bright late-morning sunshine. The temporary half-darkness reminded him of the strange sight that had faced him as he had bounded in fury out of the caravan: Darren Eames gibbering in the moonlight on the grass like Nebuchadnezzar and then standing up and pointing – not at Gareth but at something, or someone, near him – and then buckling forward as though kicked in the arse by the back legs of a cart-horse before collapsing to lie as still and as cold as a carcass of pork.

He recalled Angharad dressing hurriedly – a sight only slightly less arousing than the reverse process had been; his drive to the public telephone; summoning the ambulance; finding her waiting for him and his attempt to arrange another meeting; her driving off before the ambulance came; his excited circuits of the field in the silence afterwards, trying to calm himself, feeling himself gradually detumesce; tripping over the crash-helmet; sitting with a large whisky in one hand and the copy of *Dark of the Moon* in the other . . .

Rising, he tugged the sheets of his bed tidy and briefly smelt again the whiff of her perfume. Shaking his head, he dressed hurriedly in corduroy trousers, tee-shirt and sweater for the caravan was colder than the sun promised. While preparing his breakfast of bread and honey he glanced over at the red crash-helmet he had put on the table. He guessed it must belong to Eames. He had heard a motorbike being ridden off – probably by Platt – before he went to summon the ambulance. Holding a slice of bread in one hand, he picked up the helmet in the other, pinching the brow-ridge between finger and thumb. He was surprised at how heavy it was, and how cool. He set it down and cupped his palm over the crown to test it for the warmth it should have absorbed from the sun's rays though the window. His first impression was confirmed: it was distinctly cool to the touch, cold even. Pushing the rest of the bread into his mouth, he placed both hands on the helmet's smooth sides. It was uniformly chill, though one side had been in the sun. He chewed thoughtfully.

He remembered involuntarily the feel of Angharad's hip-bones under his palms and closed his eyes in a sudden confusion of emotions: lust to possess her again to the finish without interruption; shame that he had betrayed a man who had been good to him; dread that she might tell Winterman; anxiety at what rumours might be spread by Eames and his cronies if, as seemed probable, they had been listening outside; unease about the cause of the lad's strange condition; excitement at what he continued to learn from *Dark of the Moon* . . . He opened his eyes, sighed and moved the helmet off the table on to a window seat. He did so by putting his hand inside it and balancing it on the extended tips of his fingers.

He stopped walking as he was setting it down. His hand felt suddenly, increasingly, cold. He withdrew it and picked up the helmet again in both hands. He peered inside, unsure what he was expecting to see. Holding it upside down with his left hand under the crown, he dipped his right inside again as into a goldfish-bowl. Again there was the faint, then sharper, sensation of chill in the flesh and even the bone of his fingers. He snatched his hand out and the chill faded. He tried once more to assure himself that he had not imagined the effect. He was sure now he had not.

He juggled the helmet lightly from one palm to the other like a football, thinking. It was absurd . . . And yet . . . He put the helmet up on a shelf near the sink and decided he would have to consult Winterman again. A visit would also, per-haps, reveal Angharad's attitude to what had happened between them last night. The thought of discovering that it had been for her merely a casual carnal interlude was unbear-able to him – he wanted her to be wanting him again. He found himself wondering, as he shaved, whether she had allowed or even encouraged her husband to make love to her afterwards. He was gripped by such a spasm of unexpected jealousy that he cut himself in a tender spot just under the point of his chin.

CHAPTER TWENTY-THREE

WINTERMAN WRIGGLED THE POINT OF HIS BEARD DOWN INTO THE CLEAVAGE BETWEEN ANGHARAD'S BREASTS. HE FELT THE WARMTH OF HER PLUMP thighs clamp around his floating ribs and her arms cradle his head. The sun was not warm enough through their bedroom window to prevent his bare feet feeling a little cold as they protruded from under the duvet.

'I love,' he murmured drowsily, 'making love on Sunday mornings.'

'You love it any time of the day, any day of the week.'

He rumbled agreement back at her and sighed. 'You were late last night.'

'I took a shower before coming to bed. You were already asleep.'

'How were Toby and Jocelyn?'

She hesitated before replying. 'Curious.'

'As in "odd", or as in "inquisitive"?'

'Both. They were in a funny mood – tense. As if they'd had a row just before I arrived. But very inquisitive, while trying not to seem so. They wanted me to talk about your book. I ended up wishing you'd come with me. Or gone instead.'

'What did they want to know about my book?'

'Oh . . . all sorts. Toby was most taken with your theory about the Riots, and the Lincoln Curse, and all that.'

Winterman lifted his head and shifted some of his weight on to his elbows. He was about to comment but had second thoughts. 'And how was Gareth Burden?'

'Tense also. Quite an evening, really.' She widened her green eyes at him provocatively and wriggled underneath him. 'Slide higher up the mountains, you old goat!' She hooked her hands under his armpits and tried to tug him higher up the bed.

He complied. Their mouths collided and he felt her left hand caress the fine hair at the nape of his neck while the fingers of the right slid through his thicker, curlier hair to stroke his scrotum. He sighed with pleasure as the ball of her thumb tapped his already swollen shaft towards bone-hard readiness. Slithering her lips free from his kiss, she whispered in his ear, 'Or should I have said "old donkey"?'

He entered her with the single, easy, eager, blunt thrust that he knew never failed to excite and astonish her. 'You decide,' he mumbled, moving his forearms to their favourite positions under her shoulderblades and the narrow base of her spine.

'Donkey!' she gurgled happily. 'Oh, definitely donkey!'

'And was Gareth Burden more donkey than goat?'

She stopped sliding the soles of her tiny feet up the backs of his legs and pulled her cheek away from his. He continued his insistent plunging, watching her out of the corner of his eye. Her anxious stare changed to a quick frown and then a disbelieving smile. She began to shake her head. 'You mean you intended . . . ?'

He suddenly quickened his pace and increased the pressure of his arms until he heard her gasping at the force of his possession. 'How was he, Gwenhwyfar?'

'Too slender!' she panted and he sensed her quiver with excitement at his use of her second name that he reserved especially to signal the start of the slow but unstoppable approach of his spurting seed.

Winterman turned to face her dressing-table mirror. Behind the reflections of perfume bottles and aerosol sprays he watched the dipping lunges of his pelvis between the rounded curvatures of his wife's legs. That terrible movement had always fascinated him with its beautiful combination of power and purpose. Unwilling and unable to hold back any longer, he heard himself grunt, grunt and grunt again.

'He didn't do that,' she said eventually, nuzzling her mouth against his ear. 'We were interrupted.'

She told him about the screaming outside the caravan and how Gareth had found one of his pupils. He listened in silence.

'But, if we'd been able to finish,' she continued, 'I suppose he could have given me a child. We didn't take any precautions.'

'And wouldn't that have been what you wanted?'

'You know it's your child I want.'

'I know, but I'd happy for it to be his.'

'Why?'

He took so long to reply that she asked again as he was starting to answer.

'Because I've chosen him for you.'

'I don't need a lover,' she scolded, hugging him, 'with you for a husband.'

'I've not as your lover that I've chosen him. But as your husband.'

She tried to sit up but he continued to press her down into their bed.

'We don't have much longer together, Angharad my dear. And you've a task to perform. Without me. You'll need Gareth to do it.'

He rolled off her abruptly onto his back and stared up at the ceiling.

'What "task"?' she began. 'When?'

'Let's get dressed,' he said. 'He'll be here soon. I'll explain everything to both of you together.'

CHAPTER TWENTY-FOUR

'HOW CAN I BEGIN TO EXPLAIN MY RESERVATIONS?' said the prior. 'THE VIOLENCE WOULD ATTRACT NATIONAL — IF NOT INTERNATIONAL — MEDIA coverage and you are surely not ready yet for the sort of civil unrest that could erupt.'

'This experiment,' drawled Fingerwight expansively, 'would last for only a short period – an hour at most.'

'And how do you propose to limit it to such a period?'

'By recalling the entity with the formula that you will provide.'

The Prior snorted and then laughed drily. 'You seem unaware that recall may not be possible.'

'But, surely, during the New Year Riots – '

' – the gargoyle-sprite was eventually recalled but with immense difficulty and then only by an expert.'

'What's his name? Can he be contacted quickly?'

'He died during the transference of the Imp. Contact is, I suppose, still possible through the agency of some of our mediums but hardly likely to be of much use to you.' The Prior thought that Fingerwight was having difficulty in interpreting his smile.

Fingerwight was not smiling. His narrow face showed signs of sudden strain. 'I must have the means to run a trial.' He spoke in the tone of a man who has just realised that he is about to be disappointed and finds the sensation unfamiliar. 'You don't understand the pressure to succeed that is imposed on all Front members. I must also remind you that you have entered into an agreement with us. My superiors are not going to be pleased to learn that you have broken it.'

The Prior's face became stern again. He remembered the agreement only too well.

'And you no doubt think every day about your daughter. It is at our Winchester office that she works as a secretary, isn't it?'

'I am fully aware, Mr. Fingerwight, that Penelope is virtually a hostage.' The Prior paused, flushing. It was only when he felt able to speak without his voice quivering that he went on, stiffly. 'I did not say that I was refusing to enable you to run a trial. I meant that a trial involving the Imp – especially at such short notice – poses such problems as to be too dangerous to all involved, yourself especially, to be contemplated. I could, however, and if you insist, I will, provide you with a, er, less powerful entity.' He stood up and paced thoughtfully towards a potted fuchsia. 'Though even that,' he murmured, rearranging the fall of its lax stalks, 'in a secondary school, could have effects beyond our complete control. Adolescent minds have powers and potentials we still do not fully understand.'

Fingerwight sat forward. He had learned from his dealings with teachers that it was most effectual to allow people with a complaint to talk themselves out.

'This school, St Cuthbert's,' continued the Prior, 'does it

have any pupils whom one could call maladjusted in any way? Any with a history of violence, or with anti-social tendencies?'

'It's an ordinary comprehensive,' said Fingerwight.

The Prior stroked a fuchsia bloom with a fingertip, making it oscillate delicately. 'Meaning that the answer to my question is No.'

'On the contrary, as the word implies, that type of school contains an almost complete cross-section of society – for the area it's serving, that is – so we can be certain it has a fair percentage, mainly boys, of course, who will be criminals soon after leaving it, if they aren't already.' He smiled as he watched the Prior's puzzled old face turn away from his flowers. 'Precisely the state of affairs that the Front will rectify, given time.'

It was the Prior who smiled then. He had met people like Fingerwight before and had only contempt for their pathetic faith in the possibility of human improvement. 'Come with me,' he said. 'I think I can help you.'

CHAPTER TWENTY-FIVE

'I NEED YOUR HELP,' SAID GARETH. HE SAT DOWN AT THE LONG PINE TABLE IN THE KITCHEN WHERE WINTERMAN INDICATED A CHAIR.

'You'll join us for lunch?' he asked, going on without waiting for an answer to explain that Angharad was still dressing. 'Long lie in!' he added, watching Gareth's face as it coloured.

He brought out a large jug of orange juice from the refrigerator and set it on the table along with a couple of tumblers. 'Nothing like the natural juices!' he boomed, enjoying Gareth's increasing discomfiture, as he poured them both a drink.

Gareth was glad to turn to face the door when Angharad swept in, wearing a deep green track-suit. He stood up awkwardly to greet her, half-sitting again before she invited him to and then rising to his full height and colliding with the back of a chair as he stepped aside for her.

'Gareth's agreed to stay for lunch,' announced Winterman. 'He has something to tell me.'

Gareth tried to read the look on Angharad's face but she

avoided his glance and, without comment, busied herself with a fruit-bowl and a cheese-board.

'Darren Eames was out at my caravan last night,' he said. 'I heard what I thought was an imitation of a werewolf baying the moon but when I got out there and found him on the ground, I realised he wasn't pretending. Some sort of fit. He's in hospital now. I had to phone from the farmhouse for an ambulance.'

'He won't be pestering you again for a while, then.'

Gareth grunted agreement and went on to describe the extraordinary symptoms of terror that Eames had displayed. 'I've never seen anything quite like it. Something had given him a unprecedented shock.' Winterman continued to listen in silence. 'Before I finally turned in for the night I went out again for a last look round and came across what I presume was the crash-helmet he'd brought with him.' As Gareth went on to tell him what he had discovered about the crash-helmet, Winterman's face became steadily more grave. Noticing him, Angharad paused from tossing a salad in olive oil.

'Darling!' she said in what sounded like surprise. 'You looked suddenly . . . ' She turned back to her preparation of lunch.

'What?' he asked. 'Worried?'

'Old,' she said smiling. 'Cheer up, it's Sunday morning.'

'Where is it?' he asked Gareth quietly.

'On the back seat of my car. I brought it with me because I thought you'd want to test its, er, properties for yourself.'

'I'd like you to bring it in later.'

Gareth nodded in silent agreement and smiled nervously at Angharad. Even the track-suit seemed a size too small for her. He looked back at Winterman to see that he had been watching the way he had looked at her. He drained his orange-juice.

'So that we can enjoy our meal together,' said Winterman, suddenly brightening and clearing away the tumblers, 'let's remove at least the anxiety of uncertainty.' He reached into a cupboard and brought out three wine-glasses. Filling them from an already opened bottle of Frascati on the sideboard, he handed Angharad and Gareth a glass each and took a mouthful from his own.

'I know what happened,' he said after a noisy swallow, 'in your caravan last night, Gareth. Notice I said in it, not outside it. In fact,' he held up his free hand as Gareth began to speak, 'you could say I arranged for it to happen. You see, ever since your interview for the job at St. Cuthbert's, I've realised that you are the person to take over from me.' He sat down opposite Gareth while Angharad continued to stand between them at the head of the table, fiddling with the salad. 'I sensed your interest in, and aptitude for, the occult. I could see that you found Angharad more than just attractive. And she you. This may seem cold-blooded and abrupt. It's both. We've not a lot of time for explanations and I knew when I married her that I couldn't expect too many years in her bed. No dear, you know that's true!'

As Angharad and Gareth exchanged glances for the first time during his speech, Winterman took another, deeper, pull at his wine.

'But now I'm certain I won't be able to live with her much longer.' He extended a restraining palm at her. 'No, please, let me explain.'

'Good God,' protested Gareth, 'you're not sixty!' He felt a

heady amalgam of emotions: relief, excitement, embarrassment.

'Hear me out, both of you. I didn't say I expected to die. Though I might be killed. And to prevent that I shall have to disappear, giving the impression to those who are going to want me out of the way that I've permanently obliged them.'

'And who would want you dead, pray?' asked Angharad. Gareth had grown very quiet and was watching Winterman intently as though trying to discover exactly how he was performing a conjuring trick.

'You're both aware of the increasing political prominence over the last few years of the Albion Front?'

They nodded.

'I was reading up on them long before they started making the news bulletins. They're planning a coup d'etat. Their strategy is to increase public disorder to such an intolerable degree that the class of people who would have opposed a right wing revolution – and the loss of civil liberties that it would entail – will actually come to welcome it, when the Front promises to deliver Law and Order.'

'How are they going to orchestrate the public disorder?' asked Gareth. 'Won't it be too obviously the work of paid rowdies?'

'They've enlisted the services of an occult organisation that claims descent from the Knights Templar. Until about ten years ago they were a relatively harmless group of cranks who met in the upstairs rooms of pubs to dabble in Kabbalistic magic. Then they elected a Prior – as they term their leader – who had developed some magical techniques of his own. Quite a genius, in his own way.'

'How do you know all this?'

'I'm myself part of what you might call a rival company. And I too have developed techniques of my own.'

'You mean you've improved on *Dark of the Moon?*' Gareth leaned forward, his forearms on his knees.

Winterman smiled and nodded. 'The Neo-Templars have, it seems to me, rediscovered the magical process of releasing petrified demons. That is one of the reasons they now call themselves Tophetim. One demon in particular, I personally believe, was invoked by the mediaeval Tophetim to foment the hatred against the Jews in the Lincoln pogrom at the time of the murder of Little Saint Hugh. It was an exorcist belonging to the order of the Gilbertines of Sempringham – possibly with the assistance of some friars – who eventually petrified him again – in what we quaintly call the Imp.'

Gareth was nodding too, as if understanding for the first time the complicated solution of a mathematical problem.

'Are you two sharing a joke at my expense?' broke in Angharad. 'A fifty-five year old Deputy Head is to be assassinated by the Latter Day Knights Templar? And because he's found out they're conspiring to have the Government replaced, he's arranging to have himself replaced?'

'With the effortless succinctness of the sceptic you have brilliantly summarised the situation, my dear. So baldly put, it does, I admit, seem absurd. That absurdity vanishes, however, when you know, as I do, how seriously the Albion Front take the Tophetim and the lengths to which the Tophetim will go – and have gone – to acquire the control they need in occult matters. I've not given you the Prior's name. It would surprise you. He's a well known figure in the county. You may not believe in demons yet, my love,' he said to Angharad, 'but I assure you he not only believes, he trembles. What's more to the point,' he continued, draining his glass, 'he knows that someone else, outside his order and probably hostile to him, also knows. When he is sure who that person is he will try either to recruit or to eliminate him.'

'Will you be able to drop out of sight before he finds out?' asked Angharad.

Winterman shrugged. 'I can only hope so. Your best defence, both of you – for you may be in danger by association – is to feign ignorance. Show as little interest as possible from now on in the psychic. I know that won't be easy for you, Gareth. Steep yourselves in the carnal. I'm sure you'll both enjoy that. Let them think you're glad I'm out of the way. They may even come to suspect that you removed me.'

Gareth looked at Angharad. She was breathing heavily but silently. She returned his glance with a brief widening of her green eyes.

'And get her pregnant,' added Winterman.

Gareth was so astonished that he concocted a sneeze to mask his total bewilderment. 'What did you say?' he asked automatically, knowing that he had not misheard.

'I seem unable to father children,' said Winterman. 'Despite her acquired scepticism, Angharad has inherited through her Celtic ancestry – Welsh on her father's and Gaelic on her mother's side – a clutch of genes that will, combined with yours – Cornish father and Irish mother – produce the children who may rescue this country from the mess into which it will sink for a generation. Yes,' he suddenly glared from Gareth's face to his wife's, 'the Front will probably succeed at first. My function is to try to see to it that, if they do it, they do so without the help of the Tophetim.'

'How did you know about my ancestry?' asked Gareth.

Winterman's face became softer again. 'I know your family tree better than you do. Another hobby of mine that I'm going to have more time for, it seems.'

'What is the likely date for this coup?' asked Angharad.

'I can't be certain but I'd say the New Year.'

'And when are you planning to leave me?' Her voice was resonant with several strings of meaning.

'As I may already be under surveillance, I intend to lead them into thinking that I suspect nothing, so I'll go to school tomorrow as usual.'

They both waited for him to complete his statement but he seemed content to avoid their gaze.

'And?' prompted Angharad eventually.

'Oh, I shan't tell even you, my dear, when I'm going, or where.'

'Why not?'

'They're very good at making people talk. Best not to know.'

'But surely,' Gareth protested, seeing the sudden look of fear in Angharad's eyes, 'the Front have some very senior politicians in their ranks now – ex-Cabinet Ministers.'

'It's not the Front that I'm primarily worried about,' said Winterman. 'It's the Tophetim. Now let's try to enjoy our meal.'

During lunch Winterman explained further details of the secret financial arrangements he had been making to support Angharad in his absence. Gareth sat directly opposite her. The more he studied her face – the rather deep-sunk eyes and the slightly prominent cheekbones – the more he realised how her beauty lay not in closeness to any ideal but in her uniqueness. He had never seen another woman remotely like her. There was also about her an air of serene indifference that he found unexpectedly attractive. She combined with this the almost insolent aura of those who are always capable of doing or saying the totally astonishing thing. The thought crossed his mind as she slid the salad bowl across the table towards him. As he reached to take it he felt the warm pressure of what must be her heel against his testicles and the movement of her toes against his lower abdomen. He somehow managed to bite a radish in half without cutting his lip.

After rearranging the linen napkin across his lap, he seized her foot firmly in his left hand, thumb down the arch of her instep and fingertips digging into her sole. Responding to the pressure which was too fierce to be ticklish, she leant back in her chair and slowly clawed her fingers into her hair, pulling it tight above her tiny, neat ears. Gareth wondered how Winterman would respond if he announced that he wanted to take her to bed there and then. In the light of his astonishing declaration earlier he could hardly object. It occurred to him that Winterman might at any moment suggest it himself. The feel of her foot, the flavour of the wine, the conversation, the whole bizarre situation were exciting him so much that he did not trust himself to speak.

Then he remembered his reading of *Dark of the Moon* and his experiment with its methods. He remembered Darren Eames's face and the lad's terror which had outdone anything he had mentally planned for him. He remembered the crash helmet that he had brought with him. He looked up to see Winterman putting down his wineglass and smiling at them.

'Perhaps you could fetch me that helmet, Gareth,' he murmured. 'I want to be on my own when I examine it but Angharad will,' he paused slightly, 'keep you company.'

Gareth released her foot and stood up. He felt light-headed. The wine partly explained the sensation but he knew he was in the throes of a challenge to his orthodoxy that was making his mind reel. As he walked with exaggerated care out into the afternoon sunshine, he repressed the niggling doubt that Winterman and his wife were sitting at their table secretly laughing at the success of a carefully contrived hoax. His conviction that Winterman was essentially serious, how-ever, made him reluctant to harbour such a suspicion. As soon as he picked up the crash-helmet off the back seat of his car and felt its sinister weight between his fingertips all his doubts evaporated.

CHAPTER TWENTY-SIX

A S SOON AS HIS HANDS FELT THE WEIGHT OF THE STONE GARGOYLE FINGERWIGHT KNEW THAT HIS EFFORTS TO SECURE THE POSITION OF LIAISON officer for the Albion Front with the Tophetim had been worth all the time and effort in commitment and favour-currying. The numbing coldness of the stone and its strange mass awed him. Never what could be termed a spiritual man, he recognised with an emotion that for him came close to humility that he was on the edge of an area of experience too big to be explained by the system of belief in which he had been reared and educated. He felt an excitement and a dread and a peculiar whetting of that appetite for the occult which had after many years of dabbling and scepticism brought him to this moment.

'Was this what was used in the New Year riots?' The roof of his mouth was dry. He handed the stone figure back to the Prior with an odd reluctance that belied the relief he felt as soon as it left his grasp.

'No. This one has never been used before.' The Prior replaced it carefully, almost reverently, into a linen wrapping over which he then drew a leather pouch. 'It's the result of a transference from a gargoyle in a churchyard in Yorkshire in which three children were murdered. Several months apart, I may add. The boy responsible for the murders was never caught. He went "missing'. Hundreds of young people aged sixteen do. The Police are still looking for him in the King's Cross area. He was actually in one of our houses in Lincolnshire all the time. Until fairly recently that is.'

'Where is he now?'

'About ten feet under the mud of the Wash. He was too unintelligent to respond to the training but clever enough to be able to remember too much about us.' He shook his head as if in regret and then his tone grew suddenly brisker. 'I do hope, Mr. Fingerwight, that you will be able to follow the procedures exactly. Precision is of vital importance in these matters. Contrary to popular impressions, the occult is very far from being a vague art practised by aery-faery vegetarians who wear beads and sandals: it is an exact, and exacting, science.'

He handed him a piece of pasteboard inside a polythene sleeve about the size of a postcard. 'It is only necessary to whisper or murmur the words. At whatever volume you speak, however, you must intend them to be effective. Do you think you will be able to do that? You'll be wasting your time, if you can't. Intention is everything.'

Fingerwight began reading aloud to himself the words on the card.

'Just read them silently now!' said the Prior, his voice suddenly rising and becoming tight with anxiety. 'Read them as if they were cooking instructions on a packet of soup, to gain information.'

'You mean I mustn't read them, now, as if I were giving instructions?'

'Precisely.'

'How important is the form of words?'

'Immensely.' The Prior smiled and then broke into a chuckle. 'Forgive me – I was just recalling the English of the church service I attended earlier. Many people nowadays who ought to know best about the importance of the form of words seem to have lost, or deliberately abandoned, their belief in its power. But more important even than the proper words in the proper places is, as I said, the proper intention of the speaker. I ask you again – will you be able to summon up the required intensity of intention?'

Fingerwight looked at the card again and rubbed the edge of his index finger along the throat-line of his beard. 'I think so.'

'You must be more certain than that. I think I should ask one of my subordinates to accompany you.'

'Won't the Head of the school think it odd my having an assistant? Advisers usually operate singly. He knows me. Will your man be able to pass as an educational administrator?'

'The man I have in mind is very resourceful. Sufficiently so, I'm sure, to pass himself off as an ex-teacher. After all, he has only to get himself into the building. Once the sprite is out, no-one is going to be worrying about a human visitor's qualifications.'

'What will happen?'

'Impossible to say with certainty. But it'll be something you'll never forget. I advise you to stand near a doorway and move as soon as possible to a position from which you can observe, unobserved.'

CHAPTER TWENTY-SEVEN

THE YOUNG DOCTOR PEEPED IN THROUGH THE OBSERVATION PANEL IN THE DOOR OF THE WARD AND THEN TURNED TO THE WOMAN BESIDE HIM. HE gestured to her to approach the door. As she looked in at the two beds and their supine occupants his eyes roved slyly over her figure as she stretched up slightly towards the glass. She seemed to him on this closer examination to be in her early to mid thirties though her clothing was more that of a casually but fashionably dressed teenager. He realised that she must have borne her sons very young. He glanced at the record-card in his hand.

'You may go in by all means, Mrs Eames, but they are both under heavy sedation. We've put them together partly because they're brothers and it will help you with the visiting and partly because,' he paused and cleared his throat, 'they seem to show exactly the same symptoms.'

'What is the matter with them, duck?'

She shifted her seven stone back onto her high heels and smoothed the seam of her jeans from her hips down to her mid thighs. Her accent suggested to him that there was little point in giving any explanation which involved using too many words of more than two syllables.

'We're not sure. We've done tests. There doesn't seem to be anything phys-, anything wrong with their bodies. Heart beat fine, though a bit slow. The trouble comes when they regain consci-, when they come round, as they do from time to time.' He paused and watched her worried face as it nodded at him. 'Then they show all the signs of . . . fright. A fear so strong that the only escape from it seems to be back into the coma. Most puzzling. And they complain of severe headaches.'

'Darren often gets migraine! Do you reckon it could be that, duck? He eats a lot of chips, you know. I tell him they're bad for him but you can't make them listen, can you? Do you reckon it could be that – too much chips?'

'I hardly think so, Mrs Eames – '

' – or chocolate. Jason's always been a bad 'un for chocolate. They do say chocolate's bad for migraines, don't they? His dad was bad for it as well, come to think. Do you reckon they've got something from him?'

'I really couldn't comment. Will Mr Eames be visiting, by the way?'

'You must be bloody joking, duck!' she laughed harshly. 'He's in Berwick-on-Tweed, isn't he? We never see him.'

'I'm sorry. I wasn't aware . . . '

'Don't feel sorry. I'm not!'

'Has he been gone long? I mean, can he be contacted, if – '

'Oh, God, he's been gone over two years, duck! Went off with an eighteen-year-old. Well, she'll be twenty now.'

'I'm sorry,' said the doctor again, looking back down the

corridor in the hope of seeing a nurse with whom he could strike up a more medical conversation.

'Yeah!' growled Mrs Eames, nudging him in the arm to regain his attention. 'I found him with her on the rug in front of the fire when I came back early the night they had to cancel the Bingo. Only night they've ever had to call it off. She used to be Jason's girlfriend an' all. Little tart!'

The doctor was uncertain whether to smile or frown.

'Do you reckon that could have caused my eczema?'

'I'm sorry? Ah, Nurse! A moment, please.'

'My eczema. Finding them like that. The shock of it, I mean.'

'That's something you should discuss with your G P, Mrs Eames. Now, if you'll excuse me, I have other patients to see. You can visit, remember, at any time.'

He left abruptly, gesturing backwards at her through his stomach to the nurse and raising one eyebrow.

Mrs Eames sat down slowly on the wooden bench that ran along a recess in the corridor wall. She stared in front of her, seeing yet not seeing the nurse's narrow waist. She was remembering how she had paused at the living-room door and looked through the crack between the hinges, resting her forehead against the sharp edge of the wood. Mandy had been a skinny little slip of a thing, flat-chested but pretty, with long thin thighs. They were wrapped around his thick waist and he was going at her so hard it was no wonder she was making so much noise that they had neither of them heard her coming in. She reckoned they couldn't have heard Darren either. It had only been when she had seen him on his knees, peering around an armchair that she had run in, shouting and kicking herself . . .'

CHAPTER TWENTY-EIGHT

W HEN GARETH RETURNED, HOLDING THE HELMET
BY ITS CHIN-STRAP, HE FOUND ANGHARAD ALONE
AT THE TABLE. SHE WAS ALREADY LOOKING AT
him so fiercely that he bumped into the table edge as he paced
towards her.

'Where's Sidney?'

'Preparing to examine that. He said to leave it on the
table.'

He set the helmet down carefully as though it might
scratch the varnished pine.

'I don't know what to say,' he began. He unbuttoned
his shirt collar and revolved his chin. 'Your husband's some
character!' He tried to chuckle but the noise came out as a
clearing of the throat.

She stood up and tossed her hair back. 'You'd better wash
your hands after touching that.' She nodded at the kitchen
sink. 'I'll be in the bedroom opposite the head of the stairs.'

Unable to speak, he watched her saunter out of the room
with one backward glance at him as she reached the door.
Her eye contact was broken by a slow downward glance over
his body to his feet. After drying his hands on a small green

towel that lay on the draining-board, he followed her. At the door he paused to look back at the helmet. The house was very still. He thought he could hear the faint throbbing whine as of a distant electric drill. He could not locate the source of the noise but, as he continued to stand in the doorway, he became more convinced that it was emanating from the helmet. He dismissed the thought and allowed his mind to brim full with images of what Angharad was doing above him, and what she was going to do.

He swayed slightly and put finger and thumb to the bridge of his nose. Part of him was telling himself to walk out now and drive away. More of him was propelling his feet towards the staircase. After all, Winterman had virtually instructed him to make love to her. He paused at the foot of the stairs. That was the trouble. Until now his women had always been unattached. This was different. And yet, how much of a marriage could it be? Was Winterman impotent? Was their desire for a child the explanation of their conduct? He started climbing the stairs, concentrating on the brown and green patterns of the carpet. At each step he felt his pulse quicken. At the top he was almost breathless. In the bedroom doorway he stopped breathing altogether for a moment and leant his forehead against the gleaming white paintwork.

He saw Angharad before taking in anything else. She was lying on her side on a large pine four poster bed that faced the door. The sunlight flooding in from the open casement window to his left enhanced the milky whiteness of her naked flesh. He noticed next, as if by contrast, the almost excessive greenness the room: carpet, wallpaper, curtains – all different shades of green, the silk bedspread the darkest.

The only other colour was the tawny pine of the built-in, louvred wardrobe that ran the length of the wall on his right.

'Shut the door.'

He pushed it to behind him and exhaled.

'There's a bolt. We don't want to be disturbed.'

He twisted back without moving his feet and slid it home. It was of brass and he was not sure whether it was the sight and feel of its easy movement which made him lightheaded or the perfume he was inhaling.

'I have to know something.' He moved to the foot of the bed, gripping one of the posts with both hands and leaning his forehead against its smoothly turned wood. 'Are you doing this for yourself, or for Sidney, or for me?'

'Can't it be for all three of us?'

'Would you be doing it if he didn't know?'

'Take your clothes off and I'll tell you.'

'I'd have preferred it if you'd let me undress you.'

'As you did in your caravan? You ripped my underclothes so badly that I've had to throw them away.' Her eyes widened in mock reproach.

'Sorry.'

She sighed and rolled up onto her knees. From behind a pillow she tugged out a pair of striped cotton pyjamas. As soon as she pulled on the jacket Gareth realised they must be Winterman's. The thought excited him so much that he almost overbalanced as he pulled his trousers down. As he tugged off his shirt, she squirmed about on her back, thrusting her rather heavy hockey-player's legs into her husband's pyjama trousers. She fell back into the pillows, laughing, and lifted up first one leg and then the other. About nine inches of cloth hung limply from her hidden feet. She was tying the waist sash into a bow when he came to lie naked alongside her. She pointed her arms up at the ceiling and waited for the sleeves to crumple down to her elbows before taking his face in her hands.

He looked down at her from where he had propped himself up on one taut arm the better to take in the full length of her body. It was the sort he liked best: even under the folds of the loose cotton the curves of her breasts, hips and thighs inflamed him as did the heat of her skin through the thin cloth under his swooping hand. His fingertips found the core of her warmth as he slid his hand through Winterman's flies.

As in his caravan, he covered her swiftly and entered and filled her wet readiness with a greedy lunge. She started whispering in his ear as he started to move.

'Gareth, I feel . . . fertile.'

'If that's what you want.'

'That . . . And this . . . Plough me!'

He increased the violence of his thrusting, expecting her to cry out that he was hurting her but she kept on rhythmically repeating 'Plough me!' in his ear until she was shouting the words and slapping the small of his back with the palms of her hands in time with her squeals. Twisting his head on the pillow he saw the short, rapid movements of his penetration reflected in the dressing-table mirror being gradually eclipsed by Angharad's cotton-clad thighs as she raised and spread her knees to receive him more deeply. He knew that what was giving him almost as much pleasure as her glowing softness beneath and around him was the knowledge that she was making so much noise that, wherever he was in the house, Winterman must hear her.

CHAPTER TWENTY-NINE

SIDNEY SET THE CRASH-HELMET ON A SQUARE OF WHITE LINEN SPREAD IN THE EXACT CENTRE OF A SMALL PINE TABLE NEAR HIS DESK. HE PULLED UP A STRAIGHT-backed chair and set it to face the back of the helmet. Before sitting down, he paced unhurriedly round the table, looking at the red plastic from all angles, humming to himself. When he drew level with the visor for the third time he slowly stretched out his left hand and reached his stiffened fingers, thumb extended upwards, under the brow-piece. He sucked in his breath through the corners of his mouth and snatched back his hand. Placing his hand flat on the linen, he slid it forward again between the cheek-pieces. This time he left it there a few seconds longer but removed it again rapidly. He moved on round to sit on the chair and began massaging his beard with his right hand.

Placing his elbows on the edge of the table, he joined his hands, as if in prayer, and inclined his head until his deepening frown touched his knuckles. He remained in that position, with his eyes closed, in silence for about five minutes. When he opened his eyes, they were bright and his forehead was smooth.

He crossed to his desk and punched a number on a trim-
phone. Waiting, he stared up at the pine-boarded ceiling and
listened to the faint but rhythmic pulsing above him. 'Mark?'
he said suddenly, turning his whole attention to the voice at
the other end of the line. 'Sorry to disturb you on a Sunday
but I'll be brief. It's possible my phone is already tapped and
probable it will be soon . . . They've started. At least they've
successfully transferred the Imp . . . Yes, I have some physical
evidence here of his transitional presence. I can't be totally
certain but, if my ability to discern spirits is what it was, then
it's the Imp all right. I may have to shapeshift very soon now
at short notice so, as arranged, I'm sending Angharad to you
as soon as it becomes necessary . . . No, he'll be with her. You
can trust him; he's certainly the one. He's turned up at precisely the right time. If, from now on, I feel it's insecure to use
the telephone, we'll have to fall back on our telepathy . . . Yes,
ten o' clock . . . You know I never say goodbye.'   Breaking
the connection, he stood up, took the helmet in both hands,
tossed it up in the air to spin like a football and caught it,
crown downwards. Taking it then by the chinstrap, he went
out into the garden to where Gareth's car was parked on the
gravelled drive under a eucalyptus tree. He tossed it onto
the back seat and straightened up with a sigh of relief.

Pacing back across the lawn, thinking to himself that he
would probably never give it the final cut it needed before
winter, he paused and looked up towards the roof of his
house. Through the open window of his bedroom he heard a
familiar prolonged wail, spiralling up through three tones,
that he knew must be coming from Angharad's blushing,
stiffened throat and, blending with it, an unrestrained male
bellow of relief and release. Trying not to listen to the over-

lapping sighs of fulfilment, he forced himself to walk slowly indoors, muttering to himself: ' "And we have started too!" Winterman muttered to himself.'

CHAPTER THIRTY

'KEEP STILL, YOU YEAR TEN BOYS!' BELLOWED
WINTERMAN. 'AND QUIET!' HE CLOSED HIS EYES
BRIEFLY AND EXHALED THROUGH HIS TEETH.
Shaking his head, he expelled from his mind the imagined
picture of Gareth Burden anything but still between Angharad's legs and the memory of her filling their bedroom and
garden with her cry of satisfaction. The assembly hall was
nearly full. Only that new Technology teacher's class was to
come and he could see them now traipsing in, being shushed
at the door by a fussing Forbes.

There fell over the five hundred or so pupils that intensifying hush that he managed to achieve every morning
immediately preceding the Head's arrival on stage. In his
relatively short period as Deputy he had perfected the art of
holding the whole school still for long enough to hand it over
to the Head as totally attentive as possible. Things only went
wrong if he mistimed matters. The longer the Head took to
appear after the hush had fallen, the more difficult it became
to maintain it. He could manage it but only he knew the
expense of will-power it required. This morning he could see
the Head chatting in the entrance hall with the Gender

Adviser, Fingerwight – a man whom Winterman had always found it easy to dislike – and some other official in a three-piece suit whom he had never seen before. He snapped his fingers at a Year Seven girl he had spotted starting to pirouette vacantly in the front row below him. She stood to attention, flushing as the Head came on stage, hitching his academic gown more securely onto his narrow shoulders.

'Sorry, Sidney,' he muttered out of the corner of his mouth. 'Officialdom here in strength.' He nodded surreptitiously down towards the hall doors where Fingerwight and his companion had sidled in alongside the Year Seven form-teachers who were standing at the ends of the ranks of pupils.

Winterman smiled bleakly and went to stand at the other end of the stage near the piano while the Head proceeded to announce the morning's hymn. The Music teacher played through the first few bars, paused, smiled briefly at Winterman's equally brief appraisal of her cleavage, and began the first verse. The school joined in without conviction or enthusiasm. Winterman's eyes scanned the singing faces. A movement by the door caught his attention; Fingerwight had bent forward to shift a briefcase from between his feet. Winterman looked back from him into the ranks of Year Nine where he caught sight of a tall boy with glasses – Leonard Wright or Liam Ward or something – poking the corner of his hymnbook into the nape of the neck of the raven-haired girl in front of him. He continued to stare at him until the lad became aware that he was being observed. His face became at once grave and he began flicking his hymnbook about as at an imaginary wasp, frowning furiously.

Winterman looked away again, satisfied that the boy

would settle down. He noticed now that Fingerwight's companion was joining in the second verse of 'He Who Would Valiant Be' with the sort of gusto that a member of an amateur choral society might be expected to display, though what he was holding in his hands did not appear to be a hymnbook. The hymn ended more quietly than it had begun and the Head gripped the sides of the lectern in his bony hands. He waited for the rustle of closing hymnbooks to subside and began his address.

He had a habit of pausing for effect at the end of every phrase for a count of about three seconds, believing that this mannerism made his utterances more accessible to the resolutely bored teenagers standing in gently swaying rows beneath him. He combined this peculiarity of delivery with a Wearside accent.

'I suppose,' he began. 'That you are wondering. What I am going. To talk to you about. This morning.'

An ironic sigh of anticipation droned briefly from one of the more intelligent forms in Year Ten. Winterman raised one eyebrow as he tried to identify the exact source of the disturbance.

'I dare say. If I told you. That I had no idea. You would all be. Pretty disgusted.' He paused for an endless count of ten, nodding to himself knowingly. A ripple of something dangerously like a giggle flickered across Year Nine faces like a breeze over a cornfield. 'You expect me. Of course. To have prepared. My little talk to you. And you have. Indeed. Every right. To expect that. And I!' His voice suddenly rose to a shriek. 'Have a right. To expect. Certain things from you!' He stabbed an extended arm at the middle of the hall.

Members of staff began to exchange glances. Though he

Winterman's Company

had not been Head for very long, they could not once recall
him raising his voice. They watched fascinated, galvanised
from their usual Monday morning torpor into sharpened
attention, sensing that something rather more exciting was
about to be said.

'I have the right. To expect. Not to overhear. Foul language. On my school's corridors. I have –'

'Bollocks!'

There was a simultaneous intake of breath by the whole
school so sharp and loud that Winterman found himself
incongruously reminded of a moment in his youth during
of performance of Handel's *Messiah*. At some point in the
Hallelujah Chorus the massed choirs had sucked in air
together just like that before exploding into a sunburst of
sound. But the school held its collective breath. It was
momentarily stunned, for the voice that had yelled the devas-
tating profanity had been a teacher's. It was moreover a
teacher, they realised to their swelling excitement, who was
supposed to be Head of the Religious Education Department.
It really was Mr. Jones who had done it. Heads began craning, as one, to seek his face.

He was standing towards the front of the hall alongside
his form who were now gazing at him with a fascinated
horror that was mingled with a delicious sense of anticipation
that he might shout something else at any moment. Instead of
adding further comment, however, he was beginning to climb
up the wall-bars in nervous little spasms of clutching and
slipping. His face, as he twisted it over his shoulder to glare at
the assembled school, was very red but his expression suggested that this was not from any sense of shame. He seemed
to be experiencing great difficulty in breathing.

The Head had taken one pace backwards when the bombshell had burst upon him. His face was ashen and his knees, Winterman could see, were shaking under the hem of his gown as were his fists which were clenched so tight that the knuckles reflected the overhead strip-lights. He staggered as though a heavyweight boxer had punched him with professional expertise in his solar plexus. Turning his head towards Winterman, he mutely appealed for help to extricate him from this disaster.

Winterman realised that the best chance of retrieving the situation lay in the stunned silence continuing. He felt his anger at the helplessness of his position swelling. He knew that if he were standing within reach of Jones he would prevent him from speaking again by, if necessary, knocking him unconscious. This knowledge developed with a rapidity and intensity that surprised him into an aching desire to go down and do precisely that. As the thought set his legs in motion, some instinct made him aware that Fingerwight was watching him.

A commotion in the middle of the hall reclaimed his attention. The girl who had been pestered by the boy with the hymnbook had turned round and was apparently trying to scratch his face. The boy was moving backwards, slapping her extended arms away. Then without warning he lunged forward and punched her full on the jaw. To Winterman's astonishment the boy began kicking her semi-conscious body before it was flat on the floor. The boys on either side of him joined in. In turn they were attacked by the girl's friends.

He could hear the Head's voice somewhere to his right asking feebly what on earth was happening. 'Can't you bloody well see?' he snapped over the swell of noise that was spreading through the five hundred children. He had to suppress an urge to run over to the Head and knee him in the testicles. 'Stand still!' he bellowed instead. 'Stand still, all of you!' He was light-headed, not so much from the effort of shouting as from the realisation that a sort of dam had burst in his mind, allowing a torrent of resentment to flood out. He found himself absurdly remembering trivial incidents which he thought his magnanimity had long buried. He even felt angry again at how he had been passed over by the school governors for the Headship which they had decided to give instead to this pompous wimp who was shuddering slack-jawed beside him.

As he lowered his hand from his temples he saw that a dozen fights had broken out among the pupils. Some were between boys whom he knew were enemies and had old scores to settle but others were between knots of girls who were turning upon current rivals. The noise in the hall now resembled that made by a football crowd when the home team is pressing and it can smell a goal coming. He could hear Tomkins, the Head of Science, screaming abuse up at Jones who was now abseiling along the bars above him. Snarling back, Jones swung a suede-shoed foot and caught Tomkins under the point of his bearded jaw. His head snapped back and he fell heavily into a row of jeering boys.

The Head had advanced to the very edge of the stage and was stretching out his arms like some prophet in a Hollywood biblical epic. He broke off from this pose to lean forward to listen to what Mrs Buckfast, a Biology teacher whom he was trying to persuade to take early retirement, was earnestly shouting up at him.

It was when he saw the look on her face as she grabbed

the Head by his purple tie and yanked him off balance that Winterman realised what was happening. He recalled that the last time he had seen such an expression on a human face had been in an illustrated edition of Dante's *Divina Comme-dia*. The Head fell onto his head and did not rise from where he sprawled among wrestling Year Sevens. He would have been unable to do so even if he had remained conscious for Mrs Buckfast, with an agility that belied her fifteen stone, had hurled herself upon his back and seized him by the ears. In an apparent attempt to flatten his nose she began to pound his face down into the polished parquet flooring.

Winterman's sudden insight made him search again for Fingerwight but he and his companion were no longer standing by the door. He looked out over the seething mass below him. Almost all the pupils had now split up into punching, kicking and scratching pairs. All those that were distinctly audible, and they were the younger pupils nearer the front, were shrieking violent obscenities. Through the windows he saw adults passing by on the pavement about fifty yards away stopping to stare in through the railings. A few were edging their way uncertainly towards the main entrance. It seemed that every member of staff was struggling with a colleague or a pupil. Jones was now swinging from an exercise rope, lashing out with his feet at the heads of all who came within range.

Winterman saw Gareth Burden's Citroen pull up in the car park at almost the same moment he caught sight of Fingerwight and his friend watching him from the wings. They were standing back to back, feet together, hands clasped across the solar plexus. Any doubt he had about the cause of the mayhem vanished. He looked back to where they had been standing and saw the opened briefcase propped up against the wall.

He jumped down off the stage, landing on the balls of his feet. Using the impetus he had gained, he put his head down, hugged his arms around his chest to make himself less of a target for restraining hands and shoved his way through the Year Sevens towards the door. His bulk brought him half way there with ease but eventually the press of bodies forced him to resort to grabbing children and twisting them aside out of his path. The more they obstructed him the more violent he grew in hurling them aside. He knew what was happening to him and tried to resist the almost overwhelming urge to punch and maim anyone who opposed him. The children's blind determination to injure whoever they were fighting at that moment enabled him to work his way nearer to the briefcase. Someone tripped him when he was about four fighting pairs distant and he went down heavily on one knee. To his horror the two boys into whom he fell, momentarily separating their thrashing arms, both continued kicking at each other as though his intervening body were not there. He struggled up, his temples humming and his chest tight with an inward pain, while they continued their venomously single-minded struggle.

He caught sight of the briefcase again and grabbed its handle. As he straightened up he collided with Ms Patterson, a Year Seven tutor who taught French. He had always thought her attractively shaped though he found her florid face rather plain and her conversation tedious. He had not recommended her promotion to Head of Lower School on the grounds that he felt she lacked sparkle and rapport with the younger pupils. Somehow she had found out. She looked up at him now through the rose-tinted lenses of her owlish spectacles, smiled strangely as though reading his mind and to his dismay brought up her shapely knee with stunning accuracy into his testicles.

The glancing blow that her thigh struck the side of the briefcase lessened the full force of the attack she intended but the pain she managed to inflict made him buckle, retching, at the waist and knees. As his head came down level with her shoulders, he heard her screaming into his ear: 'You hairy, sexist pig!' Recoiling from her advance, he sensed the madness boiling up inside him. When he was able to straighten up he was going to batter this impudent little fart into a bruised mess of bone and tissue. Through his watering eyes he saw Gareth Burden in the doorway, round-mouthed in disbelief at what he was seeing. He felt the heavy briefcase slipping through his fingers but he clutched at it again and hugged it under one arm. He staggered past Ms Patterson, fetching her a sideswipe to her cheekbone with his free elbow that knocked her into the wall-bars. Above her the once more abseiling Jones obligingly stamped on her skull. Without looking back to see if she had hit the floor, Winterman tumbled past Gareth through the double doors into the entrance hall and shouted to him to follow.

'Into your car now!' he snarled. 'Just drive!'

Gareth paused by his 2 cv's door to listen in dismay to the uproar throbbing from the school hall. When he saw pupils starting to run down the main corridor he ducked into his car and started the engine. He reversed all the way out of the carpark straight out onto the main road and did not look at Winterman until he had engaged top gear. As he tugged on his safety-belt, Winterman struggled to master a persistent pain, trying to think up answers to the seething questions he knew Gareth wanted to ask. He clutched the briefcase as though it contained the proceeds of an armed robbery, eyes screwed shut, face pale, forehead damp with sweat. Gareth drove out to the roundabout on the ring-road and pulled off into the first lay-by. Switching off the engine, he waited in silence for Winterman to speak.

Winterman inhaled and held his breath for longer than he had dared since leaving the school. 'They've started,' he hissed as he exhaled. 'Sooner than I expected.' He nodded, more in confirmation to himself of a private conviction than at Gareth. 'Thank God I warned Murdoch yesterday. We must move quickly now.'

'Is it the Front?'

'And the Tophetim. The Front couldn't have achieved that result alone. You just missed a riot back there every bit as intense and nasty as the big New Year eruption. There'll be more. Bigger. Worse. And not just here.'

'I overslept,' said Gareth. 'Fortunately, I suppose. How do they do it, exactly?'

Winterman flipped back the flap of the briefcase and pulled out something wrapped in linen. He partly unfolded the cloth.

'Good God!' muttered Gareth.

' "On the contrary!" said Winterman,' said Winterman. He looked down briefly at what looked like a cross between a horned wildcat and a lizard, quickly bound up the stone figure again and thrust it back into the briefcase.

'Do you mean that's one of their petrified demons? How did you come by it?'

Winterman told him. Gareth listened solemnly.

110

'Fingerwight?' he whistled. 'Can't say I really know him that well.'

'Take my word for it, he's dangerous. They all are. I think he may have wanted me to take it.' He sighed and put the briefcase down on the rubber mat between his feet.

'Did he see me drive you off?'

'Not sure. Doubt it.'

'So he's unlikely to come looking for it at the caravan? Assuming he wants it back.'

Winterman nodded, his eyes flickering up to the left but focussing on the middle distance as he calculated rapidly. 'Yes,' he said eventually. 'He'll want it back. But we need it too. We must hide it there, or near there, for now. Can we go at once? I'll explain what you must do, as we drive.'

Before they could pull out into the traffic they had to wait for a fire-engine to shrill past on their side of the road, followed at brief intervals by three ambulances, all with blue lights flashing. They left the ring-road as soon as Gareth found the exit that led him to the country lanes in which they felt safer.

'I want you to take Angharad in tonight,' said Winterman as Gareth straightened up the steering-wheel and settled to cruising at a steady forty. 'Keep your eyes on the road! If any vehicle tries to pull up in front of us, get round it somehow, even if it means going off the road.' He pulled his safety-belt across his broad chest for the first time since he had leapt into the car. 'They'll almost certainly visit my house tonight and I don't want her there while I try to keep them out.'

'Do you want me there?'

'I'd rather you were protecting her. I've made my house

111

safe against the sort of attack they'll be able to mount – at least while I'm in it. Keep her with you in the caravan, until it's time for you both to go into hiding. I'll let you know, at the last minute, when that is and where to go.'

Gareth grunted agreement.

'But I've other preparations to make that'll keep me busy. This means I'll have to ask you to perform the other task that must be done soon.'

'You want me to come and collect her?'

'No, I'll send her to you. You mustn't be seen now at my house more than is necessary. Things have moved on since I said that you should not show too much interest in the occult.'

'*Tempora mutantur et nos mutamur in illis.*'

'I think that your knowledge of Latin will serve only to deepen your understanding of what is happening. For what you have to do, however, English will suffice.'

'And what do I have to do?'

'A service to the community which will also test the seriousness of what, up to now, has perhaps been merely a flirtation with the unseen world: I want you to exorcise the school.'

CHAPTER THIRTY-ONE

F INGERWIGHT WAITED UNTIL THE OLD MAN HAD FINISHED RANTING. HE HAD NOT IMAGINED THE PRIOR CAPABLE OF SUCH SUSTAINED ANGER. HE SAT STILL, rubbing the tender bruise under his beard. 'I understand your concern,' he purred, 'but cannot help feeling that you're overlooking what we've gained from this morning's exercise.'

' "Gained?" ' snapped the Prior, sitting down heavily.

Fingerwight raised a deprecatory palm. There was an intensity of malevolence in the old man's pale blue eyes that was almost alarming. 'Yes. Gained. The effectiveness – and therefore the repeatability – of the method of release has been corroborated, as has the virulence of the entities with which you are capable of providing us. You've not seen the evening news bulletin?'

The Prior shook his head wearily and with some exasperation as if unwilling to explain how obvious it should be that such mundane activities were far beneath him.

'The Police had to be called in eventually. The school was set on fire and has been closed until further notice. About half the pupils and staff had to be treated as outpatients. Several have been kept in hospital under observation. The Headmaster is in intensive care. Seemingly, he was severely beaten up.'

'We've known for some time, of course,' said the Prior, in what seemed to Fingerwight an attempt to regain the initiative as his normal air of calm returned, 'that such sprites have the power to increase the physical strength of those they influence, even adolescents.'

'Ah, no!' smiled Fingerwight. 'I should have said. It was a teacher who attacked the Head. The pupils were too busy beating each other or wrecking furniture and equipment throughout the building. It was a teacher too who punched me on my way out.' He touched his chin gingerly again.

The Prior nodded slowly. 'I see. I suppose I shouldn't be surprised. That sprite – indeed all of them – will seek out harboured resentment and use it.'

'An effect that has enormous political implications,' murmured Fingerwight happily. 'And there is also the confirmation that this Winterman is the interloper. I've no doubt about it now. He knew what was happening, after the initial shock. And he managed to control his own violence constructively. As did the assistant you provided me with. I'm glad he was able to instruct me how to develop an immunity.' He cleared his throat. 'Yes, it was Winterman who made off with the replica in the briefcase. I watched him.'

'You watched him?'

'And would have followed him if there hadn't been a sudden surge of pupils towards the stage and hall doors. But there's no need for concern; he'll be under surveillance from now on. When we're ready, we'll pick him up. We'll hold off for a few days until we can observe who his contacts are. Then collect the lot of them.'

'We want that replica back as soon as possible.'

'But as it's now only a replica, what's so important about it?'

'Don't you understand yet – even after witnessing the release – what we're dealing with?' The Prior began to pace up and down his conservatory. 'The sprite should have been revoked before you left. It will only return to its replica, or to the original gargoyle from which it was transferred.'

Fingerwight frowned and then asked hesitantly: 'Then where . . . ?'

'Still in the school! I suggest you use your influence at County Hall to keep it closed until we've repossessed the replica. There's surely nothing to be gained at this stage from further disruption. And you must inform us as soon as you have moved against this Winterman. He could be very dangerous to all of us.'

'A low priority meddler, surely?'

'On the contrary! His ability to escape from the riot with the replica, unharmed, suggests to me that he knows more than you think. He may even . . . ' He paused in mid-stride. 'He may even possess the knowledge to enable him to revoke the sprite himself. And release it again at his own convenience.'

'Then you regard his elimination as a matter of urgency?'

'Elimination?' The Prior looked own at his slippers. 'Not necessarily. Such a man might be more useful fighting with us rather than against us. Does he have any family?' The irony in his tone was enough to embarrass Fingerwight into a brief blush.

'I believe he married the widow of the former Head of the school. Not very long ago.

115

'Ah, Corbett! I remember. Yes, of course, a little redhead.' He sat down again, thoughtfully, his eyes flickering like a lizard's. 'My wife knows her better than I do. Seem to remember she advised her before the wedding to sell the house and buy a new one.' He paused and scratched his nose. 'But she didn't. Always a mistake, that, I think.'

CHAPTER THIRTY-TWO

'I
T WAS A MISTAKE TO GIVE HIM TIME TO PACK HIS
WIFE OFF,' SAID TEMPLE, HIS VOICE SHRILL WITH
COMPLAINT.

'I wouldn't mind at all!' growled Springfellow softly.

Temple looked across at him from where he sat behind the wheel of his Volvo and sighed.

'No,' said Springfellow again but more loudly, 'I wouldn't mind doing that myself!'

Both men looked through the windscreen of the parked car at the scene being played out in the doorway of Winterman's house. His wife was making a great show of kissing him goodbye. A taxidriver was carrying a suitcase and a travelgrip down the drive towards a waiting Sierra. Long after he had stowed the luggage in the boot, Winterman was still hugging his buxom young wife to his middle, swaying her to and fro. They finally broke apart and she tripped off towards the taxi, waving over her shoulder half way down the drive.

'Let me know how your mother is,' boomed Winterman after her. He waited until she had slid, flashing her teeth and smooth knees at the driver, onto the back seat before waving once at her and closing the front door abruptly. The bright security light stayed on.

'What do we do now?' asked Temple.

'Follow instructions.'

Temple covered his eyes with his hand when the Sierra's headlights illuminated them briefly as it turned in the road thirty yards away.

'But she might have it in one of those suitcases.'

'We were told to search the house.'

'It's not there. I can feel it's not there. Can't you?'

'Then we'll have to get him to tell us where he's put it.'

'How do you propose to do that?'

'Tell him that the taxidriver is one of ours and has just driven his very rapable little wife to a place where she'll be held – by a lot of very big men – until he tells us.'

'I think you're underestimating him. Unless he's a very stupid amateur – ' Temple broke off and pointed towards the house. 'All the lights went off. Just then, as you stopped speaking.'

The two men exchanged glances in the light of the street lamp. Springfellow consulted his wristwatch. He jerked his head to indicate that he wanted Temple to accompany him as he stepped silently out of the car. Together they walked the short distance to Winterman's front gate. After a momentary hesitation, as though each were waiting for the other, they strode up the path. Springfellow rang the doorbell.

A light came on in the hall and then an external one high up on the corner of the house. The front door opened and to their surprise they saw an old man of about seventy, almost bald, buttoning up a fawn cardigan with a shaking, blue-veined hand. They frowned at each other before Springfellow spoke first.

'Good evening,' he began. 'Is Mr Winterman at home? Could you tell him we'd like a word?'

The old man looked from one to the other, his eyes screwing up tighter behind his rimless spectacles. 'Are you Jehovah's bloody Witnesses?' he asked in a surprisingly firm voice.

'Er, no, sir,' said Temple, actually starting to laugh as the irony involved in the question momentarily distracted him. 'Most certainly not. We're friends of Mr Winterman. Perhaps you could tell him we're here. He's expecting us, you see.'

'I'm sure he is,' grunted the old man. 'But he doesn't live here. You've got the wrong house.' He jerked his head to his right. 'He lives next door.'

'We're so dreadfully sorry to have disturbed you, sir!' said Springfellow, tapping Temple on the elbow before he could reply. He flashed a bright smile at the old man, who was already starting to shut the door, and turned on his heel.

Temple followed him, twisting round several times in the drive to look back at the house in bewilderment. He felt a sickening sense of disorientation as he used to as a boy when he jumped off a rapidly spinning playground roundabout. Back on the pavement he waited till his ears stopped roaring and addressed Springfellow in a furious whisper. 'Now what? Who the hell was that? You said there were only Winterman and his wife living there.'

'That's not his house,' said Springfellow emphatically.

'Don't talk rot! I've been watching it for the last two hours, long before you arrived. We both watched him saying goodbye to his wife in the front doorway.'

'Let's try this one,' said Springfellow, refusing to argue. He began to walk up the drive of the house next door. There were lights on in the front room and the hall. Temple rang the bell, breathing deeply in an attempt to force himself to appear calm. A girl of about twelve answered it almost at once. Her left arm was in a sling and two strips of sticking plaster held a large square of lint against her forehead.

'Is Mr Winterman in?' asked Temple, his heart sinking at seeing a child but beaming down at her until his jaw muscles felt sore.

'I'm afraid you've come to the wrong house,' she said. She raised her slender right arm and pointed it importantly across her flat chest to her left. 'He lives next door.'

'Who is it, Melanie?' asked a man's voice from inside. 'There's an awful draught!'

Temple thought he noticed the Neighbourhood Watch sticker on the glass of the porch side window fractionally before Springfellow seemed to.

'Come on!' muttered Springfellow urgently, backing away.

Temple turned around to frown after him but stayed obstinately in the light from the doorway. A middle-aged man appeared beside the girl, wiping a pair of spectacles from his florid face in a controlled gesture that nevertheless hinted at repressed annoyance.

'What can I do for you?' he asked in a tone that did not sound at all helpful. 'Go and help your mother clear away,' he said to the girl.

She went without argument and with an alacrity that suggested the man was accustomed to being obeyed.

'Er, I'm a little confused,' mumbled Temple, rubbing his

face with a moist palm. The throbbing in his forehead had started again. 'I'm looking for Mr Winterman's house and I was told he lived here.'

'I distinctly heard my daughter tell you,' said the man, frowning, 'that he lives next door. Are you trying to sell double-glazing or something? Because if you are ... ' He allowed his intensifying frown to complete his sentence.

'I'm sorry to have troubled you,' said Temple, retreating and holding out a palm in a pacifying gesture. 'Our mistake. Good night.'

'Good night!' echoed the man, remaining in his doorway until Temple had rejoined Springfellow on the pavement.

'Back to the car!' hissed Springfellow under his breath.

'No!' moaned Temple. 'We've got to try the first house again now. If we don't, he's just the sort who'll call the Police.'

'Do as I say!' snapped Springfellow with sudden venom.

Temple was so taken aback by his tone that he followed him along the pavement to the Volvo. He could see Winterman's neighbour peering out at them through his venetian blinds.

'Drive off!' ordered Springfellow. 'Don't wait about. Drive off now!'

'But, our instructions ... ' protested Temple, switching on the engine.

'Inadequate. We'd get nowhere. Pull up again once you're out of this estate.'

'I knew which house it was. We both watched him standing in the doorway. He must have persuaded that old fart to join him and answer the door. That's the only possible explanation. That and the fact that this is the sort of estate where they don't like numbers on their doors. Just look at these houses!' he hissed, turning on to a main road. 'The more they look subtly different from each other, the more they are the same. Why don't we go back and insist on seeing him?'

'Because we'd be wasting our time. You were right. I've underestimated him. We're up against a magician. He's put his home under protection – by ensuring anyone trying to find it is totally disoriented. I've come across this sort of thing before. We've no chance of gaining access until after midnight at the earliest.'

'And by then he'll be gone?'

'Almost certainly. The Prior,' he added thoughtfully, 'is not going to like this.'

Temple pulled in to the kerb under the orange glare of high sodium lamps. He was sweating and his throat was prickly dry again. 'We should have followed the taxi,' he whined.

Springfellow shook his head. 'What would you do, if you were in Winterman's position? You have the replica. You know that whatever was contained in it has been released, but not revoked and bound again. You're a magician – probably of long standing and considerable skill. You know where the sprite is . . . ' He looked at the trembling Temple, his face expressionless in the glare of the lights.

'I'd try to revoke and bind it.'

'So, we'll drive to the school and wait.'

CHAPTER THIRTY-THREE

NGHARAD SET OFF ACROSS THE FIELD. THOUGH THE
NIGHT AIR WAS COOL SHE FELT HOT AND FLUSHED.
SHE REMEMBERED THE DRIVER'S EYES IN THE
mirror flickering over her, assessing, guessing, knowing. He
had seemed to know how to find Gareth's caravan, had even
asked was it the one belonging to the teacher with the 2CV.
She recalled her last visit to the caravan and its cramped bed,
and Gareth doing to her what she had found herself hoping,
the first time she had set eyes on him, he would do - stripping
her without a word once she had let him lead her by the hand
into his bedroom, mounting her as she fell backwards onto
his bed, and stabbing without foreplay and without shame
into her slippery readiness. The universe had condensed for
her then into that pool of dim light, the roar of the pressure-
lamp and the shuddering of the caravan beneath her as he
seemed to probe up closer to her pounding heart with each
thrust.

She set down her bags and thumped on the door. He
opened it at once, pulled her up the steps by both hands,
ducked down onto the grass to lift up her luggage and closed
the door on the night. The curtains were drawn to, lamps lit

and a gas fire glowing. There was a whiff of whisky. She saw the bottle of White Horse on the table and a tumbler two fingers full. The spirit was on his breath as he kissed her neck while she unbuttoned her coat. She twisted in his arms to kiss his mouth but he put an extended index finger across her opening lips.

'I have to go out soon,' he said.

'What do you want me to do?'

'I want you to stay here and, whatever you do, do not open the door until you're certain it's me back again.'

'Sidney asked me to remind you about the crash-helmet.'

'It's in this cupboard,' he said, sliding back a panel that hid a compartment under the wall seat. 'But just leave it there.'

'Is it dangerous?'

'Only if you put it on.' From the same cupboard he took out what looked to her like a doll swathed in linen. 'Has Sidney had time to tell you what happened in school this morning?'

She nodded. 'It's started, hasn't it? I've had what you might call my briefing. God!' She shook her head as if to clear her hair of water after a swim. 'I wouldn't say no to a drink of that! What are you going out to do?' She stared at the object that he was setting down on the table before starting to look for a clean glass for her. Her widened eyes suddenly narrowed. 'Sidney doesn't expect you to . . . ?'

'He spent most of this morning instructing me. As you'll recall,' he added, smiling archly as he poured her a whisky, 'he seems genuinely anxious, I'm very glad to say, for me to take over almost all of his functions.'

'Fancy being a Deputy Head, do you, then?' Her Welsh

accent surfaced as she took the drink, trying not to smile back.

He shook his head. 'To my completed career in schoolteaching!' he announced, raising his glass and almost draining it. 'It is, I suppose, as good as over. At least until this business is finished. And God knows how long that will be. Now, while you're waiting for me, you could double-check the text of *Jejune Incest* here for typing errors. Or there's a rather intriguing book there on the shelf, written by your husband.'

She reached behind her and picked up *Dark of the Moon*.

'This is by H I Emsvir,' she said, frowning.

'I know. A pen name of Sidney Winterman. He's very good, when it suits him, at hiding his identity. Work it out. I did – just before you arrived. Now,' he added, finishing his whisky, 'lock the door behind me.'

CHAPTER THIRTY-FOUR

FROM HIS BEDROOM WINDOW WINTERMAN WATCHED THE VOLVO DRIVE AWAY. HE RETURNED TO THE HOLD-ALL THAT HE HAD PUT ONTO THE BED AND SLIPPED in a few last items. He had left a space at the top of the bag to accommodate the replica of the gargoyle-sprite when Gareth returned with it. He hoped he would come before midnight; by first light the following morning at the latest he must be on his way.

He went through into the bathroom to complete the last few stages of his preparations. After clipping off most of his beard with scissors, he shaved himself smooth, taking his sideburns away well above the ear. By means of a henna-based preparation he managed to make his now greying hair closer in colour to his wife's chestnut. He thinned out his bushy eyebrows to about half their thickness, using Anghar-ad's pencil to alter further their distinctive outline. He tried on a pair of old horn-rimmed spectacles that he had last worn as a student and looked at the result in the mirror. He sighed in satisfaction at the way in which the planes of his face had already been subtly changed. While his hair was still drying he combed it forward, Roman style, over his forehead and trimmed it to a severe fringe.

After collecting and flushing down the toilet all traces of hair-clippings, he stripped off and changed into a set of clothes that in colour and fashion were extremely different from his habitual browns and greens. The dark blue suit that he pulled on, bought from an Oxfam shop, gave the impression that he was underweight. He winced at the striped shirt and ice-blue tie. The final touch restored to his features their normal ironic smirk. He leant heavily on the crutch and practised a few steps around the bedroom. It was the sort that has a bicycle-clip-like support just above the elbow and a plastic grip further down the tubular steel shaft.

A former pupil, now working for the County Hospital, had obtained it for him. Winterman had improved upon the crutch's usefulness by introducing into the end of the tube a spring-loaded metal spike about six inches long. On removing the rubber stop and releasing a catch located under the grip, this spike sprang out and, thus locked into position, became a bayonet which in a few seconds transformed the crutch into a lethal weapon.

He had chosen to disguise himself as a cripple in the belief that most people seldom look into the faces of the handicapped: they see their white sticks, their guide-dogs, their wheel chairs; they remember most vividly, he hoped, their crutches. No-one looking for an active man in his mid-fifties, he reasoned, known to be fond of taking walks in his casuals, would look twice at a cripple in city clothes. Satisfied that his disguise would serve until he had safely reached his haven, he laid the crutch on the bed, picked up the telephone extension and dialled the number of St. Cuthbert's other Deputy Head.

'Hello, Nancy. Sidney here. What news of Colin?' He listened inattentively, glancing at himself in the dressing-table mirror and smoothing his hair down in its new direction, while she twittered on about their Head Teacher's injuries. Timing his moment at a pause while she drew breath, he cut in.

'Listen, Nance old girl, I'm going to say this once. As you know, in Colin's absence I'm Acting Head. In his absence and mine you are. I'll be absent tomorrow, so the school's yours. County Offices will contact you about when we'll be able to re-open for pupils. Use your judgment. I should guess that by the time it's all made ship-shape Colin will be back. What's that . . . ? Of course you'll manage . . . I don't know when I'll be back, Nancy . . . Something, tell him, that really can't wait . . . No, a personal problem I have to attend to; Angharad's left me . . . Good luck, Nancy!'

He hung up in the middle of her astonished intake of breath. 'Boring old cow!' he muttered. Nancy lived in a world where there was no room for problems that could possibly prevent one from arriving at school at half-past eight every working day. In her thirty-five years of teaching the most cataclysmic interruption of her schedule had been a puncture in her nearside front tyre that had cause her to arrive, she once told him at length, at a quarter to nine with a wheelrim mangled beyond repair. Now, for a day or so perhaps, she could pretend she was in charge of the school to which she had dedicated her every waking thought for over a quarter of a century. At the thought of the school, he began to pace the bedroom, visualising Gareth moving in its empty darkness.

CHAPTER THIRTY-FIVE

U SING THE KEY THAT WINTERMAN HAD GIVEN HIM,
GARETH LET HIMSELF IN THROUGH A SIDE DOOR OFF
THE YARD. HE GLANCED AT HIS WRISTWATCH AND
confirmed that it was just before ten o' clock. It had taken
him five minutes to cross the playing fields from where he
had parked his car. Winterman had stressed that he should
begin the ritual of exorcism and binding on the hour. He had
been fascinated to learn that this is the time when white
magicians and spiritual healers all over the world offer up
most of their prayers, for it is then that the atmosphere of the
planet is psychically charged with maximum potential for
the success of a good enterprise.

As he walked down the low-ceilinged corridor, oppressive even in daylight, towards the hall, he felt in the almost
total darkness a profound need for whatever spiritual support
might be available. As he approached the entrance-hall
through the still pungent smell of burnt wood and paint the
sense of something waiting for his arrival grew more intense.
When he stepped out into it he saw in the light of car headlights passing on the main road the double swing-doors into
the assembly hall standing open, one inward, one outward,

like a shattered valve. He had to stand still and breathe deeply to master a sudden desire to use the master key that he was still clasping in his fist across the roots of his clenched fingers to open the front doors and run. He looked outwards towards the sane normality of the vehicles on the road. Winterman's Peugeot, still parked outside, looked as inviting as a bathtub of hot water after a long, blistering tramp. Winterman had already given him a set of its keys. To drive off in it now to a quiet pub would be so easy. He could ring up from there and say that he felt that the school was being watched. He could even return with the replica and announce that he had performed the ritual, when in fact he had not . . .

Although he was standing only about ten yards from its doors, it took him almost two minutes to enter the hall. He recalled feeling this sort of leg-weariness as he climbed the final few yards to the cairn on the summit of Snowdon last Easter. He had to breathe through his mouth and his vest was itchy with cooling sweat. Checking his watch again, he saw that it was just gone ten. He clenched his teeth, put down his head as if against a gale and shouldered his way into the hall. When he was five strides in he pulled up and tightened his grip on the figure now locked under his left armpit, crushing with it the urge to flee that almost overwhelmed him again.

He unwrapped the stone figure and moved into the centre of the hall. He set it down on the parquet floor and stood back a yard from it. He kept turning round to look into the four corners of the hall, unable to shake off the sensation that someone was edging up behind him about to tap him on the nape of his neck. Memories of childhood nightmares flickered across his mind: suits of armour that reached down into your bed to embrace you to death; old women with pointed teeth who slid under the sheets with you and bit your throat just under the angle of your jawbone; spiders big enough to have faces like stoats . . .

'Unclean spirit!' he yelled. 'In the name of Gabriel I summon you; . . . in the name of Michael I command you; . . . in the name of Raphael I bind you; . . . in the name of Uriel I keep you. Depart now from this place and come to the stone prepared for you!'

He remembered to stand still, erect, heels together, head bowed, elbows close to his ribs, hands clasped, fingers interlocked, eyes shut. Drawing a deep slow breath, he began the last phrase, the final syllable of which he would draw out into a steady reverberating hum for as long as he had breath in his lungs: 'I ask this in the name of Jesus the Nazareeee . . . '

In the caravan he had managed, after practice, to hold the note for forty-five seconds. Here, with something very near terror constricting his chest, he felt he had achieved thirty.

' . . . eeeene!' he gasped, sucking in the damp air of the hall which still stank of smoke, sweat, dust and polish. He opened his eyes and stared at the replica. Was it his excitement or had it indeed briefly glowed? Was it still glowing now? He stepped closer to it and saw that it really was shining with a now intense creamy-white light. He felt dazed and stupid and then as his head cleared he simultaneously realised that the light was from the beam of a powerful torch and that the noise he could hear was glass shattering.

He turned towards the windows on the side of the hall furthest from the main road. More glass was shattered and he thought he could make out the shape of a man behind the torch. Unsure whether he had succeeded, he snatched up the replica and with its linen shroud trailing from his shoulder ran for the doors and the dark corridor.

He heard a curse behind him, more tinkling of glass and the sound of something very physical dropping heavily to the wooden floor. He was about twenty yards down the main corridor when he saw another flashlight fifty yards off and coming towards him. He slithered on the tiled floor and turned up the staircase to the English rooms. At the head of the stairs was the small stockroom. Transferring the replica to his left hand, he dropped the master key in his haste, knelt and swept it up again almost before it hit the floor and fumbled it into the lock. He sucked air deep into his lungs as the door opened. He was about to close and lock the door behind him when an idea flickered across his mind like the pleasure of an unexpected gift.

He stood still and listened. He heard firedoors banging halfway along the corridor and sharp voices. There were at least two pursuers – Albion Front, or Tophetim, or both? They had met outside the Graphic Design room and realised he must have turned off the main corridor. He thrust the replica onto a shelf alongside ancient unread copies of *Prester John* and stepped out onto the landing. Swiftly but silently he unlocked the glass-panelled door of the nearest English room. He strode across the room to the windows that overlooked the front lawns and main road and yanked open the catch of one of them. Then he ran back, catching his thigh a painful knock on the edge of a desk. He left the door ajar and had reached the stockroom again when he heard footsteps racing up the stairs.

He slid behind the door, closing it noiselessly. He was breathing deeply but silently through his mouth. He locked the door and turned at once to the window which looked out onto the flat roof over the boys' toilets and cloakroom. As he eased it open he heard the handle of the stockroom being tried. Then there was a grunt and a cry from further away. He heard the door of the English room being flung wide and feet crashing in.

The window was small and was going to be difficult to squeeze through even without the replica in his hands. He could still hear his pursuers crashing about in the classroom and exchanging orders as they discovered the opened window. He tugged off his waxed cotton jacket, slid the replica into its poacher's pocket, rolled the coat tightly into a cylinder and dropped it from his fully extended arm the short distance to the bitumen-coated surface of the roof. Twisting around in the confined space, he wormed his way out feet first and dropped onto the roof with his feet landing either side of the jacket. As he unrolled it and pulled it back on he heard footsteps clattering down the stairs. Relying on the fact that they were assuming he had escaped over the front lawns, he swung over the edge of the roof, hanging on by the guttering. He dropped into the yard and as soon as his feet hit the tarmac started sprinting for the playing fields behind the main building.

The weight of the replica both slowed him down and confirmed that the ritual had been successful. After climbing the low perimeter fence with difficulty he peeled off his jacket and stood for a moment, slick with sweat and fighting to regain his breath, one arm heavy on the roof of his car.

He looked down the suburban road. Most of the houses were on the side opposite the playing fields. Further down there were bungalows on both sides. At this time of night most of the householders' cars were in garages or on driveways. There were three vehicles parked out in the road under the street lights: a Cavalier and a Polo outside a house with a lot of lights on at which there sounded to be a party in progress, and what looked like a B M W parked facing the main road in a relatively unlit spot between two street lamps. He squinted at it as he wiped sweat out of his eyebrows. It looked as if two men were sitting inside but at that distance they could as easily be headrests.

He unlocked the driver's door, folded up his jacket, heaved it onto the passenger seat and slid in behind the wheel, still watching the B M W During the last fifteen minutes he had astonished himself. He had not thought himself capable of such quick thinking and such calmness under pressure. As he turned the ignition key, he found himself wishing that he had already swapped cars with Winterman. Until he drew level with the B M W he kept in low gear. There were two men sitting in it, one of them smoking. He drove on and, as he braked at the junction with the main road, looked in his mirror. The B M W was accelerating away from the kerb.

CHAPTER THIRTY-SIX

'YOU LET HIM, AND HIS WIFE, GET AWAY?' HISSED THE PRIOR.

SPRINGFELLOW LOOKED AT TEMPLE BEFORE replying. 'In a sense, sir, no. It wasn't Winterman at the school.'

'Then who? Has he an accomplice? Where does this end?'

'The man we caught a glimpse of in our torchbeams was not Winterman.' He looked again at Temple for confirmation. Temple nodded. 'He was younger,' continued Springfellow. Moved very quickly. I think he knew the building, so I'm assuming he's a member of staff at the school whom Winterman has recruited.'

'Recruited? To what extent?'

'He was performing a ritual involving the replica, sir,' said Temple.

The Prior slapped the edge of his desk with such force that Springfellow was glad he had not been the one to break the news. He sneaked a glance around the study in which they were sitting. He had the feeling that not many people were interviewed in here. It was almost like being in a bed-room. There was a cloying scent as of incense or of joss-sticks.

'And we can therefore also assume,' snarled the Prior, 'that he will have taken the replica, with the sprite rebound in it, back to Winterman – who, you're sure, had protected his house with total efficacy?'

'It was as if it wasn't there, sir,' said Springfellow.

'Will this accomplice be able to gain access, then?' asked Temple, suddenly hopeful.

'Of course he will,' snapped Springfellow, delighted to administer the rebuke at what he had made to seem Temple's crassness, 'if Winterman admits him. What do you want us to do now, sir?'

The Prior pressed his fingertips against his eyebrows, flattened his palms against his cheeks and breathed deeply. He maintained the pose for so long that Springfellow glanced at Temple, inviting him to make the false step of passing comment.

'Discover who this accomplice is,' said the Prior. 'Let me know as soon as you do. But do not act against him until I have decided how you are to proceed. Is that understood?'

They both nodded, avoiding his fierce stare.

'You had better return at once to watching Winterman's house.' His tone of voice suggested that they should leave without further questions. They stood up. 'And expect to see another team of watchers. The Front have told me that they will investigate Winterman "in due course". I think that they will already be watching him. The replica would be as dangerous to us in their hands as in his now. Fingerwright knows how to release.'

Temple hesitated in the doorway of the study. 'Sir,' he

asked, 'if we have to make the choice, which is it the more important to secure – the replica or its exorcist?'

Springfellow watched the Prior carefully, hardly breathing as he began nodding and narrowing his eyes as if contemplating for the first time the value of an unexpected present. He fought to suppress a spasm of excitement as the old man said exactly what he hoped he was going to say: 'Neither. On second thoughts, if it's possible, the best prize would be Winterman's wife.'

CHAPTER THIRTY-SEVEN

"WELL DONE!" bellowed Winterman,' bellowed Winterman, taking the replica in its linen binding from Gareth and stowing it in his travel-grip. He zipped up the now tightly packed bag and lowered it onto the floor off the kitchen table. 'But you shouldn't have drunk any whisky. I should have stressed that.'

'I suppose you did, really,' said Gareth, leaning against the table and shaking his head in disbelief at the change in Winterman's appearance.

'How do you mean? There was no time for me to tell you everything I'd have liked to pass on.'

'*Dark of the Moon* mentioned your preference for a twenty-four hour fast before an exorcism – food and alcohol.'

'Did you say "your preference"?'

'I did. You are Emsvir, H I Emsvir?'

Winterman laughed. 'Good! I've chosen well. Yes, the book is mine. At the time I wrote it I had to adopt a pseudonym, for various reasons. Now it's a disguise, for obvious reasons!'

'When can we expect to see you again?'

'Can't tell you. You'll have to manage with an intermediary. Now listen, this is my last instruction and I daren't commit it to writing. When it becomes impossible to stay – and you will have to be the judge of that, though I should say it'll be sooner rather than later – you are to escape to the Isle of Mull, making sure you're not followed there. Go to my greatest friend, Dr Mark Murdoch. He'll be expecting you. He runs a hospice called Calman House just north of the village of Dervaig, though he regards his main purpose in life as being to oppose the works of the Tophetim. You can trust him with your life. And Angharad's. You'll have no option, anyway, by the time you reach him. Have you understood that, Gareth?'

'Dr Mark Murdoch, Calman House, Dervaig, Mull. And he'll be expecting Angharad as well?'

'Yes . . . You must never abandon her – do I have to tell you that?' Winterman's face and tone became so severe that Gareth flinched.

'Of course not. I had my doubts about leaving her alone tonight.'

'I doubt they've connected you with me yet. Were you followed here?'

Gareth hesitated long enough for Winterman to repeat his question with an anxiety in his voice that Gareth found disturbing. 'I'm not sure,' he admitted. 'A B M W pulled out of Eastern Avenue not far behind me. It followed me down the Skellingthorpe Road but I think I lost it in the Birchwood estate, after a bit of back-doubling.'

He paused and watched Winterman stroke his tender

chin. 'By the way,' he began rather awkwardly, 'will Murdoch regard Angharad as . . . as my wife?'

' "I'll have to let you find out the answer to that," chuckled Winterman,' said Winterman drily. 'Suffice it to say, for the moment, that he's a devout Roman Catholic. Convert. Best of the tribe. Or the worst – depending on your viewpoint.'

Gareth avoided his laughing eyes. 'Should I get back to the caravan now?' he asked.

'Not yet. I need you to give me a lift.'

'Where to?

'Manchester Airport.' He laughed aloud at Gareth's surprise.

'Where are you flying to?'

'Nowhere. I'm picking up a rented car I've booked. But if anyone follows us, I want to give the impression that I'm leaving the country.'

'Wouldn't it be an idea for Angharad and me to rent a car too? They may well be intending to follow your Peugeot's movements.'

'No!' he insisted abruptly. 'You must use my Peugeot – and nothing else – to take Angharad to Mull.' His tone and voice relaxed again as Gareth nodded in agreement. 'It's protected, you see. Like this house. Years of use and hours of – let's say charm. Not absolutely impregnable, I suppose, so drive carefully.'

Gareth sighed and began to walk about to try to dispel a sudden sensation of chilliness of the sort that usually presaged for him the onset of flu. 'I only wish you'd been able to protect my caravan as well,' he muttered.

CHAPTER THIRTY-EIGHT

'WHY ARE WE GOING THIS WAY?' ASKED TEMPLE IRRITABLY. HE WAS TIRED AND HIS HEADACHE WAS CIRCLING BEFORE TOUCHDOWN.

'To see if that taxidriver's back on the rank,' murmured Springfellow.

'Which tax- ?' began Temple, pausing to sigh at his own dullness. 'You mean you took his number?'

'But of course.' Springfellow flashed a predatory smile. 'Pull up here. We're in luck. He's parked over there. Give me five minutes while I make us even luckier.'

Through his Volvo's windscreen Temple watched him lope over to the taxi, lean an arm on its roof and begin a conversation with the driver. He shook his head slowly, wincing at the ache between his ears, and observed with disgust and admiration the ease with which the banknote changed hands. The driver spoke animatedly from behind his steering-wheel for another half minute, his hands gesturing directions through the wound-down window, his lighted cigarette zig-zagging like a butterfly under the tall street lamps. Temple also noticed the gesture he made as Springfellow turned away. It involved an encouraging raising of his fore-arm and a clenching of his fist.

Springfellow seemed excited as he slumped back into his seat. His armpits already stank of exertion but there was a new whiff of tension about him not unlike the odour in the air after an electrical short-circuit.

'Take the Sleaford road,' he drawled confidently, his grin more than ever like a shark's.

Some fifteen minutes later they pulled up just past a gate into a large meadow. Temple could see a caravan in it with one lighted window.

'She's on her own,' murmured Springfellow.

In the darkness of the lane Temple assumed that the noise he was making was caused by licking his lips and sucking. 'How do you know that?' he asked.

'Because the taxidriver told me that when he dropped her off here earlier there was a 2cv parked outside the caravan. He's seen the car before during runs he's had to make out this way. Belongs to a teacher. It's not there now.'

'And you reckon that its owner is the man who was in the school earlier?'

'Almost certainly. He's Winterman's accomplice. He'll be delivering. Then rushing back here. As I should be, if she was waiting for me. Won't he be frustrated when he finds her gone?'

'What if she won't come with us?'

'She'll come,' he scoffed. 'I want you to be searching the caravan for any evidence of his identity, or anything that ties him in with Winterman. We can sort him out later.'

'And what'll you be doing?'

Springfellow seemed to be enjoying the delay in answering. 'She's just my type!' he said, drawing out the words in the chill air. 'Small, but very, shall we say, mature.'

'You're not proposing to . . . ?' Temple gasped. 'Think of the complications!'

'If the Prior wants to "talk to" her,' sneered Springfellow, 'she's as good as dead. You know he daren't reveal his identity. As soon as we take him to her, she'll realise his involvement. No, once she's told him what he wants to know, he has to dispose of her.'

'But surely . . . ' moaned Temple.

'It's happened before,' whined Springfellow impatiently. 'He usually lets me,' he paused as if to choose his words, 'enjoy myself before doing what's necessary. Pleasure before business, you might say. He prefers so many things back to front.'

He slid out of the car and then ducked his head back under the roofline. In the dim glow of the courtesy-light his teeth seemed yellow. 'Cheer up! You can have her too, when I've finished.'

CHAPTER THIRTY-NINE

A S THEY APPROACHED THE OVERHEAD LIGHTS OF THE INTERSECTION OF THE A1 AND THE M62 WINTERMAN TWISTED ROUND TO CHECK THROUGH THE REAR window that the B M W which had followed them from Lincoln was still in position about five hundred yards behind.

'I think we can assume they'll be shadowing us till we leave the motorway,' he said. 'I doubt they'll try anything while we're on it.'

Gareth grunted in reply and concentrated on feeding the little Citroen into the fast-moving west-bound traffic. Winterman had slipped into the car in darkness, cramming an old trilby onto his head as they had driven through the estate out on to the ring road. Gareth had spotted the B M W closing on them as they reduced speed to pass through the village of Doddington. It had kept a discreet distance behind until the A1 and then he had lost it among the hundreds of headlights moving north.

He squinted back now at the glare in his mirror but soon gave up trying to identify their pursuers. There was little point in worrying until they reached Manchester Airport. Once there it would be time to start becoming anxious about the likely success of the plan that Winterman now began to propose. He kept the willing engine steadily thrumming at seventy. Winterman, once satisfied with his plan, kept up an equally steady drone of advice, with background information, about Angharad's past, her present preferences, and likely future reactions to living without him.

'How can you walk away from a woman like her?' asked Gareth.

'I'm not walking. I always knew it would come to this. You surely know what it's like to recognise a pre-imagined pattern taking shape before your eyes? I mean, you and she came together like two magnets, didn't you?'

Gareth sighed agreement.

'Good. Make the most of it. Carpe diem! It's all on the calendar.'

The signs for the airport began to loom out of the patchy fog. Gareth eased himself into a more upright sitting position, forcing himself towards a greater alertness. He dreaded the long drive back alone but feared more the possibility of being shadowed again by men who could not intend him much other than harm. He wondered how he was going to cope when Winterman had gone.

'Psalm Ninety-One,' said Winterman, interrupting his thoughts. 'You should learn it off by heart. Ideal for situations like this. I've put it on tape for you. Listen to it on the way back.' He reached into a pocket and slipped a cassette into the player under the dashboard.

Gareth found his way to the terminal entrance. Winterman tugged his travel-grip off the back seat and rested it across his knees, fiddling with the sword-crutch between them. As he pushed open the door, the B M W pulled up

146

directly behind them. Winterman stepped out and, after slamming his door, stood with his back to the cars. Gareth glanced in his mirror and felt an almost delicious sense of stillness seep over him. He changed into reverse, revved up and let in the clutch fiercely. The Citroen leapt backwards, its rear bumper over-riders smashing up into the B M W's head-lamps, shattering them.

Gareth stepped out unhurriedly and paced round the front of his car to the pavement, coming to stand by the B M W's nearside door, leaning against it as the passenger started to try to get out.

'I say!' said Gareth loudly enough to attract the attention of even more bystanders than had been drawn to the noise of the breaking glass. 'Are you all right? I really am most dread-fully sorry! Could have sworn I was in first gear.'

The driver had climbed out and, swelling his shoulders to fill out his flack-jacket, was examining his headlights. He looked up murderously from their ruin at Gareth who was continuing to obstruct the passenger. Gareth glanced over his shoulder and with a mixture of relief and regret saw Winterman's back vanishing into the terminal building. He grinned and ran back to his car.

'Aren't you going to take his number?' he heard someone shouting at the B M W's driver whom he saw in his mirror standing, arms on hips, watching him drive away.

CHAPTER FORTY

═══

SPRINGFELLOW BALANCED THE JEMMY WHICH THEY
HAD USED TO BREAK INTO THE SCHOOL ACROSS HIS PALM
AND SLID ITS TIP UNDER THE RUBBER-LINED FLANGE OF
the caravan's door just beneath the lock.

'Always slide it in gently before the rough stuff,' he
whispered.

'I can't see the point of what you intend to do!' hissed
Temple.

'There's nothing to beat it,' sighed Springfellow. 'That
moment when they give up and let you in. They all do.'

Temple snorted in disgust and stared up at the starlight.
The outline of their car was visible through a gap in the
hedge. He wished he were in it, driving away.

'Once we're in,' said Springfellow, leaning back and brac-
ing himself, 'you close the door and see it doesn't open. I'll
drop this so I'll have both hands free for her.'

'I thought you were planning to brain her with it to save
time,' sneered Temple in a furious whisper.

'You still don't understand,' chuckled Springfellow,
giving a preparatory tug on the jemmy. 'The struggle first is
half the fun!' He wrenched once and the door sprang open.

Tossing the jemmy inside in front of him, he plunged up and in. Temple followed close behind, grabbing for the edge of the door. As he fumbled it shut, he heard the woman's shriek as she recovered from the first shock. He turned to see her rising from where she sat at a small table that was heaped with sheets of paper.

She was not much taller than five foot, splendidly proportioned, if slightly plump, with a mass of coppery hair set off by the pale grey silk of a blouse with a deeply cut collar that just revealed the cleavage between her prominent breasts. As she came around the corner of the table – he wondered where she was trying to go – the curve of her hip was accentuated, as was the swell of her calf muscles when she rose on to the toes of her bare feet.

'Who are you?' she whimpered.

Without a word Springfellow hooked his fingertips under the silk of her blouse collar and ripped savagely downwards and outwards. Gripping the torn cloth, he yanked her towards him. As she staggered forward off balance, he sidestepped smartly for his bulk, caught her in an armlock around her neck with his right arm and pulled her down until her head was at his waist's height. His other gloved hand he thrust between her legs from behind, rucking up her skirt and clutching her intimately until her shock-stiffened face began to wrinkle in pain.

Throttling her with his arm and pinching her with his fingers, he propelled her towards the door of the bedroom. 'Open it!' he panted, turning his face, blotched and swollen with arousal and effort, at the astonished Temple.

He obeyed as if hypnotised, but frowning; the woman was beginning to gurgle alarmingly under the pressure of

Springfellow's forearm. They staggered through and fell together on to the divan, Springfellow heavily on top, crushing out of her what little breath she had left in her small body. He swayed up off her, releasing her neck, but using his grip between her legs to rotate her onto her back.

Temple leant against the jamb of the bedroom door, watching everything despite the disgust that was vying with excitement, his head throbbing. In the light from the living-room he looked on at Springfellow's powerful shoulders oscillating rhythmically as though in tune to a marching song as he systematically ripped off the woman's clothing. Moving to one side to let in more light, he caught a glimpse of rounded white arms writhing and the curved mass of a breast. He heard the shredding of silk and Springfellow's snorts of pleasure and moved abruptly back into the lighted room, looking back once again over his shoulder. There was a sudden pause in the flurry of limbs and he caught the insect whine of a zip. At the sight of Springfellow's pale, muscular buttocks above his sinking waistband, Temple turned away again to begin his search.

He went first to the table, riffled through the papers on it and saw to his surprise sheets of neatly typed poems. His eyes flicked up to the shelves running just above head height around the walls. Seeing nothing of interest, he dropped onto one knee and slid open the fitted cupboards under the seating. He looked down, reached in and pulled out a red crash-helmet. He stood up slowly, his eyes widening, his brain seething.

Even the young woman's continuing squeals and moans of protest could not distract him from a swift but detailed examination of the helmet. Holding it by the chin-strap, he dipped his fingers inside it, withdrawing them as if from a pan of boiling fat. He remembered having as a child some warts frozen off his fingers by the application of liquid nitrogen. The strange sensation of the chilling heat of burning ice rushed back into his consciousness. He recalled his mother comforting him as he cried afterwards on the way home. His mother had been a redhead like . . .

A louder, deeper yell from the bedroom made him spin around. The woman had managed to hurt Springfellow enough to be able to slide off the bed. She staggered as far as the door and seized its frame in both hands, about to propel herself into the living-room. What clothing remained on her was in tatters. Her breasts were heaving. Scratchmarks on her abdomen were trickling blood into her pubic hair. She swayed like a drunk in the doorway, her gaze fixed on Temple in silent appeal.

Springfellow appeared behind her, standing on one leg and kicking his trousers free from his other ankle. As he kicked, he chortled and hooked his now untrammelled hairy leg around her narrow waist. Watching his Implike stance and the greed with which he seized her breasts from behind and heaved her back up against his chest, Temple felt his stomach heave.

'What have you got there?' asked Springfellow over the woman's naked shoulder.

'Something I was not expecting to see again,' said Temple, holding up the crash-helmet, but saw at once that Springfellow's desire for Winterman's wife was too overwhelming for him to be able to think very long about anything else.

Springfellow dropped his leg to the floor and spread his feet. Temple could not look away from between the woman's bare legs: for a mad moment he imagined that from some- where Springfellow had sprouted another wrist and fist. He blinked to confirm what it was that was pointing its crimson tip at her navel. If Springfellow violated her with that as energetically as he clearly intended to by the way he now jerked her off her feet, Temple realised that this dainty little woman could be half dead before they took her to the Prior.

Springfellow's plough-horse strength tugged her back into the bedroom. Temple watched again from the doorway as they bounced together on to the mattress in a parody of a boisterous game. Springfellow's hands were clawing in her hair. He was tugging her to one side and twisting powerfully from under to mount and possess her. As she fought to draw breath to scream his bulk was suddenly, athletically, all poised above her. His knees were nudging her taut thighs apart. While one hand twisted her hair into a rope, the other was rooting under her writhing buttocks, lifting and aligning. He was grunting and snarling and ducking his head away from her clawing hands. From her determined grunts Temple imagined her trying to tighten herself as she felt Springfel- low's thick rigidity gain a brief purchase, fractionally with- draw; push harder, tug back; find the gap again, suck away; start to penetrate, recoil; invade her for a sharp, chafing inch and swell there. Her increasingly frantic writhings suggested to him that she knew she was at any moment going to weaken, slacken, open up, moisten, yield. All her resistance seemed suddenly to focus into a last cry of defiance and refusal.

It helped Temple make up his mind. He walked through into the bedroom with the crash-helmet held high in his outstretched fingers like an archbishop with a crown. Springfellow was oblivious of everything but the pleasure he was deriving from the pain and outrage of the young woman beneath him. She had squirmed as high up the bed away from him as she could but her head was now rammed up against the headboard and Springfellow's fingers were squeezing her hamstrings to force her knees up and apart.

Temple leaned over and slipped the helmet on to his frenzied partner's head. He knew what it would do but pressed down and wrestled it firm when he felt him begin to try to twist around to see what was happening. He did not have to hold it for long. Springfellow was motionless for a few seconds, whimpered once, then bellowed. Temple released him and stood back.

He looked quickly at Angharad who was watching in disbelief as the man who had seemed set to bruise the neck of her womb withdrew his hands from her knees and sat back on his haunches like a dog. Temple could not see his face from where he was standing but knew from the noise he was making that the sight of it would be terrible. Springfellow arched backwards in a spasm, as if a live electric cable had been thrust up his anus. He crashed off the bed, kicking backwards into the living-room. They watched him on his back on the floor, obscenely thrusting up at thin air, his eyes rolling at the ceiling, his gloved hands clutching at the sides of the helmet.

Temple moved alongside the woman and she flinched away from him.

'Cover yourself with this,' he said, throwing her Gareth's silk dressing-gown that he had pulled down from behind the door.

She obeyed him in dumb gratitude, while he wondered how long it would take before Springfellow stopped screaming.

'THOU SHALT NOT BE AFRAID OF THE TERROR BY NIGHT; NOR FOR THE ARROW THAT FLIETH BY DAY; NOR FOR THE PESTILENCE THAT WALKETH IN darkness; nor for the destruction that wasteth at noonday,' Winterman's voice was saying as Gareth slotted into a parking space outside the Hartshead Moor services and released his seatbelt with a yawn. 'A thousand shall fall at thy side, and ten thousand at thy right hand; but it shall not come nigh thee.' He switched off his engine and then the cassette player. 'Only with thine eyes shalt thou behold and see the reward of the wicked,' he said aloud to himself before stepping out of the car into the chill wind. He reckoned he now had the whole psalm virtually off by heart.

After a quick cup of coffee which he drank at the head of the steps to the restaurant, watching the faces of everyone who came in, and a brief refuelling during which he felt exposed and observed under the high lights, he set off again, fairly sure that no-one was following. A few reassuring glances in his mirror as he wound the Citroen up to seventy were enough to relax him. All the way from Manchester to here he had spent more time looking in his mirror than through his windscreen. He even began to feel confident enough to start mentally congratulating himself on his resourcefulness in smashing the B M W's headlights. He held the car at its maximum speed, heedless now of what such treatment might do to the engine. Winterman's old Peugeot was waiting for him, and then a long drive up to Scotland. He had decided after leaving the airport – and recalling the looks on his pursuers' faces – that it would be safer if they left as soon as possible. And after that . . .

He squirmed himself more comfortable in his seat and tried to review his position. He squeezed the steering-wheel in controlled delirium at the realisation that from being one week an unmarried, unexceptional teacher of English and Latin whose most compelling interest in life was editing a poetry magazine, he had rapidly acquired a wife, experience as an emergency exorcist and a commission in an anti-satan-ist, anti-fascist crusade. All this meant, he knew without a rag of regret, the loss of his job and the end of his career but, if Winterman were to be believed, he faced, were he to cause the opposition too much trouble, the loss of his freedom and possibly the loss of his life.

He pondered again how sincere had been Winterman's wish that he should father a child on Angharad. He wondered whether he might already have achieved that objective. He recalled the details of their last untrammelled and enthusiastically consummated coupling with such vivid-ness that he became achingly ready for the next.

The miles droned by. Vibrations numbed his perception of his weariness and heightened his feverish arousal. In a warm cocoon of anticipatory desire he slipped through the night at seventy miles an hour towards the fondly recollected curves and softnesses of a woman he wanted to possess as totally as Winterman had explained to him a demon could penetrate and cleave to stone.

He saw the glow in the sky as he turned off the Sleaford road. He stumbled out of the car towards the gatepost and leant on it, staring in incredulity and mounting panic at the flames. Despite its ferocity, he could see that the fire was past its peak. The framework of his caravan was vaguely discernible in the incandescent glow that forced him to turn his face away as he approached.

He heard the distant belling of a fire-engine. He shrank from questions, explanations. There were no answers he could give. Was she in this inferno? What had happened here? What was he to do now? His mind refused to close around the implications. He heard the fire-engine approaching. He ran back to the Citroen. Its engine was still running as he had left it when he leapt out. He decided it was wiser not to be present when they arrived. As he drove off down the lane, it occurred to him that it might even be to his advantage for as many people as possible to believe that he had perished in the fire.

The intrusive mental picture of Angharad burning to death overwhelmed him again and he slapped the steering-wheel in anguish. He suddenly knew that he loved her. But surely, however the fire had started, she could have managed to get out? Then where was she? Unless someone had come before the fire? Someone who had started it? The Front? Or the Tophetim? He heard the fire-bell stop its ringing. In his mirror he could still see the glow that now resembled a fine sunset. If it was the work of arsonists, had they done it believing him to be inside, or knowing he was not? If they wanted him dead, did they already know enough about Winterman's intentions? If they wanted him alive, what were they trying to frighten him into doing? Did they hope that, in despair, he might now lead them to Winterman?

Seeing the entrance to a bridle-path in his headlights, he slowed down and reversed into it about twenty yards so that he would not be seen in the headlights of a passing car. He switched off and sat still in the silence, trying to calm his boiling brain and decide what he must do next. Remembering what he had read in *Dark of the Moon*, he forced himself to breathe regularly and deeply as he thought about Angharad. He found he could not think of her as being dead. Encouraged, he grew increasingly confident that she was still alive. He willed her to think of him.

Suddenly, as on a screen behind his forehead, he saw her face. Her eyes were closed in concentration. He became deliciously aware that she was seeing him. A smile steadily broadened the line of her mouth but her eyes remained closed. His mental camera pulled back to reveal her lying on the double bed that she and Winterman had shared – the bed on which he had shared her with Winterman. He noticed to his surprise that she was wrapped in what seemed to be his own dressing-gown. It was as he started the engine and began to bump forward on to the road that he knew he had seen out of the corner of his mental eye the shape of a man in the bedroom doorway. Shutting his mind on the thought, he drove for Winterman's house as though the country lanes were the motorway.

CHAPTER FORTY-TWO

THE NIGHT NURSE WHO WAS RECORDING DARREN EAMES'S TEMPERATURE ON THE CHART AT THE BOTTOM OF HIS BED LOOKED UP IN ASTONISHMENT at the two brothers who had sat up together in their adjoining beds. She backed away towards the door of the side-ward and called out for the Sister to come and witness what seemed to her a miraculous simultaneous recovery from deep coma.

When the shapely young Sister arrived the two women stood in the doorway and watched the two youths staring in disbelief first around the dimly lit ward and then at each other.

'Where the hell are we?' demanded Jason. 'What's been happening?'

Wayne turned and gawped at the nurses who were now approaching them. Noticing the narrow waist and curved hips of the elder one as she came around the corner of his bed, his face slackened with sudden memory and he slumped back on to his pillows, rubbing his eyes.

Jason began to swing his long legs out from under the sheets but the younger nurse advanced on him, clucking.

'Which one of you's getting in with me, then?' he asked.

'Fetch Doctor, Nurse,' sighed the Sister brightly. 'This looks like a complete recovery!'

CHAPTER FORTY-THREE

FINGERWIGHT PUSHED THE AERIAL BACK INTO HIS MOBILE PHONE. DESPITE HIMSELF, HIS HANDS WERE STILL FAINTLY TREMBLING; MS MILLINGTON'S ANGER was effective even at a distance. He stepped out of the passenger seat and walked round to where his driver was busy fitting a spare bulb into the headlight. As Fingerwight stood over him, he looked up enquiringly while casually brushing shards of glass off the front bumper with his gloved hand.

'We're to find and eliminate at our convenience,' muttered Fingerwight, looking back into the lights of the airport terminal building, which seemed so normal and welcoming. 'They're obviously on to us, so they're a danger now. She said we can't risk waiting too long to see what they do next.'

The driver nodded in evident agreement and satisfaction. He straightened up with a grunt and dusted himself down purposefully. 'Which one first?' he asked through closed teeth.

Fingerwight went to sit in the passenger seat again. 'Since we must assume,' he drawled as the driver settled himself behind the wheel and tried the headlights, 'that Winterman has left the country – at least temporarily – we'll go after

Burden. He'll almost certainly turn up at the school when it re-opens. Teachers are so unimaginative and habit-bound. He probably reckons he's safer while he's in a public place. So there's no immediate hurry. We'll pick the best moment. It's Winterman who bothers me.'

The snarl he heard could have been the driver or the engine starting up. 'Why so worried,' asked the driver, 'if he's on his way to Canada or somewhere? If he's any sense he'll stay there. At least until Christmas. Though I suppose,' he chuckled savagely at his own irony, 'he'll be back for the New Year, if he's worked out that things will be starting then.'

'If he does that,' said Fingerwight, as they pulled out into the airport traffic and moved towards the exit, 'he'll miss everything.' He grinned as the driver twisted his close-cropped head briefly towards him. 'Keep this quiet, but Millington told me that one of the reasons she wants them out of the way sooner rather than later is that we're all set to go for it in November.'

CHAPTER FORTY-FOUR

———

GARETH SHRANK BACK INVOLUNTARILY AS WINTERMAN'S FRONT DOOR OPENED WITH A JERK AND HE SAW A MAN'S FIGURE IN THE UNLIT hallway.

'It's all right!' came a hiss. 'I'm protecting her. Come in quickly.'

The door was shut behind him noiselessly. He smelt armpit sweat and heard the man whisper: 'She's in their bedroom, resting.'

'Who are you?'

'Sam Temple. We nearly met earlier this evening at your school. It's as well we didn't.'

Gareth held himself in check again. The house was in darkness but from the light of street-lamps filtering through the lace curtains he was beginning to make out the man's features. He began to speak.

'Explanations later,' Temple interrupted. 'She seemed to be expecting you. She needs you. I'll be down here.'

Once in the unlit bedroom Gareth heard Angharad writhe on the bed and then flinch upright as he came to sit beside her. He spoke her name and they hugged each other wordlessly for a delicious moment of relief. He listened without interruption as she tearfully told him everything: the men bursting into the caravan out of the night; what one of them had done to her and what he almost did; the one called Sam Temple and the helmet . . . He waited until her shuddering had subsided.

'Do you think we can trust this Temple?' he asked.

'We must,' she said. 'He's probably in more immediate danger than we are, now he's changed sides. He'd better come with us to Mull.'

Gareth shook his head. 'It's too risky.'

'He's dead if he doesn't find somewhere to hide. And he could tell Dr. Murdoch such a lot.'

Gareth stood up and moved to the window to peer down at the street. There was no sign of movement.

'Setting fire to the caravan, with the other man's body wearing the helmet still in it, was his idea?'

'Yes. But I had time to bring out our luggage. And *Jejune Incest*.'

He gasped and came back to join her as she slipped off the bed.

'I'd forgotten all about it.' He was astonished and delighted at the renewed ferocity with which she hugged him. 'I was just crazy to know what had happened to you.' He pulled her face against his chest.

'I'm all right now. The other one . . . Believe me, he didn't . . . '

'Was he Tophetim or Front?'

'Tophetim. They were the two after you in the school, Temple told me. He's had his doubts for some time. Seeing what had happened there this morning, with children, helped him make up his mind. What the other one tried to do to me settled it for him. He thinks we must run to earth as soon as we can. Please, Gareth! The three of us should be able to make it.'

He patted her shoulder-blade, warm through the silk of his dressing-gown. 'We have to take Sidney's car. He was insistent about that. But it's still outside the school.'

'Let's all drive there together, transfer our baggage and start north. Please! I can sense them closing in.'

'Better for me to go alone and come back for you here.'

'No!' she half shouted. 'I'm not letting you leave me again.'

He waited until the protest and panic had ebbed out of her voice and breathing. 'All right, darling. We'll go together. Is everything ready?'

She nodded and stood back from him.

'What about Temple?' he asked. 'He can hardly have any luggage with him. And we can't risk waiting for him to pack a bag.'

'Do they know yet that he's defected?'

'They'll soon guess as much, I should say, when neither of them reports back and it's confirmed there's only one body in the caravan. But he'll have to be the judge of that. Come on then!'

They saw Temple's bulk at the foot of the stairs. Gareth switched on the hall light and saw from Temple's haggard and anxious face the answer to his question before he asked it. He found it difficult to believe that such an otherwise ordinary, nondescript, bland middle-aged man, whose body stank of fear, could be involved with a movement as uncompromising as the Knights Tophetim.

'I want to thank you,' he began, holding out his hand. 'I'll admit I have to trust you. I hope I'll become able not to have doubts about you.'

Temple shook his hand vigorously in evident relief. 'Mrs Winterman has told me that you have a friend in Scotland who can provide you with a refuge. An associate of her husband – on Orkney, I understand?'

Gareth started to look at Angharad but managed to turn his gaze back to Temple's red-rimmed eyes.

'I could be of invaluable assistance to them both, I can assure you. They seem to have found out what my . . . my former associates were up to. Will you, I beg of you, take me with you? I presume you must realise that you dare not stay where either the Tophetim or the Albion Front can find you? I was sent to your caravan to bring Mrs Winterman to our Prior. He would, if I'd obeyed him, be now extracting from her what he wanted before giving her over to his knights and esquires for them to do to her what Springfellow intended. After they'd finished, her body would have been dismembered and fed to the pigs on our farm – '

'For God's sake!' snapped Gareth, putting his arm around Angharad's shoulders. 'They could still reach us! Do you have to – ?'

'I do, because I want you to be quite certain what you're up against. If they try to capture us, are you ready to try to stop them? I mean, have you ever killed a man?'

'Of course I haven't!'

'Do you have a weapon of any sort?'

Gareth shook his head. Temple looked at Angharad who was checking the bags. She had pulled a long fawn raincoat over the dressing-gown.

'Is there anything here?' he asked. 'Anything at all that he could use?'

'There's a hammer among the tools under the stairs,' she said, fastening her belt. 'Please, let's go.'

'I'll follow you in my car,' said Temple, 'until we're sure we're not being tailed. Could you fetch him the hammer, please?'

While she rummaged under the stairs, he spoke to Gareth in a furious whisper. 'You must not let them take her alive. If you have to kill her – a swift blow,' he pointed to a spot just above a line between his ear and his eye, 'here.'

Gareth told him about Winterman's Peugeot. Temple nodded.

'Good!' he said in a more relaxed, normal voice. 'They won't be expecting you to go back to the school. The Prior should be starting to wonder by now where Springfellow and I are but his first move will be to send someone to check the caravan. Then I think they'll come on here. Thank you.' He hefted the two-pound hammer in his hand before passing it to Gareth. 'It would be a mistake for our cars to be found together, so you leave yours at the school while I drive on to a spot where you can pick me up.' He glanced from Gareth's face to Angharad's. 'I'm trusting you too, you see. Have you thought of a route?'

Gareth looked hard at him, trying in the short time available to gauge again the man's sincerity. 'The A1. Safer from ambush than minor roads. I managed to take Winterman to Manchester Airport on the motorway.'

'Where's he flown to?'

'Do you need to know?'

'Can we contact him?'

167

'No. We must wait till he contacts us.'

Temple sniffed, his face working, mind calculating.

'We'd better go,' said Gareth, glancing at Angharad's face. 'You know where the A 15 joins the bypass? Pull off on the north side of the roundabout and wait till we join you. Don't try to go home to pack a bag or anything like that. Do you understand?'

Gareth's tone of resumed authority hardened as he felt Angharad's grip on his forearm.

'Very well,' sighed Temple. 'There's a lot of stuff I'd like – but let's not waste any more time.'

Angharad put out the light and they carried the three travel-grips and the briefcase to Gareth's Citroen. She pulled the house door to behind her and did not look back. He reversed into the road without switching on his lights and drove off at once. At the junction with the main road he paused and looked around for other cars before putting on his headlamps.

'You feel we can trust him?' she asked.

'You told me we'd have to.'

'You're not answering my question.'

'He certainly has the opportunity now of letting them know where we'll be. Will he change his mind?'

'He daren't, after what he did to his former colleague.'

He kept peering into driveways and side-roads, con-stantly checking his mirror, beginning to wish the Citroen's engine were quieter. 'I liked the bit about Orkney.'

'That was a bit of insurance. You could still leave him waiting at the roundabout, if you're not sure.'

He whistled in admiration on a long outbreath. 'You bounce back, don't you? Are you sure you're not hurt?'

'I expect there'll be some bruises later. And my belly's scratched. By my own nails. He wore gloves. The whole time.'

He reached across and squeezed her forearm. 'You'll be able to stretch out and sleep on the back seat of the Peugeot. Leave the navigating to Temple.'

They drove the short distance remaining to the school without speaking. He parked by the locked gates of the rear entrance. Leaving the engine running, he fumbled with the padlock key on Winterman's key-ring. When he swung open the gates he was thrilled and encouraged to see that she had already slipped behind the wheel and was driving the Citroen through. He hesitated, debating whether to lock the gates behind them again or not. He decided it would be wiser, though his heart was thumping with anxiety and impatience by the time he had done it and his mind swirling with the continuous pressure of making decisions.

He jumped in beside her and directed her on around the narrow tarmac path that ran around the school. She switched off the lights without him telling her to as they approached the front car-park and they coasted up alongside the old blue 504, almost black in the light of the street-lamps. The odd car passed but no pedestrians as he transferred the bags from one boot to the other. Before he locked the Citroen, he reached back inside to extract Winterman's cassette from the player and slipped it in his pocket while Angharad started to unlock the front gates. As soon as she swung the second heavy gate back over its retaining catch, he started the Peugeot's engine on the first turn of the key. He moved through gingerly, only half engaging the unfamiliar clutch, put on the handbrake and jumped out to help her shut the gates. As he bent forward to click the padlock shut again he saw her out of the corner of his eye look up abruptly just before he heard above the noise of the engine slightly racing on half choke the scratch of another car's tyres braking to a sudden halt.

CHAPTER FORTY-FIVE

THE CLERK AT THE CAR-RENTAL DESK LOOKED UP AT THE MYOPIC FIGURE LEANING ON A CRUTCH.

'YOU DID REQUEST AN AUTOMATIC, DIDN'T YOU, sir?' she asked sweetly, consulting a form.

He nodded patiently while she scanned a computer v d u. After some key-tapping which matched the sound of his fingernails on the gleaming counter, she beamed up at him. 'No problem, Mr Emsvir. I'll have someone escort you to your vehicle right away.'

Minutes later. Winterman was driving west on the M56. As dawn was breaking he reached his cottage outside the hamlet of Pwlldefaid on the westernmost tip of the Lleyn peninsula. Before succumbing to the temptations of the thick duvet on the pine bed, he poured himself a large Lagavulin from the decanter on the Welsh dresser in the low-ceilinged living-room and, sipping at his glass, made a one handed telephone call.

'Thought I'd catch you at your dawn devotions,' he said.

'I was just about to begin the second Sorrowful Mystery,' chuckled Mark Murdoch softly.

Winterman caught what he thought might be the trickle of rosary beads against Murdoch's mouthpiece.

'I've gone to earth,' he said.

'I hope you find the extra supplies that I arranged for Bleddyn to lay in to your taste?'

'As always. The malt is excellent.'

'So early?'

'So late, for me. I've driven through the night.'

'You had to leave in haste, I presume.'

Winterman told him briefly about what had happened in the school and how Gareth had helped him escape. 'They followed us, but we shook them off.'

'You're quite sure of that?'

'Wouldn't be proposing to go to sleep, if I weren't, charmed though the cottage is. The roads round here aren't, though, and it's too easy to be pinned down on a promontory.'

'Bleddyn's been told to ring you if any vehicle starts down the road to the cottage. He misses nothing. It's good we can still talk by telephone between Wales and Mull – at least for the moment. Don't forget Bleddyn still has his pigeons, if all else fails.'

'The cottage is charming as well as charmed – a wonderful atmosphere. I'll be able to recharge here. I've important work to do.'

'When do you begin?'

'I'll wait for my disappearance to be reported and for the ripples it'll cause in the local media to subside – Deputy Headmasters are soon forgotten. You've managed to provide everything I said I'd need for the work?'

'It's all there.'

'It'll take a few days. And there's one more item I must obtain myself.'

'The silver candlesticks were the hardest to acquire. The crystal is Waterford. I hope you know what you're doing, Sidney.'

'One more glass of this Lagavulin and sleep till tomorrow morning.'

Winterman put down the receiver before his old friend could ask any more about the one thing that he still required.

CHAPTER FORTY-SIX

═══════

GARETH DID NOT KNOW WHETHER TO FEEL RELIEVED OR ANXIOUS WHEN HE SAW THE POLICEMAN WALKING TOWARDS THEM. AS HE APPROACHED AT his steady, almost casual, pace it occurred to him that there must be some supporters of the Albion Front in the Police and very probably a few active members operating under cover. The policeman – a sergeant he now saw – seemed slightly shorter than average and Gareth stiffened, feeling the hammer in the inside pocket of his jacket as he realised this might be an impersonator.

'Do you mind telling me what your business is here, sir, at this time of night?' The bland East Midlands voice was neutral, and vaguely familiar. He turned away from Gareth briefly to nod at Angharad.

'It is late, isn't it?' Gareth heard himself saying genially as he straightened up and dusted his hands and trouser thighs. 'But that's what we teachers have to put up with. I teach here, and this lady is the Deputy Head's wife. We're just back from a school trip.'

'Day trip, sir?'

'Er, no. We've been doing some Geography field work up in the Lake District.'

'So you won't have heard about the fire here earlier today?'

'Fire?' asked Angharad, moving closer to Gareth. 'Was anyone hurt?'

'There were plenty hurt, madam. But not, apparently, in the fire. Seems to have been some sort of riot. School's closed until further notice.'

'Good God!' said Gareth, rubbing his jaw in what he hoped was a convincing display of astonishment. 'I wish you'd come past ten minutes ago; I could have told our pupils not to come in tomorrow. Still, I suppose their parents will know all about it.'

'Didn't they tell you anything, sir? When they picked up their children?' The sergeant looked slowly from Gareth to Angharad.

'No,' said Gareth quickly, clearing his throat and trying, despite his sudden weariness, to think faster.

'We arrived ahead of schedule.'

The policeman said nothing but looked thoughtfully at the Peugeot.

'Most of the pupils were Upper School; they made their own way home,' continued Gareth, nodding to Angharad to get into the car. 'Now, if you don't mind, Officer, we'd like to get home too.'

The sergeant looked blankly at him for a moment and then turned to look at his striped Escort which was drawn across the front of the Peugeot.

Gareth smiled and opened the driver's door. 'For a nasty

moment there,' he laughed, 'I thought you were going to charge us with breaking and entering, or something.'

'As a matter of fact, I was,' replied the policeman.

Gareth paused in the act of sitting behind the wheel, his stomach sucking down towards his pelvis.

'Until I recognised you, Mr. Burden. We met at the New Parents' Evening at the start of term. You probably won't remember me but you teach my lad English.'

Gareth snapped his fingers. 'Of course! Daniel Perkins, 7 w. Writes amusing poems, computer buff, short blond hair, big ears.'

The policeman chuckled, trying to disguise his evident pleasure. 'Sorry to delay you, sir! Just making sure.'

'Don't apologise, Sergeant Perkins,' drawled Gareth, settling behind the wheel and suppressing the urge to scream. 'Goodnight!'

The sergeant touched the peak of his cap at Angharad and strolled to his car. They watched him in silence until he drove off and then both expelled lungfuls of air in noisy relief. She reached over and squeezed his thigh just above the knee.

'You were most convincing.'

He glanced in his mirror as they pulled away. 'He's stopped again,' he said, accelerating once he had pushed home the choke.

'So long as he's not following us,' she sighed, shrinking back into her seat and tightening the folds of her coat around the small body at which he could not resist a sideways glance. 'God, I could sleep for a week!'

At the roundabout on the by-pass he stopped long enough for Angharad to transfer to the back seat and for a very anxious Temple to jump in beside him. They were moving off when a Jaguar cruised slowly past them and appeared to be turning back towards the city. As they moved off north along Ermine Street, Angharad stretched herself out on the back seat under a rug while Temple fussed with his safety-belt. Gareth asked him to keep checking the rear window so that he could concentrate on the driving. Weariness was flushing over him now in almost delicious spasms as if he were being regularly hosed down by a jet of warm water.

'There's a fairly large car behind,' murmured Temple.

Gareth was pleased to observe that he seemed to be speaking softly so as not to disturb Angharad, whom he could hear already making the small noises of someone settling into a profound sleep. There were many questions he wanted to ask Temple but he knew they would have to wait until he felt sure that their route north was secure. 'In another mile or so,' he said, 'the old Roman road to Sturton-by-Stow joins this one at right angles. I'm going to turn off, without indicating, at the very last moment. If they stop, I think we'll know they're supposed to be tailing us.'

'And they'll then know that we know. Is it wise? Won't we be forcing their hand?'

'Yes. But I can't stand the suspense of not knowing. Besides, Winterman told me he's charmed this car.'

Temple was silent for a little longer than Gareth expected, as though his absorbing the significance of that information had involved a recalculation.

'He's also had a turbo fitted,' continued Gareth brightly, beginning, now they were at last on their way, to enjoy himself despite his tiredness. 'Whatever they're driving, they'll never be able to pass us on that road. Not until we hit the 156 to Gainsborough. But I don't think they'll try to stop us yet, not if they're Albion Front.'

'You're assuming that's who'll be after us?'

'Well, you agree that your former colleagues will still be trying to work out what happened at the caravan?'

'Yes, but they're collaborating closely with the Front now.'

'But they don't have teams of cars cruising about at night?'

'No. Though how did this one behind us know where to pick us up? Assuming that's what it's done.'

'They could have followed you and Springfellow to my caravan. And you and Angharad from there.'

'Possible. Though I noticed nothing. Did anyone follow you just now from Winterman's house to the school?'

Gareth shook his head but told him about the incident with the policeman.

'Perkins, did you say? They're closing on us.'

'Name mean anything to you?'

'There's a bell ringing, shall we say. They're moving out to overtake.'

Gareth maintained a steady sixty as the other car drew alongside, switched to high beam and swept past.

'XJ6,' said Temple. 'Couldn't see the driver clearly.'

'Two people in it,' said Gareth. 'Didn't look us over. We may have been worrying about nothing.'

'They can tail – if you see what I mean – from in front. They're probably expecting us to be heading for the M 180. I'd stick to your plan and turn off. They're slowing down a bit.'

The Jaguar was cruising about two hundred yards ahead. Gareth saw the road sign for Sturton. He knocked the gearstick into neutral, selected third gear, kept the clutch pedal depressed and let his road speed drop as he coasted towards the junction. When his speedometer read forty he let up the clutch, swung left and accelerated hard as he straightened the wheel again. He held on to third gear until the Peugeot was starting to howl before changing up to top and building up speed with a rapidity that clearly impressed the now totally still and silent Temple. When he saw the needle pass ninety he looked briefly in his mirror.

'They're reversing past the junction,' he announced. He glanced at his speedometer with a smirk of satisfaction and then again into his mirror. 'And now they've turned onto this road.' He looked over his shoulder at the dark abandoned expanse of Scampton airfield. The road ahead glowed in his headlights as straight as a runway and he had the distinct sensation that their car could at any moment take off and fly. 'I reckon we've gained almost a mile on them.'

On the back seat Angharad moaned in her sleep but did not wake up.

'Keep your eyes on the road, please!' begged Temple.

Gareth held the old car at its limit along the straight road, not even attempting to slacken speed at the crossroads with the B 1398.

'Our willingness to take risks,' he said as he heard Temple exhale deeply once they were safely over the junction, 'in our desire to avoid being caught is greater than their willingness to take risks in their desire to keep up with us. That gives us the edge we need.'

He slackened speed only slightly as they thrashed through a sleeping Sturton-by-Stow and plunged on along the straight towards Marton. The lights of the Jaguar remained about a mile behind. Just before they coasted up to the junction Gareth switched off all his lights. Temple gasped in surprise but Gareth accelerated away smoothly in the faint moonlight after turning left and south.

'Why this way?' asked Temple, as Gareth switched the lights back on to high beam and engaged top gear.

'They'll not be expecting us to turn back south. I'm going down as far as Newton-on-Trent, over the toll bridge and on to the A1. Even if they work out which way we've gone and catch us up, once we're on that, in traffic, they'll not be able to do much except follow.'

'But we'll have to sleep some time,' yawned Temple. 'You've driven to Manchester and back already; you must be dangerously exhausted.'

'But also exhilarated by danger. Any ideas?'

'Yes. It'll mean a diversion but, if we share the driving – and I suggest I take over soon – we should be able to make the Lakes in about four hours. I've a holiday cottage near Loweswater. It's not let at the moment.'

Gareth remembered that Temple believed they were heading for Orkney. His relief at the thought of a secure bolt-hole not far off his intended route to Oban almost made him admit their destination but he checked himself.

'Sounds wonderful!' he sighed. 'I can manage as far as Scotch Corner. You can take over from there.'

Apart from stopping to take on petrol and to change drivers they drove at a steady seventy through the night. Gareth woke, stiff-necked in his seat, to see first light glowing on Derwent Water as they dropped down into Keswick. Temple took the Peugeot briskly over the Whinlatter Pass and by a bewildering series of lanes until he pulled off up a wooded drive. The house was dark under pines and yews but to the south Crummock Water glimmered. As they unloaded the car they could hear rooks clattering and a neighbouring dog a field away giving notice of their arrival.

He wearily took in an impression of red carpets, wooden ceilings, lots of wall-lights and a faint smell of damp while Temple went to switch on the oil-fired central heating. The boiler's roar was faintly audible in the double bedroom to which he led them.

'Some of my married guests complain that the mattress is too soft,' he said before wishing them a good sleep.

There was a bathroom en suite and while Angharad used it Gareth stripped to his vest and confirmed that Temple's guests were right. He felt so weary that he turned onto his side under the duvet and surprised himself hoping the Angharad might do the same.

He drifted back into consciousness to feel her arms around his waist and her lips warm under his ear. He twisted around languidly and spread his legs. She rolled between them, her hands prodding at the still taut muscles of his shoulders and upper chest.

'I don't think we're going to be able to do this in Dr Murdoch's house,' he murmured.

Her hips paused in their slow exploratory grinding and she pulled her mouth away from his neck. 'Are you serious?' She started moving again.

'Perfectly,' he said.

'How's that?' she whispered, quickening the pace of her hips gradually but very perceptibly.

'Perfect.'

'Can we stay here a few days?'

'As long as you want. Don't stop.'

Nor did she, until she felt him some ten minutes later pull her down closer against him and then grow limp around and inside her and fall asleep so quickly that she thought for a crazy, wild moment that he had died of a heart attack, just as Corbett, her sixty year old first husband, had done one morning in the excitement of mounting her for the third time since taking her to bed early the night before.

She rolled onto her narrow back in the snug dimness and surrendered herself to the pleasure of settling to sleep as October daylight grew brighter behind the thick muslin curtains. She looked forward to being woken by his comfortable weight – so much lighter than the oppressive sixteen stone of Corbett – even if not as satisfying yet as Sidney's demanding bulk. Closing her eyes, she massaged the skin above her secret hair where she was sure the cells of their baby were already exponentially dividing.

'Grow safe, little body,' she murmured, 'grow strong . . .'

CHAPTER FORTY-SEVEN

'THE BODY OF CHRIST!' SAID THE PRIEST, PLACING THE HOST ON WINTERMAN'S PALM.

'AMEN!' HE RESPONDED, SO LOUDLY THAT AN alter boy, with hair as red as Angharad's, day-dreaming in the sanctuary looked up startled from his thoughts as if he had been rebuked.

Winterman covered the host on his left palm with the fingers of his right hand and stood to one side to make way for the next communicant. Instead of consuming the wafer, he closed his left hand around it and raised his empty right hand to his lips. Facing the tabernacle behind the altar, he crossed himself emphatically and returned to his pew. While kneeling next to the wall, he carefully slid the consecrated wafer into a small box that had once contained some cuff-links which Angharad had bought him soon after he proposed to her a few weeks after Corbett's funeral. The sharp snap of its shutting lid briefly attracted the attention of the old woman in a black lace mantilla who resumed her place at the end of the pew. He smiled back at her brightly. She returned his greeting shyly as if, he hoped, casually wondering for a moment who the red-headed stranger might be and what business or pleasure had brought him here to Pwllheli for a weekday Mass at the very end of the tourist season.

During the drive back to the Lleyn cottage Winterman felt his excitement mounting: now he had everything he needed except perhaps, he thought, the courage to dare. He had to keep reminding himself to check his mirror for any car that might be tailing him. The late October sunshine that was making a Mediterranean out of the Irish sea lifted his spirits but he was sticky with sweat from an inner heat by the time he pulled up outside his retreat.

He locked all the doors and went up to the workshop whose dormer window peeped out towards Bardsey Island. Removing the water-colour of Aberdaron, he unlocked the wall-safe set into the granite blocks of the north gable and removed the linen-wrapped bundle. He set it down on the pine table alongside the small box that he had been carefully constructing since his arrival. As he remembered how he had melted down the silver altar-candlesticks to provide the backing for the four mirrors, he smiled in satisfaction. Lifting the hinged lid of the box, he looked inside and saw his unfamiliar face reflected back at him perfectly. He unwound the linen from the small stone figure. Moving unhurriedly and with precise, painstaking movements, he began to bind up the gargoyle again in the long bandage that he had fashioned from an altar-cloth. He wound the cloth tightly until the figure became a cocoon with only a small, lozenge-shaped area on its abdomen left bare. He arranged the folds so that it would fit snug and flush into the box prepared for it, packed firmly enough not to move. The foot or so not required he cut off with scissors. Closing the lid, he reached for the brass screws. He worked them down into their predrilled holes with his fingertips before tightening up with a screwdriver. Pausing, he dried his sweating forehead with the remnant of altar-cloth.

In the centre of the lid he had drilled a hole about the diameter of ten-pence coin. A threaded brass collar had been fitted into it. He removed the cuff-link box from his pocket. He made the sign of the cross slowly, from forehead to navel, from shoulder to shoulder. He opened the box and stared down at the pale white disc. In the silence of the room he could hear a pulse thumping in his left temple and waves breaking on the shore. He closed his eyes briefly but even before he opened them his hand was moving towards the silver cylinder about the size of four ten-pence coins placed on top of each other.

With a pair of tweezers he picked up the wafer and laid it on a small block of wood. Using a thick sewing-machine needle, he pierced a hole through its exact centre. The day before, he had cut a thin aperture into the cylinder. Into this he slotted the host, exhaling slowly as he watched it disappear completely, apart from the thin white line of its rim. With the aid of a two-pronged fork that he fitted into two small sockets in its face he then screwed the cylinder tightly into place in the lid of the box. Stepping back, he leaned straight-armed against the edge of the table and sighed down at the object that now resembled a cigar-box that some young photography enthusiast had converted into a simple camera. The small hole in the cylinder's centre winked at him in the sunlight through the window.

CHAPTER FORTY-EIGHT

THE PRIOR'S DOG SLUMPED AT ITS MASTER'S SLIPPERED FEET AND CURLED ITS LIP AT FINGERWIGHT WHO WAS SITTING IN THE CHAIR OPPOSITE, SUPPRESSING a yawn with the back of one hand while fiddling with a sherry-glass in the other.

'Is there any real doubt in your mind?' asked the Prior.

Fingerwight shook his head. 'From what we've been told by a fireman – who's one of our members – they found the remains of only one body in the caravan. Male. Then, by a piece of luck, a policeman – who's one of our unofficial members – on routine patrol came across Burden with Winterman's wife. A car was put on to them. It reported that they picked up a man at the roundabout on the Brigg road. He wasn't hitch-hiking. Our contacts in the Police have since reported that a car found abandoned near the roundabout belongs to your man Temple.' He paused and coughed. 'But, somewhere near Gainsborough, they managed to, er, shake off the tail I put onto them. I'm afraid we've nothing to show for a very late night – lost all three of them.'

'For the moment,' drawled the Prior.

Fingerwight stopped sipping his sherry and looked at him sharply.

'Temple's commitment to us, we knew, was uncertain. That is why we have been testing him so hard. But he could become one of our best. I trained him personally.'

'You mean he's assisting them to escape only in order to discover where they're going, and who's behind them?'

The Prior smiled. 'Oh, at the moment he no doubt firmly believes that he has joined them against us. But when the time comes, he will resume his allegiance.'

'You seem very sure of that.'

'When I trained him, I put him under very deep hypnosis.' The Prior sniffed his sherry complacently. 'He's a divided man but, when he hears the call, he'll integrate and return.'

'But how will he hear the call?'

'We can summon our own.'

'Are you intending to,' Fingerwight paused fractionally, ' "summon" him before November?'

The Prior's eyes narrowed; he did not like the sound of the inverted commas that Fingerwight's voice had put around his chosen verb. He did not, come to that, like anything at all very much about Fingerwight. 'If it looks,' he continued smoothly, 'as if these unexpected adversaries that we are encountering are going to move against us before that date, then yes. In the mean time, we see great advantage in his remaining with them. We have to think of what life will be like after the coup. We shall, of course, want to identify and then eradicate all traces of resistance.'

Fingerwight nodded, apparently appeased. 'You know your man. I only hope you've not miscalculated.

He finished his sherry and set his glass down beside a pelargonium in an orange plastic pot. 'So warm and peaceful in here, for October! No-one watching us would ever guess what we have been discussing. That is what I find most stimulating about this whole venture!'

CHAPTER FORTY-NINE

'RESTFUL AS IT'S BEEN HERE FOR THE LAST TWENTY-FOUR HOURS,' SAID GARETH, POURING FROM THE TEAPOT, 'I WANT TO MOVE ON TONIGHT, AFTER A good meal to set us up.' He strolled to the window and looked out at the slopes of the mountains swooping down to the lake that was molten steel now in the afternoon light. His legs ached pleasantly after the walk on the fells with Angharad.

'How long do you think it will take us to Thurso?' Temple looked up through the steam off his mug of tea.

'We were never going to Orkney, Sam,' said Gareth. 'Sorry. Just a little deception – until we were completely sure of you.'

Temple looked away from him at the mountains. 'I understand.'

'You must realise how difficult it has been for us,' persisted Gareth.

Temple attempted a weak smile.

'If it makes you feel better,' continued Gareth, 'I can tell you now: we're going to Mull. But not from Oban. I'm driving round to Lochaline. There's only one road in to the ferry

189

and we can be more certain we're not being followed. It's a short crossing to Fishnish. No need for bookings, or names on forms, or car registration numbers, or any of the sort of specifics we want to avoid.'

'What's our route from here?' He checked himself and grinned. 'I'm just interested. If you feel able to tell me . . .'

'Back on to M 6, A 74 up to Glasgow, across to Stirling, Glencoe, Corran ferry over to the Morvern.'

'Long way round!'

'Often the safest. About six hours, from here to the Lochaline ferry.'

'And after that?'

Gareth avoided his glance and sipped his cooling tea. 'Not long. We should qualify for a late breakfast.'

'But will I be welcome?'

'I know next to nothing about our host. Don't worry. I'll explain, as will Angharad, how much you've helped us.'

Temple nodded slowly and then suddenly shivered.

'What made you decide you'd had enough?' asked Gareth.

Temple poured them both a second mug. They both listened to the water being drawn in the upstairs bathroom and the faint shudder of Angharad's feet on the boards above them.

'At first I was fascinated by what I learnt about the powers – the self-development – that the Occult can bring. Have you ever experienced that particular lust?'

'Not fully until I met Winterman.'

'I thought to begin with that the Tophetim were little more than a coven of Kabbalistic warlocks. Dabblers. Then I discovered that they'd got runaway children virtually in imprisonment. Boys mainly – a lot of the esquires are bisexual – but there was one little girl . . . '

Gareth waited for him to regain control of his breathing.

'When I say "little', she must have been about fifteen years of age. But she wasn't . . . big enough.' He cleared his throat. 'They'd suspended her in a harness from a beam in the Commandery cellar. The twelve members of the exclusive coven I was trying so hard to join . . . raped her in pairs.' He looked quickly away from Gareth's darkening face out at the shadows sliding down the mountain slopes. 'Simultaneously.'

'And what did you do?'

No answer came immediately. Gareth watched him weeping noiselessly.

'My initiation,' he continued, sniffing, 'was to prepare her for them.' He hesitated, examining his fingertips, as if searching for splinters. 'With Vaseline.' He shrugged. 'And then to watch, without protest or interference. When they'd finished – and it took a long time – they told me that, if I ever informed on them, they'd track me down and hot-collar me.'

'Hot what you?'

'Kill me in the way King Edward II was murdered. It's their standard method of executing deserters.'

'But surely? If I remember rightly, didn't they kill him by . . . ?'

'Yes. And the Tophetim are quite capable of that.' He stood up from where he was leaning against the sink. 'Believe me! I know that that is what is waiting for me, if they ever catch me.'

Gareth was silent for a while. 'What became of the girl?' he asked, as he drew down the kitchen blinds.

'She's a prostitute in Nottingham now, apparently. Earn-

ing more than you do, I shouldn't wonder.' He tried to smile
as he dabbed at his eyes with a tissue that he had drawn in
useless shreds from the trouser pocket of the corduroys into
which he had changed. He made a throwaway gesture, as if
dismissing the memory. 'Strange, that's the one thing I've
never been able to bear. I had suspected appendicitis once. My
doctor tried to give me an internal examination. Couldn't. I
just seized up. They seem to know what each member's
deepest, most primitive, most private dread is. I suppose they
discover it during the hypnosis you undergo when they screen
you for membership. The Prior himself hypnotised me.'

'Who is he?'

'A prominent local businessman but, as you're new to the
county, his name will mean little to you. Best you don't know
it, I assure you.'

Gareth nodded, sensing Temple's genuine reluctance at
that juncture to reveal any more information of that sort. 'But
why are they so carnal-minded when they're supposed to be
interested in supernatural things?'

'That puzzled me too at first. But I came to learn that the
distinction we make between the physical and the spiritual is
not really valid.'

'Isn't it?' Gareth could not keep out of his voice the note of
ager curiosity.

'No. Didn't Tertullian, of all people, writing about the
orgasm, of all things, say: ... *in illo ipso voluptatis ultimae
aestu, quo genitale virus expellitur, nonne aliquid de anima
quoque sentimus exire?*

'Say that again.'

Temple obliged.

' ... in that very fervour of the last pleasure,' translated

192

Gareth, 'in which the generative slime is thrust out, do we not feel that something goes out from the soul also? But doesn't it rather depend on what you mean by "soul"?'

'Yes, I suppose the key word is soul. We know what flesh is – but is the soul, as we call it (what the Greeks called *psyche* and the Romans *anima*) closer to the carnal or to the spiritual? Perhaps I should have said that the distinction we make between the physical on the one hand and the psychic, or astral, on the other is not so great as we think. It's apparently, from what I was learning, only a matter,' he broke into a laugh, 'did I say "matter"? – of a difference in vibration. The psychic can interpenetrate the physical; that is to say: mind animates matter. But a psychic body cannot penetrate another psychic body – except, of course, in the way that a physical body can penetrate another physical one.'

'Are you telling me that on the psychic/astral level there is bodily activity? Supernatural sex?'

'That's right. But without the reproductive element.'

'Pure pleasure?'

'Or impure pleasure. The Tophetim are experimenting with demons and sprites and elementals, in order to gain physical advantages. That's another reason I decided that I had to get out, if I could. But I knew I had to wait until I could join forces with a white magician who could afford me the right level of protection.'

'And what made you think you'd found one?'

'When I saw how Winterman had protected his house and regained control over the entity released at your school. That one, by the way, was a murderous elemental spirit that feeds on resentment, some sort of salamander – it's no accident that we talk about "burning resentment". I'm also pretty certain that Winterman's colleague on Mull is another such magician.'

Gareth put down his mug and rubbed his face in his palms as though washing vigorously, massaging his eyelids with his fingertips. 'I still find it strenuously difficult to believe that all this has happened to me – so much in such a short interval has shaken my whole concept of time itself.'

'You mean you'd like to wake up in a few minutes and find it's really Monday morning and that you've a week's teaching ahead of you?'

'No,' Gareth chuckled archly, 'I don't think I said that!'

CHAPTER FIFTY

WINTERMAN SWITCHED OFF THE TELEVISION AND RUBBED HIS CHIN. AS HE SHAVED IN THE BATHROOM, HE COULD NOT PREVENT WHAT HE had heard on the local evening news disturbing him: a child-molester was active in the Caernarvon area. Seemingly, he enticed children into his car – it was thought to be a Cortina – with the offer of sweets and then assaulted them. Parents were being warned to keep their children indoors after school and to escort them to and from evening activities until the man was caught.

He shaved with particular care for the second time, dried himself thoroughly and set to work with the talcum powder. When he was satisfied with the smoothness and pallor of his skin, he tried on the wig. Nodding at himself in the mirror in satisfaction, he applied the lipstick and blusher.

Some ten minutes later he undressed fully, squirted himself with perfume and dressed again in the clothes he had stored in the wardrobe for just such an expedition as he now had in mind. The effect of the two-piece navy-blue costume was finished off by a brimless straw hat of the same sober colour. The raised heels of his shoes were already giving him a mild ache in the small of his back as he struggled behind the wheel of his car, readjusting his false bosom and trying to remember to keep his knees together as he swung his legs in. On the seat beside him he placed an object in a leather case with a strap attached which a casual observer would probably have thought was a large camera.

The thirty-five mile drive to Caernarvon took him just over an hour. He parked in the Square, hung the supposed camera from his neck, locked up the car and walked at a leisurely pace in the direction of the castle. He strolled a short distance beneath its massive walls, allowing his subconscious to direct his footsteps. It was about seven-thirty and virtually dark. His sense of smell located the fish-and-chip shop first. Remembering to shorten his stride and keep it short, he crossed the road towards its welcoming lights and joined the short queue.

Three places in front of him was a boy of about six years of age. After being served he lingered for a while in the doorway, looking up and down the street. He eventually went out, turning left, as Winterman ordered a bag of chips. He felt confident that the glances he received from the other customers had more to do with his English accent than either the pitch of his voice or his appearance. He hurried out after the boy from whom he had sensed emanating most powerfully those vibrations that announce to a sensitive a natural victim and saw him again about fifty yards ahead. He felt strangely elated, all his senses honed, the heels of his slightly pinching shoes echoing off the high stone wall on his left, the greasy pungency of the chips hot in their paper mingling with his perfume. His sixth sense was howling at him that he had been right to come, and to come here, for he

would soon be provided with the opportunity to test his
ingenuity and his handiwork.

He was excited not only at the prospect of eliminating a
specimen of a species of pervert that he had always found
particularly loathsome but also at the chance of finally proving that his extensive research had been worthwhile and that
his original theory was valid. All his reading and theorising
over the last decade had brought him to the conviction that
the physical and the psychic were not so totally different as
many had hitherto supposed. There were laws of astral physics too and he was soon, he hoped, going to prove it. When he
exorcised the sprite trapped in the replica inside the box that
he had designed, its way out would be blocked by psychic
forces from which its very nature recoiled – blocked except
for the narrowest of escape routes. When a spirit abandoned
its dwelling, it normally diffused somehow and the process,
though rapid, did involve duration. When, however, the
escape channel was narrow, it must pass out in a certain
direction and, as it were, under unimaginable pressure, like a
jet of water through the narrowest of nozzles. If commanded
to go, not to the place appointed to it, as in an orthodox
exorcism, but to the nearest refuge, it must enter and occupy
any psyche in its path that was predisposed to receive it.
The speciality of the gargoyle-sprite imprisoned in the replica
contained in the box bouncing gently against his false bosom
was – as had been demonstrated at St Cuthbert's – to produce
a violent rage and an irresistible urge to burn. In the case of
the pupils and staff of St Cuthbert's the burning had been
transitive; their rage had eventually led some of them to start
fires in the school. Winterman intended the words of his
exorcism to result in something more intransitive; the

inherent evil of the child-molester was to be the fuel of his own destruction.

He had become so absorbed in the recapitulation of his theory that he had lengthened his stride and drawn closer to the little boy. As he stopped walking to allow him to draw ahead, he saw the Cortina pull out of a sidestreet and begin to crawl in first gear on the wrong side of the road towards the child. The driver, who seemed not to have noticed Winterman, wound down his window and accosted the boy. Over the noise of the car's engine Winterman could faintly hear the driver's coaxing demands in Welsh. The boy stepped back towards the wall as Winterman crossed out into the road, out of the glow of the car's headlights, and walked down the centre line. The man said something else more forcibly and opened his back door, inviting the boy to climb in. The child shook his head and began to back away, looking anxiously back towards the security of the chip-shop. The rear door blocked his route home. The driver then shoved open his own door until its edge almost scraped the wall.

Certain now that he had what he had come to find, Winterman moved with the unhurried swiftness of resolution. Dropping his parcel of chips on to the road, he strode around the back of the car and fell in through the open door onto the rear seat. As he slammed the door behind him, the child ran off down the pavement.

Winterman watched the driver twist round and stiffen in astonishment at the woman pointing a camera at him. He knew it would be the last thing the man would see in his earthly life before a blinding redness bored into his brain through the centre of his forehead. This then happened with such force that the man was jerked forward off his seat. The back of his skull shattered the windscreen as his spine collided with the gearstick. As soon as the stench of burning began, Winterman uttered the words of recall.

He sat rigid on the back seat, watching what was now the corpse spreadeagled across the fascia beginning to smoulder. At the sight of the first flicker of magenta flame, he slid off the seat, opened the door and left it ajar to help fan the flames. He walked steadily away in the direction from which he had come. As he turned the corner of the street, he turned to see that the inside of the car was illuminated by a ball of fire and that some men who had stepped out of the chip-shop were running uncertainly towards it, shouting.

He was already back in his own car and reversing out of his parking space when he heard the fire-engine through his open window. He took a last look at the castle, as any tourist might, and drove off west.

CHAPTER FIFTY-ONE

GARETH SMILED WITH THE PLEASURE OF RELIEF AS HE BACKED OFF THE FERRY UP THE RAMP ONTO MULL. HIS MEMORIES OF HOLIDAYS ON THE ISLAND WITH his parents were wholly delightful. He swung the Peugeot through a slow quarter circle, ducked to look at the peak of Beinn Bhuidhe above the pines and turned onto the track up to the main road. There had been a shower and the road was slick in the early morning sun. He wound down his window and listened to the tyres hissing. Angharad beside him was looking more relaxed than at any time during the long drive. On the back seat Temple was yawning and glancing back at the Nissan and the Land Rover that were following them along the road to Tobermory.

Soon after Salen Gareth turned off left up the Aros glen, cruising sedately in third gear until he reached the watershed from where they could look down the broad valley of the Bellart that sloped north-westwards towards Dervaig and the sea. The other cars had taken the main road. He pulled off the single-track strip of pitted tarmac and switched off the engine. Excusing himself, he walked a little way into the heather and stood looking around him at each point of the compass in turn. He breathed in deeply as he at last felt his muscles relaxing and exhaled even more slowly, whistling away the last few gasps through pursed lips, forcing his lungs empty until he felt lightheaded. The next inrush of peaty air made him close his watering eyes in something close to ecstasy. He began to feel ready for his encounter with Doctor Mark Murdoch and the demands that he knew must be placed upon him before he could sleep anywhere in complete security again.

In the car Angharad stretched, arching her spine off the seat. In the mirror she caught sight of Temple looking away suddenly over the moor, feigning interest in a wheeling buzzard. It crossed her mind to wonder whether, if he had not decided to act as he had in the caravan, he too would have raped her after the other one. She remembered that she had been on the point of submitting when he had come into the bedroom with that helmet. Out of the corner of her eyes she could see him looking at her profile as she half-turned towards him, suppressing a shudder at the memory of that night.

'I suppose he's counting the cost,' he said, nodding towards Gareth.

'Did he have much choice?'

'Does any of us? Yet he's left a lot behind. He can't live in obscurity as a schoolmaster any more, whatever happens. If he survives what's coming, his priorities will be changed for ever. I think he's realised that he's started on a long road.'

'He's more worried than he cares to admit about this Doctor Murdoch. Sidney he would follow anywhere – I can see that.'

'Just clearing my head,' said Gareth as he settled behind

201

the wheel again. 'There's a lot of thinking, as well as action, ahead.'

The village of Dervaig was stirring as they crept up its main street in low gear. A few children stared at them in curiosity as they waited for an old golden retriever to hobble out of their way. Temple opened the gate at the road's end and stood gazing a moment down the stony track that continued northwards. A curtain was edged aside in the nearest house as they passed through. Soon Calman House appeared through leafless oaks and hazels down on their left. They scrunched over gravel and pulled up in a paved courtyard surrounded on three sides by the whitewashed two-storied building. Two brindle Staffordshire bull-terriers sat up on their haunches by what looked like the back door.

'I think we'll wait for someone to come,' said Gareth.

A much shorter and slimmer version of Winterman, greybearded and spruce in a charcoal grey sweater and open-necked check shirt, appeared in the doorway. He said something to the dogs and they trotted off around the corner of the house down onto a sloping lawn that seemed to extend right down to the stony edge of the sea-loch.

As they stepped out of the car, stretching their limbs and looking about them at the flower-beds bright with red and golden dahlias and chrysanthemums, the evergreen shrubs nestling in lakes of grey gravel, milk-white doves and slate-grey pigeons gurgling on mown grass, they smelt coming from inside the house the invitation of frying bacon. Sniffing, they blinked in the sunlight off the white walls and squinted up at the roofs bristling with newly-painted dormer windows.

'You took longer than I expected,' said Murdoch, introducing himself. His voice was deeper and darker than his slight frame led Gareth to anticipate and as they shook hands he was at once attracted to the warm smile from the piercing brown eyes and reassured by the firmness of the dry-palmed, bone-shifting grip. Its strength surprised him for at such close quarters Murdoch seemed almost frail.

'We rested up, in the Lake District,' explained Gareth, as Murdoch took both Angharad's hands and accepted, a little stiffly but with a flush of obvious pleasure, the kiss she placed carefully on the clean-shaven part of his cheek.

'Sidney's told me so much about you,' she said, 'and this house. I'm so glad we've managed to meet at last.'

Temple had hung back and now approached, clearly nervous and ill-at-ease. Gareth gave his name and the two men shook hands. He noticed that Murdoch's eyes held Temple's for a fraction longer than politeness demands and there was a marked hiatus in the pleasantries.

'Samuel here saved my life,' broke in Angharad simply. 'We've so much to tell you.'

Murdoch nodded thoughtfully, the gentleness returning to his rather foxy features, and gestured towards the open door. 'Welcome,' he said with a reassuring second glance and shy smile at Temple, 'all of you, to Calman House.'

CHAPTER FIFTY-TWO

'LET US BRING TO MIND OUR BROTHER SAMUEL TEMPLE,' SAID THE PRIOR. HE LOOKED AROUND THE LONG TABLE UNDER THE RECESSED LIGHTS. THE other ten were sitting with their eyes fixed on a low copper plinth in the centre of the table. The silence in the cool room grew, swelled and became almost palpable. Every forehead was smooth, eyelids closed now at his command, every brain, he was confident, summoning up the face of their missing colleague. 'Let us see him sitting again in his chair in his rightful place,' continued the Prior, his voice low and parsonical.

Eleven minds were forming a picture, each one slightly different, of Temple sitting in his chair. Each member of the coven was suppressing the feelings of disgust and loathing that they felt for him at what seemed to be his betrayal of the Tophetim, for he, the Prior, had declared that he wanted him back. He knew that they preferred Springfellow, but he was dead. Without their most effective medium they were operating at a disadvantage. Temple knew too much for it to be safe to allow him to run away in the company of people apparently hostile to the Order. He waited for the silence to thicken further.

His voice at last broke it and he sensed the faint shudder of nervous surprise around the table. 'Brother Samuel!' he intoned, his voice loud, commanding, nasal and vibrant. 'Remember your vows! Remember your allegiance! Remember the punishment reserved for traitors! I command you to return to us! First in mind, and then in body. I am coming to bring you. My brothers will support me on my journey . . . '

With one part of his mind the Prior could see the youngest and most recent member of the coven part his eyelids fractionally and squint at what he thought was the now totally unconscious body of the old man at the head of the table, slumped to one side in his chair, his mouth open, saliva drooling from the corner of his mouth, his breathing stertorous. The others sat on, rigid and masklike. Part of the Prior smiled as the neophyte screwed his eyes shut again and tried to concentrate on the face of Samuel Temple.

With the rest of his mind the Prior felt himself up in clouds, thick, grey and cold. They were parting now in ragged snatches to reveal sea and shore, mountains and a narrow river running north-west to a low-sided fjord. There was a village and beyond it, among oaks and hazels, a white house with doves fluttering in its gardens. Further on, as he swooped lower, was an open grass-covered space in a wilderness of bracken and gorse and heather. In it a tall, grey-blue stone stood up erect from the sour soil. Its outline resembled that of a tall, thin, hooded figure. A man was standing beside the monolith, his hand stroking its lichen-mottled flank.

At first the man was unaware of his presence but as the

now westering sun glinted on the horizon and the bracken-covered slopes darkened, he stiffened, as if pained by a sudden crick in his neck, his breathing arrested. Slowly he turned, moving not just his head but his whole body around, his shoes shuffling in the mud and sheep-droppings at the base of the standing-stone. His eyes met the Prior's where he now stood motionless a few feet away on another, fallen, stone that was half-buried in soil and peat. The Prior smiled, without affection. Temple screamed like a woman in child-birth. In terror at the sound sheep bolted, crashing heavily through the surrounding bracken.

CHAPTER FIFTY-THREE

══════

After breakfast Dr Murdoch had shown them to their rooms at the top of the west wing. He explained that he had been expecting only two guests. Angharad's room was tiny but tastefully decorated in white with bowls of wild flowers on every available ledge and many mirrors picking up and reflecting whatever light came in from the small east-facing window that overlooked the courtyard. She expressed her delight at it and her intention to make up for a sleepless journey.

As they left her Gareth exchanged a quick glance that he saw did not go unnoticed by Murdoch, but shook his head briefly at the questioning arch of her eyebrows. He then showed Gareth and Temple into a west-facing bedroom of larger proportions and with two single beds.

'I hope you don't mind sharing a room?' he asked. 'Perhaps, later, I can arrange for something else. There are lots of comings and goings here.'

They made reassuring noises and marvelled at his unquestioning hospitality, declaring their intention to rest. Temple fell on top of the blankets and, despite yawning to Gareth something about a sense of unease and claustrophobia, was evidently unable to prevent his exhaustion overcoming him. Lulled by what he felt at once was an atmosphere of almost soporific peace and pleasantly filled by the splendid fried breakfast, Gareth fell asleep minutes after stretching out his limbs. He slept, as did Temple, until late into the afternoon.

They went down and found Murdoch pouring tea for Angharad at the kitchen table. After they too had accepted a cup Murdoch took them all on a tour of the house, explaining its layout and the functions of the rooms in the wing which he occupied. When he had insisted that they were to treat that part of the house as their own home, he unlocked a door half way down a corridor and led them through into the hospice.

The large rooms were arranged into small wards, each containing four or five beds. Most were occupied by elderly women though there were some middle-aged men and one bald youth of about eighteen. Nurses in white uniforms, some with nuns' coifs, bustled about, beaming at anything that moved.

'The nurses live in cabins down by the shore,' said Murdoch.

Temple looked distinctly puzzled. 'Everyone seems very cheerful,' he murmured, after they had left a sun-filled ward. 'Do they all have the same complaint?'

'They do indeed,' laughed Murdoch and, lowering his voice, added with a grin: 'They're all impatient to die.'

Temple looked at Murdoch as if he had just uttered an obscenity and was about to speak but thought better of it.

'You're obviously unfamiliar with the thinking of our hospice,' said Murdoch. 'They only come here, or are brought, when formal medicine has declared them incurable.

We do our best to ease whatever suffering they have left to undergo. My doctorate, by the way, as Gareth may not have told you, is in philosophy not in medicine. Which probably helps!' He chuckled again. 'We help prepare them, you see, for the next phase of their life. Calman House is a waiting-room for eternity – no more and no less.'

Temple cleared his throat and looked back into the ward at an old woman who was doing a crossword puzzle. Murdoch smiled and led the way back to his quarters. The last room he showed them was a tiny chapel. About twenty chairs faced a wooden altar on which was a silver box about the size of a pound of butter. A large crucifix hung from the ceiling on a wire. In a corner was an alcove with a statue of the Madonna and a prayer-stool beneath it.

'The wards, if I may say so,' said Temple, clearly disturbed by a set of ideas that were taxing his powers of lateral thinking, 'though most pleasant, are very bare. Do they not bring with them many personal possessions?'

'We discourage it,' said Murdoch, pausing to genuflect unobtrusively towards the altar before they moved out again into the corridor. 'We're always short of space anyway and those who do bring things invariably end up bequeathing them away before they leave.'

'Do any leave to return to their homes?' asked Angharad. 'Cured, I mean?'

'Oh, yes.'

'Even after formal medicine has declared them incurable?'

'Yes.'

'Many?'

'Three, since I've opened the hospice.'

'I see. Not many, then.'

'A huge number, surely, when you consider that, according to the experts, there ought to be none at all.'

'I'd not thought of it quite like that.'

'Please don't be embarrassed, my dear. You're not the first to have had attitudes changed here.'

Temple was looking down the corridor through the open doorway out onto the courtyard. 'If you don't mind,' he said to them awkwardly, 'I rather fancy some exercise.'

'The path,' said Murdoch, pointing north through the trees, 'will take you a good way towards Quinish Point. There's an unusual standing-stone you'll come across just off to the left but I shouldn't take too close a look, on your own. Dinner at eight.'

When Temple had gone, Murdoch invited Angharad and Gareth into his study. It overlooked the lawn that ran down to the machair between the house and the shore. The two dogs were sprawling on a rug and leapt up, eyeing the strangers eagerly.

'Now then you two!' scolded Murdoch. 'Friends! Both friends! Let them get your scent,' he added, as the bull-terriers advanced and sniffed their shins and feet. 'It's a wise precaution. They're very good-natured but once they get it into their heads that anyone in the house is not well-intentioned towards me, they can undergo an alarming change of personality. Especially you, eh, Surgeon?' He slapped the dog on his barrel-like ribcage while the bitch whined for her share of fuss.

'Why do you call him that?' asked Angharad.

'Soon after I bought him – from Thompson who teaches at your school, Gareth, actually – an intruder attacked me one

210

night. This was when I lived near Lincoln. This one tried to amputate his arm at the elbow and damn near succeeded. That's enough now!'

Gareth grinned as he watched the dogs patter off along the pine-boarded floor and slump together back onto another rug in the bay-window. He recalled his intention to buy such a dog from Thompson what now seemed half a lifetime ago.

Murdoch indicated a club settee facing a fire of logs helped along by a ring of glowing coals. He offered them drinks from a selection on an old oak sideboard. Angharad asked for a small gin and Gareth a straight whisky. He brought Angharad's glass and returned to pour himself and Gareth two thick fingers of malt in weighty tumblers. Joining them by the fire, he sank into what was obviously his favourite leather armchair and toasted their health. They sipped their drinks and settled back into the respective corners of the settee, waiting for him to speak. He took a second pull at his glass before placing it carefully on a chess table among pieces which, Gareth noticed, were about ten moves into a Ruy Lopez. He looked hard at each of them in turn before settling his gaze on Gareth.

'Lagavulin, before you ask,' he said as he saw Gareth raising his glass to his nose to swirl and sniff its contents. 'Can we trust Sam Temple?' he added smoothly as Gareth took an appreciative pull.

'I don't know,' sighed Gareth. 'He's had every opportunity to betray us but hasn't taken it.'

'Yet,' said Murdoch. 'He may, of course, have been sent to find out what I am doing here.'

'He rescued me,' said Angharad, looking down into her gin, 'from being raped by one of his former associates. In doing so, he killed him.' Murdoch listened in silence while she went on to tell him what had happened in Gareth's caravan.

'And it was his suggestion to set it on fire?' he asked when she had finished.

She nodded, draining her glass.

'And the helmet was destroyed in the fire?'

'He made very sure of that.'

'He's convinced,' said Gareth, 'that the Tophetim will kill him when they track him down. Would they? Even if he returned to them with information they wanted?'

'If he could convince them that he had planned his defection in order to benefit their Order, then . . . ' Murdoch shrugged his slim shoulders. 'But they are unpredictable. If his Prior had some personal affection for the man whom Temple killed, there might be an element of revenge. But, again, if Temple can prove his usefulness, he could survive until attitudes changed. Either way, he's a danger to us, unless we can be sure that his repentance is sincere and binding. I had not planned for this complication.' From his armchair he studied his whisky glass, picked it up thoughtfully and sipped from it.

Gareth took a longer look at Angharad than he had managed since their arrival. The malt and the fire were having their effect. He allowed his eyes to linger on the roundness of her thighs under the cloth of her dress.

Murdoch looked up at them. 'Nor had I fully foreseen the problem that you two have brought with you.' His piercing eyes challenged Angharad to stare him out and she lowered her head and blushed. Watching, Gareth experienced a strange overlapping amalgam of emotions: surprise, admiration, shame, anger and embarrassment.

'I can see,' continued Murdoch, 'that you are in love with each other. I realise now what Sidney has been planning. May I ask you to tell me something about your ancestry?' he asked Gareth.

He told him, tracing back his Cornish father's side a few generations and then his Irish mother's. Murdoch nodded as he listened, though kept his gaze fixed on Angharad who kept failing to meet it.

'So,' he gasped eventually. 'He intends you two to produce the Children.'

It was Angharad who caught the subtle emphasis on his last word. 'Why should children of ours be as important as you make them sound?' she asked, looking straight up at him at last.

'Do you believe in prophecy?' asked Murdoch.

'Not really, no, to be honest.'

'Do you believe in marriage?'

'I'm sorry?' she asked quickly, frowning in open annoyance.

From the other end of the settee Gareth felt her body stiffen.

Murdoch continued unabashed. 'Your first marriage to Corbett – was it sacramental?' Seeing her frown change to one of bewilderment, he explained what he meant: 'Was it a church wedding?'

'No. Register Office.'

'As was you marriage to Sidney, of course.'

' "Of course",' she repeated.

He ran his finger slowly around the rim of his glass. 'I'm

213

sure I'm right in remembering that Sidney was brought up a Quaker.'

'So he told me once. Not that he considers himself one now.'

'So, in all probability, he was never baptised? Please try to remember if he ever said that he had been.'

'No, in fact I'm sure I recall his telling me that he hadn't been. There was some fuss about his standing godfather to the child of a friend of mine. He never did, eventually.'

'Ah yes, a "fuss"!' said Murdoch. He paused, about to say something but apparently thinking better of it, and poked the fire into greater brightness. Surgeon came at once as if at a signal to sink in front of it and the bitch followed. They all watched the dogs settle for a few moments.

'Why do you ask?' said Angharad.

'When you took your vows to commit yourself to Corbett for life,' he said, 'and again when, after Corbett's death, you did the same for Sidney – forgive my directness but we shall achieve nothing by ducking what is important – did you mean it?'

Angharad began to answer at once but hesitated. Faced by Murdoch's intense but strangely gentle stare she coloured again. 'I meant it at the time,' she mumbled.

'I'm sure you did,' persisted Murdoch, 'but did you secretly feel that, if either of them proved unfaithful to you, you would be quite justified in breaking your vow and divorcing him?'

'Yes! Wouldn't I have been?'

He ignored her question and kept her on the hook Gareth was willing her to wriggle off. 'So you never intended,' he paused, leaning forward to emphasise the word with his extended index finger, 'total commitment?'

'I suppose not, no! I'm not a fool.'

Murdoch cleared his throat and finished his whisky. Angharad looked at Gareth in some confusion, as if for support.

'Had you hoped,' asked Murdoch, 'to sleep together as man and wife while you were here?' He turned his gaze to Gareth, who flinched from it.

' "Hoped" perhaps, yes,' he answered. 'Though I didn't expect you'd approve.'

'And I presume you've already,' he breathed in and looked briefly from him to Angharad who was scratching her knee, 'become one flesh?'

'What a quaint turn of phrase you have, Doctor Murdoch!' she said, clearly trying to laugh but not quite succeeding.

Gareth drained his glass and closed his eyes. The fire was hot on his cheeks now, the whisky snug in his stomach. He rehearsed his memories of the oneness of their flesh: in his caravan, on Winterman's bed, in Temple's cottage . . . 'Yes,' he said, opening his eyes. 'We have. And with Sidney's knowledge and consent and, I think I can say, encouragement.'

'So have we done wrong?' asked Angharad sharply. 'Have we . . . "sinned"?'

Murdoch paused before replying. 'I see that I'm not the only one to use "quaint" language when necessary.' The smile with which he followed his remark disarmed Angharad. 'Yes,' he began nodding repeatedly, 'you've sinned.'

Silently, Angharad began to weep.

'A sin from which,' he continued, 'I must ask you to refrain, while you are both under my roof. Please! Do you both promise me? I could explain why, at greater length, but suffice it now to say that the security of all of us could be endangered, if you don't do what I ask. Calman House is safe. It is protected from most of the dangers that confront us. But at a price. Do you follow me?'

'Very well,' said Gareth. He reached out his hand to Angharad. She took it with one hand while drying her eyes and cheeks with a small handkerchief with the other.

'Refrain,' said Murdoch, 'until I can marry you.'

Angharad was about to comment when the two dogs whirled up onto their feet, snarling. The door burst open and Temple staggered in, breathless but trying to speak. He stumbled forward towards the light of the fire but collapsed over the back of the settee, his hands stretching out for both Gareth and Angharad, his eyes held by Murdoch's.

CHAPTER FIFTY-FOUR

W INTERMAN STOPPED SIPPING HIS BEER, LIFTED HIS HEAD FROM HIS LUNCH OF SOUP AND BREAD AND TURNED HIS ATTENTION AWAY FROM THE WAVES' thump and hiss pulsing in through the open window.

' . . . Gwynedd Police and Fire Service admit to being baffled about the cause of the fire in an apparently stolen car that led to the death of its driver near the centre of Caernarvon last night,' the announcer was saying. 'Forensic experts have not yet been able to identify the badly charred body. We go over to our reporter in Caernarvon.'

Winterman turned up the volume on the television set and moved closer to the screen. He watched the young man in a leather jacket who was holding a microphone turn around to direct the camera's gaze at a Cortina parked in what seemed to be a yard of the police station. The paint around the driver's door was blackened and blistered. The camera panned over the shattered windscreen and zoomed in on the charred interior.

'Although foul play is not yet suspected,' explained the reporter in a marked Welsh accent, 'Police cannot tell us why, despite such a fierce fire which burnt the sole occupant of the car beyond recognition, the petrol tank did not explode. The engine compartment, too, was completely undamaged.

'Viewers may be reminded of a similar case, involving a Bangor businessman, that occurred during the New Year riots in Chester a few years ago, when his badly charred remains were discovered in his car of which only parts of the interior were fire-damaged.

'Earlier this morning I contacted at his home in Bangor, Dr Goronwy Cadwallader-Price, author of several books on parapsychology but particularly of a recent volume on the strange phenomenon known as spontaneous combustion.'

Winterman watched the talking head that suddenly filled the screen. So instant was the recognition that for a few moments he lost track of what the man was actually saying.

' . . . that in almost every case the source of combustion is within the body that is consumed. Very often only the extremities are found intact. Even bone melts. Most remarkable of all is the fact that surrounding material – carpets, chairs, beds – seem virtually unaffected.'

Winterman looked more closely at the smooth-jowled, balding head smiling rather patronisingly at the interviewer through half-closed eyelids. The last time he had seen him, the man had been shaking hands with the Prior of the Lincoln Tophetim before boarding a train that would connect with the express to King's Cross. As he had stood looking out of the open window of the train door his eyes had met and briefly held those of Winterman's who had been sitting on a bench, making rapid notes. He took out a small, leather-bound notebook and started flipping through its pages.

'For further developments,' he heard the announcer's voice saying, 'tune in to our evening bulletin.'

Winterman switched off the television and finished his beer thoughtfully. Setting down his glass and holding the notebook in both hands, he solemnly kissed the page at which he had folded it open.

CHAPTER FIFTY-FIVE

═══════

'UNDER NO CIRCUMSTANCES,' SAID MURDOCH, 'FROM NOW ON, SHOULD ANY OF YOU LEAVE THE GROUNDS OF CALMAN HOUSE. NO OCCULT FORCES can penetrate its defences to inflict harm. You will probably not have had time to notice, but there are five rowan trees planted around the perimeter. You must not pass outside the circle that links them, until it becomes necessary.

'To be frank, Sam,' he continued, 'I was uncertain whether you had broken your allegiance to the Tophetim. As soon as we met, I knew that you had had contact with evil forces. Anyone, indeed, could sense the turmoil in your mind. Gareth and Angharad have told me what you have done for them. Now that you have told us, honestly, how they are still trying to win you back there is one thing I must ask you to let me do before I can happily permit you to stay here. It will finally prove to me the sincerity of your change of heart.'

He looked across the fireplace at where Temple was sitting in the armchair opposite him, leaning towards the fire for the warmth that he seemed to crave.

'What is it?' he asked, shivering. 'God, I've never felt so cold before as I did out there beside that standing-stone!'

'I sense that you've never been baptised.'

'That's right. My parents were Rationalists – their term – my father a Communist, my mother nothing, a typical English Liberal in other words. Although I was attracted to Christianity at University, I always at the last minute shrank from a public commitment. Then, paradoxically, I became drawn to the Occult.'

'There's no paradox involved, Sam. Having come that close and missed, you'd be a prime target. You must not be exposed to that level of spiritual vulnerability again; I want to baptise you tonight.'

'Are you a priest?' asked Gareth, looking quickly at Angharad.

'I am,' said Murdoch. 'Not that it's essential for the baptist to be one. Yes, I was ordained some years ago by the Abbot of my Order. But I don't perform my priestly functions publicly in this diocese, or indeed in any other. That was felt necessary to preserve the secrecy of my work.'

'You surprise me,' said Gareth.

'We must be as harmless as doves but as wise as serpents,' said Murdoch. 'You see, when the Tribulation comes on this country, it is not inconceivable – in fact very likely – that all validly ordained priests will be rounded up and eliminated by the Tophetim and their associates. Though there are many in today's Church who make light of the Apostolic Succession, our enemies do not. They know all too well what a victory it would be for them if they could kill off every sacrificing priest. But, of course, if they don't know who all the priests are . . .' He opened his hands and smiled. 'Do you wish me to baptise you, Sam?'

They all looked at the hunched figure in the armchair. He

hugged himself to suppress another shiver and nodded. 'I do,' he said, 'whenever you think I'm ready.'

'So, as a priest, you could marry Gareth and me,' said Angharad.

'Yes,' replied Murdoch. 'When I think you too are ready.' He raised his hand towards her, pale palm outwards, to ward off her objection. 'I'm still trying to fathom out Sidney's thinking on this matter.'

'How do you read it?' asked Gareth. 'From your knowledge of him.'

'You say he encouraged you,' asked Murdoch, pausing a moment as if choosing his words, 'to make love?'

'Undoubtedly,' answered Gareth. Angharad nodded in solemn agreement. 'He even told me to ensure that I became the father of her child.'

'He seemed to have been planning the whole thing for some time,' she added. 'He spoke of having to disappear and of the need for Gareth to look after me from now on.'

'But he didn't speak as though he would certainly die,' said Gareth. 'Though he did insist that he would be unable to go on living with Angharad any longer.'

'What's his middle name?' asked Temple unexpectedly.

'Very perceptive of you, Sam!' said Murdoch.

'Arthur,' said Angharad, frowning.

Murdoch began to chuckle softly.

'And your middle name?' persisted Temple, apparently forgetting his misery as he looked at Angharad almost as if he had seen her for the first time.

'Gwenhwyfar.'

Murdoch nodded at Temple. 'The Welsh form,' he said.

'Of what?' asked Angharad, flushing in confusion at their

broadening smiles and looking as if she suspected they were having a joke at her expense.

'I'm sorry, my dear,' said Murdoch. 'Gwenhwyfar, as I thought you might have known, is the Welsh for Guinevere.' He massaged his beard in a gesture that painfully reminded her of Sidney.

'You mean,' asked Gareth, 'that Sidney thinks of himself as a sort of latter-day King Arthur?'

'He does,' said Murdoch. 'And thinks of me as his Merlin and you, so far as I can see, as Lancelot. And if he knew the full story, he'd no doubt welcome Samuel here to his Company as an unexpected but very timely Galahad.'

'Are you quite serious?' asked Angharad. 'King Arthur hardly planned his wife's love affair.'

'There's never an exact correspondence,' said Murdoch. 'Time isn't cyclic; it's more of a spiral. What was the disguise he favoured,' he asked Gareth, 'when he left you?'

'A cripple.'

'Precisely!' hissed Murdoch.

'And he has disappeared,' said Temple, 'without dying.'

'In the direction of the Far West,' said Gareth.

'So when he eventually returns,' said Angharad drily, 'what will that make me, if you marry me to Gareth?'

'The mother of the child who will rescue Britain,' said Murdoch. 'In reality, however, the priest does not confer the sacrament of marriage: the couple give it to each other. I would merely be formally witnessing a bond that, in this case, may already have been tied.'

'You spoke of children,' she said. 'And of prophecies.'

'That's right. They speak of twins, born to you, on Iona, the sons of two fathers.'

'Two fathers?' said Gareth, frowning at Angharad.

She blushed as she recrossed her legs. 'I suppose,' she said carefully, pursing her lips as though making a tricky calculation, 'that it's just about possible. Sidney made love to me,' she added with a wide-eyed stare at Gareth that left him slack-jawed and a sideways glance at Temple, 'before lunch last Sunday. Not very long before you . . .'

Murdoch coughed and Temple returned his attention to the fire.

'But Sidney told me he couldn't father a child,' stuttered Gareth. He pinched the bridge of his nose, remembering her eagerness on Winterman's bed, the bed on which shortly before his arrival . . .

He heard Murdoch clearing his throat. 'The prophecies – of the seer of Poolewe, whom Sidney and I have relied upon for years – are always extremely precise. I've never known them to be wrong. And I must say, I've never known Sidney Winterman to give up trying, even when he thought he stood no chance.'

CHAPTER FIFTY-SIX

WINTERMAN TURNED OFF THE MAIN CAERNARVON
TO BANGOR ROAD. AFTER A MILE OR SO HE STOPPED
IN THE DISTRICT OF PENRHOS. HE CONSULTED HIS
notebook and looked about him unhurriedly in the dusk at
the numbers on the gates of the suburban villas. Satisfied that
he was close enough, he locked up his car and walked down
the driveway of a grey pebble-dashed house with rather fussy
dormer windows that looked over the valley towards Bangor
Mountain and the Elidirs beyond. He rang the bell.

'Dr Cadwallader-Price?' he enquired of the balding little
man who stood frowning at him in the light from his hallway.
He adopted the Morningside Edinburgh accent whose gen-
tility he always found easy to sustain.

'Yes. Can I help you?' His tone expressed doubt.

'Almost certainly. My name is Emsvir. Our paths have
crossed – but you won't remember the circumstances. You
may, however, be familiar with my book *Dark of the Moon*. I'd
like to discuss with you some of the comments you made on
television earlier today in connection with – '

' – I'm sorry!' snapped Cadwallader-Price in a tone that

almost expressed a strange delight. 'But I don't give inter-
views without prior appointment.'

'We have,' said Winterman, his voice rising slightly to cap
Cadwallader-Price's protest, 'a mutual acquaintance. He's the
Prior of the Lincoln Commandery.'

Cadwallader-Price squinted out into his front garden and
up the sloping drive towards the road. 'You'd better come in,'
he muttered, stepping aside.

As the little man shut the door Winterman watched his
eyebrows working as he no doubt tried to recall what was
familiar about the face of this large red-haired man who
was leaning so heavily on his crutch that he was rucking up
the hallway rug. He followed him into the living-room and
was invited to sit in a comfortable chintzy armchair in front
of the open fire.

'Have you come here with the Prior's knowledge?' he
asked Winterman, sliding into the armchair opposite as
he spoke. 'You must understand that I'd appreciate some
form of identification.'

'May I speak freely?' asked Winterman, looking over his
shoulder at an open door which led into another room.

'I live alone,' said Cadwallader-Price.

'Good!' said Winterman, smiling. 'In that case I can provide you with some evidence of my authority.' He produced
from his jacket pocket a small, leather-bound notebook
which he handed to Cadwallader-Price. He took it and began
to read the names and addresses that it contained. Winterman
waited for a while, watching the man's pasty features pale
even more.

'You must know,' he began, clearly trying to disguise his

shock, 'that Tophetim do not carry lists of members around with them like this!'

'Precisely!' blustered Winterman. 'The security forces of the present government, which you and your colleagues are seeking to overthrow, would be only too interested in this little book.' He reached out his hand for it and took it back. 'They would also be interested in the information, which I could provide them with, that Goronwy Cadwallader-Price, Prior of the Gwynedd Commandery of Tophetim and Treasurer of the North Wales Branch of the Albion Front, was the man who first approached the Lincoln Commandery with the idea of collaborating in the use of demons in provoking social disorder. You have for some time known the particular potency of the Lincoln Imp. It was you, was it not, who researched the part played by the Gilbertine monks of Sempringham in eventually petrifying inside gargoyles and carvings the demons and sprites that they had exorcised? A process which, of course, the original Knights Tophetim learned to reverse.'

He paused to shift his position in the chair and test Cadwallader-Price's reaction. The little man was watching him as a gerbil might a ferret.

'You are also,' continued Winterman, relaxing and starting to enjoy himself, 'obedient to the protocol that forbids Tophetim from practising occult arts within the boundaries of other commanderies without invitation. I've been aware of your activities for some years now. I must even, I suppose, congratulate you on the success of the various New Year riots.'

'What do you want?' asked Cadwallader-Price hoarsely.

'Want, my dear fellow?' laughed Winterman harshly. 'Haven't you guessed yet? I want in!'

Cadwallader-Price seemed relieved that this stranger had partially lost the initiative. He hesitated and moistened his lips before commenting. 'Can you afford the, er, entry fee?' he asked.

Winterman reached into the poacher's pocket of his jacket and pulled out what it amused him to think Cadwallader-Price would assume was an old-fashioned camera in a leather case. 'I have something here,' he said, 'which I am sure will make a deep impression on you.'

CHAPTER FIFTY-SEVEN

IN THE PRIVACY OF HIS STUDY THE PRIOR SETTLED HIMSELF INTO HIS ARMCHAIR AND AGAIN BROUGHT INTO HIS MIND'S EYE THE IMAGE OF SAMUEL TEMPLE running away from him down a stony path. Long practised as he was in the arts of visualisation and shamanistic pathworking, he was finding it difficult on this occasion to hold the picture clearly and firmly. As soon as it focused it began to falter and fragment. Sniffing in frustration and aware of the onset of a mild headache, he stood up, set a candle in a holder on the table beside his chair, switched off the light and made himself comfortable again.

He concentrated on the candle flame. By a very great effort, involving all his considerable powers, he managed to form an image of Temple standing in what seemed to be a small, white-washed room. Three others were standing near him and two dogs, which he identified as bull-terriers, were sitting on their haunches closely observing the actions of one of the humans. His face was indistinct to the Prior but he could hear him saying something in a loud voice. The Prior listened in rising horror as he began to recognise the form of the sentences. He concentrated his will into a torch-like beam and tried to direct it at the nape of Temple's neck. There was no reaction.

'Do you turn to Christ?' he now distinctly heard the voice ask.

The Prior felt himself sweating as he waited for Temple to answer.

'I turn to Christ,' he said.

'Do you renounce Satan?'

The Prior writhed in his chair in a struggle to force himself to stay and watch. He felt himself gagging, his breath rasping in sobs through his gullet.

'I renounce Satan!' Temple was close to shouting.

Everyone there looked delighted. One of the dogs barked. The priest – it must be a priest – moved towards Temple with a copper bowl half full of water. The Prior opened his eyes and stood up suddenly in a spasm of loathing as if a very foul stench had been presented to him directly beneath his nostrils. He could not force himself to watch any longer. It was futile now. To his annoyance, but he had to admit to himself also to his relief, his telephone rang. He recognised Cadwallader-Price's voice. He sounded very excited.

'I've been approached,' he said, 'by a man called Emsvir. He wants to join the Tophetim.'

'You ring at this hour to tell me that? Is he suitable? Have you checked his background?'

'There's been no time. He came to me only an hour or so ago. But wait till I tell you what he brought with him.'

'You should come yourself to tell me. You're aware of the security problem now with telephone lines.'

'This cannot wait. We must recruit him at once. He hinted at making a direct approach to the Front himself and, though I could turn that to my personal advantage, you know where my ultimate loyalty lies.'

The Prior became silent for so long that his train of thought was eventually snapped by Cadwallader-Price asking was he still on the line. 'Very well,' he sighed. 'Outline what you've learned.'

'He has a replica of a sprite – '

' – Did you see it?'

'Will you allow me to finish what I have to say? I did not see it exactly, no. It is enclosed in a box, inside which he has placed mirrors sealed with what he terms Christian magic. There is an aperture the size of a pinprick. He knows, and can use, the incantations of release and revocation.'

Cadwallader-Price paused and the Prior pictured him waiting smugly for the significance of his news to do its work.

'What evidence did he provide of the efficacy of this . . . apparatus?'

'Yesterday in Caernarvon there was a case of what seems to have been spontaneous combustion – an as yet unidentified body charred to death in a car. Emsvir told me how the man died. There can be no doubt. The man had just tried to abduct a small boy with the almost certain intention, in view of similar incidents, of buggering him. The sprite had enough to work on, though not enough completely to destroy the body . . . Hello?'

'Go on.'

'Emsvir also had a notebook full of names and addresses of Tophetim – all over Great Britain but mainly in your Commandery. He knew all about my involvement in the Chester . . . business. He is clearly so well informed and practised in the Arts – he's written a book called *Dark of the Moon*,

I've just been looking it up – that the advantages of having him on our side must outweigh all other considerations, surely.' The tone of Cadwallader-Price's voice was almost pleading.

'*Dark of the Moon*? What did he look like?'

'What? Oh, mid-fifties. Reddish hair. Fairly heavily built. Had a limp. Needed a crutch.'

'What's he doing in your area? Where does he live?'

'He wouldn't say. But he must be staying nearby, I should say, if he was in Caernarvon last night, and here tonight, and coming here again tomorrow, as I've arranged.'

'How much did he tell you about himself? I mean, what information was he obviously pushing at you?'

'Well, he dropped his name – Emsvir – a great deal.'

'First names?'

'Yes, he kept giving both – Hamish Ian. He sounded fairly well-heeled Edinburgh to me. What's so funny?'

'The brass neck of the man!' chuckled the Prior. 'Listen carefully. When he returns you must tell him that he will be accepted on the condition that he brings his apparatus to Lincoln for a demonstration. Insist that he has no contact with the Front. And bring him yourself as soon as possible. Leave all other arrangements to me.'

'Very well, but I still don't quite understand –'

' – I know exactly who he is now, as he no doubt intended me to. Did you see that report on television of the riot and fire in a Lincoln school on Monday?'

'Yes. Is there a connection?'

'The man who stole the charged replica with which the Front, with my connivance, were experimenting was the Deputy Head at that school. He's gone missing. The local media are buzzing with the story. Also missing are his wife and another male teacher. You can imagine what they've made of that. His name is Winterman,' said the Prior in a tone of voice that suggested he was waiting for Cadwallader-Price to make some sort of connection.

'I'm sorry. It's rather late. Am I being obtuse, or something?'

'No, I suppose not,' said the Prior with a polite sigh. 'He gave his name as Hamish Ian Emsvir. That is to say: H I Emsvir. If, like me, you have the probable misfortune to possess a crossword-puzzle mind, you rearrange those letters as: H-I-E-M-S V-I-R. He taught Latin to a few lucky pupils, I'm told. A luxury, alas, in today's educational soup-kitchen. But you must have been taught some, surely?'

'A question expecting the answer Yes, I hope.' sniffed Cadwallader-Price. Of course I was!' He paused and then added: 'And of course! *Hiems* – winter; *vir* – man. But why is he letting you know that? Isn't he supposed to be in hiding?'

'He'll want to preserve his false identity – the red hair and crutch are part of his disguise – because there are the complications involved in his leaving his job so suddenly. He's worried about the Front because he knows what they're up to. And he knows that they know that he knows. He must feel that he'll be safer from them if he can join us. And now he has something to bargain with. So bring him in quietly. But be careful. He's not operating in isolation. One of my esquires – Samuel Temple – has defected and joined up with the other missing teacher, called Burden, I've discovered, and Winterman's wife. They were heading north when they realised that the Front were following them. They shook them off. I know Temple has a bolt-hole in the Lakes but I haven't told the Front that. I felt I could recall him and I wanted to know where they were going. I've been in psychic contact – he was foolish enough to go and look at and actually touch a standing-stone which, apart from being on a ley-line node, contains a petrified elemental. He refused to respond but I recognised that particular stone. Its shape is unusual. It's near the village of Dervaig on the Isle of Mull.'

'Murdoch!' hissed Cadwallader-Price.

'Precisely,' continued the Prior. 'We should have known that his "hospice" was more than he pretended. If you remember, I advised the Great British Grand Commandery, when we were informed of his reappearance, to move against him at once. But I was outvoted.'

'Is it still possible?'

'Too late now. He's protected it too well. I had just managed before you rang, with an expenditure of enormous effort – I apologise if I've seemed short-tempered – to penetrate the house psychically but I had no power there whatsoever. All I could do was observe, and that very feebly – I could only make out Temple's face. But I saw enough to know that Esquire Temple is – at least temporarily – lost to us. Murdoch has, er, baptised him. Now you must excuse me; I have to rest.'

'Of course. So, when he comes tomorrow, I shall tell him that he must accompany me to your Lincoln Commandery.'

'Agreed. But if he changes his mind on the way, kill him and bring us the box.'

The Prior hung up before Cadwallader-Price could respond.

CHAPTER FIFTY-EIGHT

———

MURDOCH COMPLETED HIS MEDITATION OF THE FIFTH JOYFUL MYSTERY, KISSED THE CRUCIFIX AND WAS REPLACING HIS ROSARY BEADS INTO A DRAWER of his desk when his telephone rang. Still holding the beads loosely in his fingers, he picked up the receiver in his free hand. The line was bad but he recognised Winterman's baritone at once.

'Mark, I'm ringing from a call-box in Caernarvon on my way back to the cottage. I think it may be insecure to use its telephone from now on. I'm negotiating to join the Tophetim –'

'What?'

'No, listen! Trust me, old friend! I have something they want. And the Front will want it too. I think it will give me access to the Imp. My problem is being able, if my plan succeeds, to bring the Imp out myself. I shall probably be asked to return to Lincoln soon. I'll continue to use the disguise I'm under now. Prepare Gareth to be ready to come to Lincoln to collect the Imp. I'll phone again nearer the time with further details but, essentially, his chance will come at the Commandery near Temple Bruer at about ten o' clock on the night I'll specify. He must wait for a firestorm and then come straight in, find the Imp – it'll be in plain view – and away with it. If he is ever in doubt what to do – and this is vital – tell him to contact me telepathically. He's read *Dark of the Moon*. What have you got to tell me, before I go?'

'One of the Tophetim has defected to us. His name is Samuel Temple. He will be of invaluable assistance to Gareth, if we can persuade him to risk his life and return.'

'Are you sure of him?'

'We are now; I baptised him earlier this evening. He helped Angharad - ' Murdoch hesitated. 'He helped Angharad and Gareth to reach here. I don't know what his motives were then but we can all trust him now – we have to. You were right. He's confirmed that they do have the Imp now; he was there in the cathedral during the transference.'

'I'm relying on your judgement. Tell Gareth that his best chance of success, once he has the Imp, is to make for the Lleyn cottage – I won't be there – hide the Imp on Bardsey Island, as you originally thought best, and let Bleddyn bring him to Mull by sea.'

Murdoch began to ask him to confirm that he had never been baptised but bleeping noises supervened as Winterman's telephone went down. He sighed, prayed silently for half a minute and went to bed.

CHAPTER FIFTY-NINE

═══

TEMPLE WAS DREAMING AND KNEW IT BUT COULD NOT AWAKEN FROM THE STATE. HE WAS IN A CELLAR. HE RECOGNISED IT AS THE ONE BENEATH THE Commandery near Temple Bruer outside Lincoln. Men were dragging him by the armpits towards a harness suspended from a beam. Leather straps began to dig into his arms and ribcage. A rubber gag was thrust between his teeth. It tasted of the stale saliva of other terrified people. In the far corner some men were heating something with a blow-lamp. Their sweating faces glowed as they kept turning towards him from their work and grinning. Suddenly the two who had tied him up seized him around each thigh while a third unfastened his belt and tugged his trousers and briefs down over his knees. He then held up a plastic funnel for him to see before walking purposefully around behind him.

Temple felt something cold and greasy being applied between the cheeks of his buttocks, fingers at his anus and then the sharp pressure of the funnel being inserted. Twisting his head back to the front, he saw the Prior standing in front of him. Although Temple was suspended about six inches off the concrete floor, the Prior's height allowed him to look

237

almost straight into his eyes. He tugged at his mouth and removed the gag. Temple knew it was not to make him more comfortable. The Prior wanted to hear his screams.

'I have always thought it strange,' said the Prior, as though he were in the middle of a lecture, 'that Christian artists have as a rule persisted in depicting the crucified Jesus as hanging high on a huge cross. In reality, he was probably suspended not much higher off the ground than you are now. Think about that, if the pain permits thought, as you die a traitor's death.'

He turned to the men in the corner and nodded. One of them advanced with the poker held stiffly away at arm's length. As he approached Temple's writhing body he held the tip of the poker briefly under his nose so that he could feel the heat throbbing off its pale-pink-hot last nine inches.

'This poker belongs to Springfellow,' the Prior informed him, smiling.

A lock of Temple's dishevelled hair slipped off his sweating brow and touched the almost white metal. The stench of its burning seared into his sinuses. The man went out of sight behind him. Temple saw the Prior's smile broaden as their eyes met again. His mouth opened to give a command. All the men in the cellar had gathered round as he began to scream the word 'No!' louder and higher and more violently at each emptying of his lungs.

Hands were gripping his shoulders. He was being shaken. He opened his eyes and looked into Gareth Burden's anxious face before falling back onto his sweat-soaked pillow.

'Promise,' he croaked, 'promise you'll never ask me to go back to Lincoln!'

CHAPTER SIXTY

WINTERMAN OPENED HIS EYES AND ROSE OFF HIS KNEES. THE RITUAL HAD TAKEN MOST OF THE MORNING BUT HE FELT THAT HE WAS NOW READY. He bowed to each of the four points of the compass and went at once to the bathroom. He showered slowly and thoroughly. After drying himself he stood in front of the full-length mirror and smeared himself lightly over most of his body with the ointment, rubbing until his skin had completely absorbed its faintly aromatic sheen. He left unanointed only his face and hands. He dressed in the blue suit, combed his red hair, picked up his sword-crutch and packed bag and went out at once to the car.

He walked a little way down the herb-garden and looked out for a while over to Bardsey Island. Turning suddenly on his heel, he jumped in behind the wheel, reminded his grinning face in the mirror that he was supposed to be crippled and drove off down the lane. He found Bleddyn beyond his kitchen-garden at the door of the spare shed that he had converted into a pigeon loft. He was feeding grain to the half dozen or so birds, murmuring encouragement to them in Welsh.

'I must be off now,' said Winterman abruptly. 'Others may come – two men with a woman.' He paused. 'A small, red-haired, very beautiful woman.' He cleared his throat. 'Help them as much as you've helped me. Dr Murdoch will tell you more, but perhaps not by telephone from now on.'

'I'll lay a fire for them, then. Goodbye, sir,' said Bleddyn, barely glancing up from his birds. 'I'll be seeing you again, I hope?' he asked slyly.

Winterman smiled. Though he looked almost fifty, there was a boyishness about the man that he found endearing. 'I hope you will. Though it may not seem that it's me you're seeing, when you see me, if you see what I mean.'

'I'm afraid my English is not up to understanding that, sir,' laughed Bleddyn.

Winterman laughed back, waved once as he turned away and climbed heavily into his car. In his mirror he saw Bleddyn standing at his low privet hedge watching him go.

In Bangor Winterman parked near the cathedral and walked slowly with the aid of his crutch to the small city's Roman Catholic church. He was a little late for the morning mass and slid into a pew behind a few old women who were standing for the gospel. He knelt throughout the reading, fingering the little cuff-link box in his jacket pocket. Thoughts of his small, red-haired, very beautiful Angharad swamped his mind and it was only the tinkle of the bell at the consecration that roused him from his memories. He remained on his knees until the distribution, going up to the altar-rail last. Returning to his pew, he stayed there only long enough to slip the host into the box, click it shut and drop it into the pocket of his waxed-cotton jacket. He half genuflected with stiff deliberation in the aisle, leaning ostentatiously on his crutch, and left before the priest pronounced the words of dismissal.

He lunched well at The Antelope, drove slowly to Cadwallader-Price's house and was admitted wordlessly. Cadwallader-Price invited him to sit down and offered him a scotch. Winterman declined but Cadwallader-Price poured himself a large Famous Grouse and drank it off almost at once with a nervous slurp.

'The Prior of the Lincoln Commandery wants to see what exactly you have achieved with the gargoyle-sprite,' he said bluntly. 'He's summoned an extraordinary meeting for tonight. We must leave soon. Will you drive us? I don't like long distances and I find it a tiresome journey from west to east coasts.'

'I insist on driving,' replied Winterman. 'I want it to remain perfectly clear to you that I am in control of the pace of these negotiations.'

'Of course!' said Cadwallader-Price, blustering and conciliatory at the same time. 'I quite understand. The Lincoln Prior, however, also sets his own pace.'

'Let him,' said Winterman, injecting into his voice as much contempt as he could feign. 'His importance derives solely from his possession of the Imp.' He looked sharply at Cadwallader-Price, who avoided his gaze. 'Come off it!' chuckled Winterman. 'We both know he has it and that its release at an appropriate moment is the cornerstone of his alliance with the Front.'

'I admire,' Cadwallader-Price hesitated, 'your intelligence. You could rise high in the Order.'

'Higher with the help of the right ally,' said Winterman softly. 'I think I will have that scotch, if you'd be so kind.'

Cadwallader-Price pounced up and scuttled over to the sideboard. Pouring a good two fingers into a glass, he set the bottle on a small table between Winterman's chair and his own.

'It will strengthen our position,' said Winterman, sipping and smiling as he allowed the significance of his use of the word our to excite Cadwallader-Price, 'if I know more precisely the timescales involved.'

'We can leave whenever you're ready.'

'You misunderstand me. I need to know, before I can think of coming with you, when the Imp is to be released.'

'The purpose of the meeting is for you to demonstrate what you have done, and can do, with the gargoyle-sprite.'

'And,' Winterman raised his voice in interruption, 'to propose a similar modification for releasing the Imp.'

Cadwallader-Price reached for the whisky bottle, his hand trembling slightly but noticeably.

'The weakness in their plan, as I see it,' continued Winterman smoothly, 'is the unpredictability of the exact effects of the release. If it can be controlled and directed, however, at specific targets . . ,' he raised his glass and his eyebrows at the same time, 'I need hardly dwell at great length on the obvious advantages.'

Cadwallader-Price swallowed his drink noisily. 'And you're sure you can construct a similar box for a demon as powerful as the Imp?'

'Given enough time, yes. That is why I must know, now, if I'm likely to be given it. If it's out of the question, then we have less to offer and our bargaining position is correspondingly weaker.' He looked hard at Cadwallader-Price. 'You'll have noticed that I've been saying "we"?'

Cadwallader-Price nodded and wiped the corners of his mouth clear of a white stickiness with the edge of his index finger. Winterman could smell the results of the churning of the man's stomach across the space between the chairs despite the overlay of whisky fumes. 'November,' he said in a whisper.

'When exactly in November?'

Cadwallader-Price cleared his throat. 'Remembrance Sunday.'

Winterman whistled on a rising note. 'I should have guessed,' he muttered. 'So they're going for the Whitehall parade.' He closed his eyes and pictured the scene: rampaging crowds, veteran servicemen at each other's throats, parliamentary figures, members of the Royal Family . . . And all on television, national and international. He drained his whisky glass.

'Does that give you enough time?'

He nodded thoughtfully. 'A month should be more than sufficient,' he said, rising and adding with a smile, 'for what I have in mind.'

CHAPTER SIXTY-ONE

'I think it best,' said Murdoch, 'if you both cross to the mainland this evening, taking my car — they will probably still be looking for Sidney's Peugeot. Book in to a small hotel near Oban and keep in touch with me from there. You're within ten hours' drive then. But if you stay on the island and the wind gets up and prevents the ferries crossing, you're no use to him. Even though you may not get close to him, or even see him, during this operation, you can always, he wants me to remind you, Gareth, keep in telepathic communication with him – if the need and the opportunity arise. Keep studying his book.'

Gareth nodded in agreement. He looked at Temple, who was sitting very close to the fire in Murdoch's study but still looking very cold. 'Are you still sure that you want to come?' he asked him.

'I'm sure I don't want to,' he said, smiling quickly. 'But equally sure that I must.'

'And what must we do if and when we have the Imp?' asked Gareth, turning to Murdoch who was smiling at Temple in admiration.

'I've been thinking and praying hard about that,' he

sighed. 'My first thought was to have you bring it back here. I had intended to set it in concrete under the altar in the chapel. But we must plan further ahead. I believe the time will come when they will invade even this place.' He looked sadly around his book-lined walls and out at the lengthening shadows on the sloping lawn.

'I thought you said that you had protected it?' said Angharad, sounding more genuinely anxious than pert.

'The spells I've woven are effective only against psychic attack,' said Murdoch. 'It is the simple, physical attack of the sort the Front would deliver that we must fear. The Law is protecting us from that at the moment but laws are changed by governments.'

'But if we succeed in robbing them of the Imp,' began Temple, 'surely . . . '

'We can only delay their rise to power, I'm afraid,' said Murdoch. 'We must believe the prophecies on all points. There is a terrible time, a great Tribulation, coming. But our delaying them is still important. Vital, in fact. It will give us the time we need to re-establish our centre of resistance in Ireland,' he paused and looked at Angharad with a smile of obvious affection, 'around the Mother and the Children.'

'Where exactly in Ireland will that be?'

'I'm not sure yet. But I do know that the Imp must be kept, still bound, out of their hands. It would be easy to drop it into the sea but I know it will be of more use, even to us, if its power is, as it were, available. Not that I should contemplate using it. Sidney has always been insistent on that point. I suppose it could prove a bargaining counter.'

'Where will it be safe from them?' asked Temple, speaking more to himself than to anyone else in the room.

'On Bardsey Island,' said Murdoch. 'Buried with twenty thousand saints to keep it company! Somewhere, Gareth, in the ruin of the abbey of St Mary. Once you're out of Lincoln, head for our cottage on the Lleyn. I'll give you the details before you leave – unwritten, so you'll have to memorise them. There's one of our Company, a man called Bleddyn, who lives nearby. He'll take you to Bardsey in his boat. And when you've hidden the Imp in a place from which you'll one day be able to retrieve it, he'll also bring you on here to Mull. After that . . . ' He shrugged and smiled. 'Man proposes; God disposes.'

He stood up decisively and winked at Temple. 'We'll leave you two alone together for a while. It's warm in front of the fire. Come along, Sam! Let me show you the peculiarities of my old Volvo.'

CHAPTER SIXTY-TWO

OME FIVE HOURS AFTER LEAVING BANGOR WINTERMAN
PULLED OFF THE ROAD AND UP THE DRIVE OF A FARM
NEAR TEMPLE BRUER TO THE SOUTH OF LINCOLN.
After parking in a courtyard, he hobbled out with his crutch
and stretched himself systematically, leaning straight-armed
against the guttering of the car and looking over its roof
towards the orange loom of the city on the northern horizon.
As they had passed through the city he had insisted on driving past his school. To his surprise there had been cars parked
outside and people walking in. Nancy, he had thought with
only a fleeting spasm of guilt, must have gone ahead with the
Careers Evening that they had planned. She would, he
reflected, adjusting his grip on his crutch; Nancy loved
Evenings.

Removing the leather-covered box from the boot, he followed Cadwallader-Price into the building. As he hobbled
along he glanced with apparent indifference at the dozen or
so expensive cars parked in the yard but, using his own
memory-system, compulsively filed away their registration
numbers in the compartment of his brain that he reserved for
temporarily holding such information.

The farmhouse itself was a two-storied structure with wings enclosing the three sides of a square. One of these had a central lantern in its roof with views over the surrounding fields. Dormer windows, four on each side, had been built as an afterthought into the steeply sloping, almost Dutch, roof. Cadwallader-Price led him up an iron spiral staircase and into a large room that ran the length of the wing. There was a fairly low false ceiling of perforated pasteboard and from somewhere droned the hum of an extractor-fan.

A very tall man in his middle sixties rose from his seat at the far end of the long centrally positioned table. As he walked towards them Winterman felt afraid for the first time since leaving the Lleyn cottage. For Cadwallader-Price he had an almost exhilarating contempt but the Prior of the Lincoln Commandery exuded a menace as palpable as a rank body odour.

Cadwallader-Price performed the introductions, using the name Emsvir and the title Prior. As the two wizards shook hands, Winterman felt that each of them was reluctant to be the first to slacken his grip. Winterman was as stiff as a swordblade. He sensed at once the Prior's attempt to draw out his power and the heightening of his own tension caused by his effort to conserve it. The Prior indicated a chair to the right of his own at the head of the table. Winterman put the box down in front of him on the polished wood, rested his crutch against the chairback and sat down with feigned awkwardness. Cadwallader-Price was offered the seat on the Prior's left.

The Prior reached under the edge of the table and pressed something. A door behind them opened and ten men, all aged between thirty-five and fifty-five filed in. Without a word they took their places behind the remaining high-backed chairs, four on each of the long sides and two facing the Prior down the length of the table. With a twist of his hand which involved collapsing it languidly from the wrist he commanded rather than invited them to sit down. They obeyed.

'Esquires,' he began without preamble, 'I am aware that I have had to summon you from your businesses and affairs at short notice, so I will be brief. Most of you know the Prior of the Gwynedd Commandery.' He inclined his grey head towards Cadwallader-Price, who pursed his lips pompously. 'The, er, stranger in our midst is Mr Hamish Emsvir. He has driven a considerable distance to be with us. I would not have brought you together if I did not believe that what he has to show us is not only of great interest to us all but also of inestimable value. It is most regrettable that Esquires Spring-fellow and Temple cannot witness what we are about to see and hear.' He paused, looking at each face in turn, challenging anyone to ask a question or make a comment. No-One did. He turned expectantly to Winterman and raised his eyebrows.

Winterman met his gaze and then glanced swiftly round the table, making brief eye-contact with everyone. To his relief the headmaster at the bottom of the table, whom he had met at several teachers' meetings, showed not the slightest suspicion of recognition. Nor did the man, sitting next to Cadwallader-Price, who had sold his house for him a few years ago. He knew from what Cadwallader-Price had told him on the long drive across England that the Prior himself had realised that Emsvir and Winterman were one and the same. His calculation that the Prior's congenital passion for secrecy and love of restricted information for its own sake would ensure he kept that knowledge to himself had so far proved correct.

He unclipped the leather casing of the box in front of him as he began to speak. 'Gentlemen,' he said in his Morningside accent, 'inside this wooden box is the gargoyle-sprite that caused the havoc at St Cuthbert's Comprehensive School on Monday.' He placed the box down on the surface of the table. There was a murmur of surprise and whispered comment.

The headmaster spoke first. 'But the sprite was released. What you have there will be just a lump of stone.' He looked around importantly, awaiting approval for the perspicacity of his remarks. None came because all eyes, Winterman noticed with satisfaction, were on the screwdriver that he had produced from the breast pocket of his suit. 'It was indeed released,' he answered levelly, 'as you say, but what you do not know is that one of my apprentices exorcised the school building the same night and revoked the sprite into this image here, using what I can assure you was the correct formula. It was, in fact,' he added as he began to unscrew the lid, 'during his attempt to reclaim this that your colleague Springfellow,' he shot a challenging glance at the Prior beside him, 'lost his life.'

The Prior's face was expressionless.

'And, I suspect,' continued Winterman, still steadily unscrewing, 'his soul.'

To his delight he could see under his eyebrows that frowns were being exchanged around the table but the implications of his choice of words seemed to be forgotten about when he prised up the lid with the tip of the screwdriver. It came loose with a faint popping sound. No-one moved. He lifted out the linen-swathed cocoon and began to unwind.

There was total silence in the room until he set the stone figure on its base on the tabletop.

He looked around, his eyebrows slightly raised, as if offering to field questions from any of the men who were now sitting back in their chairs, exhaling collectively. There were none. 'My purpose,' he continued, 'in borrowing the sprite without your permission was to enable me to prove a theory that I have held for some time now. What I wanted to achieve was a controlled exorcism. So,' he declared with a flourish, 'one takes a charged image.' He picked up the carved lump of stone and weighed it in one hand. 'One winds it first in altar cloth.' There was an involuntary intake of breath and all except the Prior and Cadwallader-Price drew back slightly from the table edge towards which they had begun to lean as they watched the movements of his hands.

He began to rewind the image, talking as he wound, looking up from time to time at their eager faces, trying to match each one to the names written in the notebook in his pocket. 'In the mean time, one has prepared a wooden box made from a disused Christian altar – or even a church pew – and lined it with mirrors.'

He set down the rewound image and held up the box, turning it in his hands through many angles. 'Mirrors of the purest crystal, backed with silver from altar candlesticks. One places the image in the box.' He did so and showed them all the snugly swaddled sprite. 'Observe that the navel of the image is exposed. The mirrored lid is screwed on.' He began to screw back the lid, aware of their close attention. He took his time, determined not to risk everything by cross-threading, speaking in short, explanatory bursts as he worked. 'Then comes the operation which none of you, I suspect, would dare perform. One acquires a consecrated eucharistic wafer.'

He paused and set down the screwdriver. It clicked against the wood of the table-top, clearly audible in the stunned stillness. Withdrawing the small, two-pronged fork from his pocket, he began to unscrew the cylinder in the centre of the lid far enough to reveal the slot in its side. 'One pierces a hole in the centre of the host with a needle,' he said. He produced a pair of tweezers and made as if to withdraw the wafer to show them. There were muffled sounds of consternation and the Prior interrupted.

'It will not be necessary to show us,' he said, evidently trying hard to conceal the anxiety in his voice.

Winterman smiled and closed his fingers around the now fully removed cylinder. 'Once one has spoken the formula of release,' he said, 'the sprite, as you all know, must obey. But it finds its way blocked by spiritual substances – and I use that highly appropriate word advisedly – so antagonistic to it that its energy is increased by what we can only assume is its self-consuming fury. Then it finds, if you'll pardon the expression, the eye of the needle. It exits under such pressure that its direction can be manipulated by moving the box. Moreover, as it cannot all escape at once, one can even retain as much of its energy as may be needed later by pronouncing the formula of revocation. That, however, is a refinement which I must confess I cannot guarantee. I have experimented with this particular sprite only once. The subject was burnt to something resembling charred toast. It's fairly obvious, by the way, from that and other indications, that the sprite must have at some time been a salamander.' He picked up the box and handed it to the Prior who, after checking that Winterman still had the metal cylinder containing the host, took it reverently in his blue-veined hands.

'The simplicity of genius!' he murmured. 'Mr, er, Emsvir, we must congratulate you!'

To Winterman's surprise the ten Esquires, joined by the Prior and Cadwallader-Price, rose to their feet and applauded him. He bowed briefly at them and slumped back in his chair. They too sat down and excited conversations broke out. The Prior let the noise run for a few minutes and then called the meeting to order again.

'Mr Emsvir has applied to join our Commandery,' he said. 'In a moment I shall ask him to withdraw while we consider our response to his request. Before he does, I must ask him to make very clear to us what he is offering in return for the privilege of membership.' He turned to Winterman again.

'I offer,' said Winterman expansively, 'the return of this gargoyle-sprite and the use of the box I have constructed. I offer my services as an Unorthodox Gnostic Christian.' He twirled the cylinder between his fingers above the tabletop for all to see. 'Without which you would find the construction of other boxes by yourselves to be difficult, if not impossible. I think I'm correct in saying, Prior, that although you yourself attend church services for the purposes of establishing a respectable persona, they never include a eucharist?'

The Prior nodded primly, as though being forced finally to admit that he had for years been wearing a wig.

'Precisely,' continued Winterman. 'But what I am offering in particular,' he paused to ensure he obtained their complete attention, 'is similarly to encase the entity that you have transferred from the Lincoln Imp.' The effect of his remark was even more eye-widening than his threatened exposition of the host. 'I shall withdraw now, as you requested, and allow Dr Cadwallader-Price to persuade you all how such a development would strengthen your position in matters anent the Albion Front.' He stood up and leaned on his crutch.

The Prior rose too and escorted him into the room from which the ten had emerged. Winterman saw that he was under the lantern. He sat down in an armchair opposite a glazed and framed Ordnance Survey map of the Lincoln district that was hanging on a wall between two windows. When the Prior had returned to the conference chamber, Winterman stood up swiftly, though still using his crutch, and tried the door in the opposite wall. It opened directly onto a staircase. Returning to the other door, he listened to the murmur of voices. The sound had that overlapping, irritating quality of a typical discussion but no individual words were distinct. He sat in the chair again with his back to the door. Surreptitiously glancing around the walls and ceiling to detect any closed-circuit cameras but spotting none, he removed the pair of tweezers from his pocket and, holding his breath, teased out the pierced host. He placed it on his palm. Moving his fingers in the space between two buttons on his shirt-front, he made the sign of the cross, put the wafer on his tongue and closed his eyes. He prayed briefly but fiercely while reaching into his pocket for the cuff-link box.

'Father,' he murmured as he swallowed the host, 'forgive me, for I know exactly what I am doing.'

Into the groove awaiting it he slotted the other host, a perfect disc with no hole pierced in its centre.

With the cylinder warming in his closed fist he went to stand, thoughtfully leaning on his crutch, in front of the map.

By way of Welbourn and Leadenham it was about twelve miles to where the A1 curved around Newark. Once on it an escaping car would be difficult to stop without attracting witnesses. Minutes later the door opened and Cadwallader-Price invited him to rejoin the others. They all stood as he entered and sat only when he had resumed his seat at the table.

'Dr Cadwallader-Price has convinced us,' said the Prior, 'that the Albion Front can be persuaded to appreciate the advantages of a controlled release of, er, what it is convenient to term the Imp. Without exception, the members of this Commandery are willing to accept you as a member, if you in turn are prepared to pledge your willingness to begin work on encasing the, er, Imp as soon as you have been introduced to representatives of the Albion Front and received their approval. Do you accept?'

'I do,' answered Winterman without hesitation. 'I have brought my materials with me but shall need a workshop.'

'Our cellars here,' said the Prior, 'have everything,' he added with a grin at the esquires, 'a man could desire.' He coughed and cleared his throat. 'Which brings me to the question of initiation.'

Winterman looked at him steadily, waiting for him to continue.

'It is our custom to involve our new members in one of our ceremonies of group, er, worship. To begin with, they merely observe. Without protest. To demonstrate their objectivity.'

' "Worship"?' asked Winterman.

'All will eventually be explained to you as you proceed through the various grades of our Order,' said the Prior.

'Suffice it to say, for the present, that you must know – even as an Unorthodox Gnostic Christian – Who it is that we worship. The purpose of the particular ceremony you will shortly be observing is to promote a corporate spirit by means of the shared possession of a woman – a woman who, in this case, is not going to consent to being so used.'

Cadwallader-Price, Winterman felt, was the first to sense his reluctance. 'Would not Mr Emsvir's commitment,' he asked, 'be considered to have been already proven by his objectivity in Caernarvon?'

'It would,' said the Prior, 'if he were applying to join your commandery. But I must insist that here in Lincoln he follows our traditions.'

Winterman glanced around the table. He sensed that each pair of eyes watching him was going to read great significance into the way he reacted. 'Very well,' he said. 'But I must ask one more thing. When exactly am I to meet representatives of the Albion Front to be assured that my efforts will indeed be used to bring about in this country the political revolution that we all, I presume, consider necessary for the establishment of the sort of society in which men like us can flourish?'

'It has already been arranged for tomorrow night,' said the Prior, 'at nine-thirty. As we have also already arranged accommodation at a Lincoln Hotel for you and Dr. Cadwallader-Price. You will discover, Mr. Emsvir,' he added with a strange laugh that sounded as if he might be choking on a fishbone, 'that we arrange things well here.' He snapped his fingers and the esquire next to Winterman handed both him and Cadwallader-Price what at first looked like large black silk handkerchiefs. The others all produced one from their pockets and began to pull over their heads what turned out to be hangman's hoods, shaped like small sacks with owlish eyeholes.

'Despite the short notice of this meeting,' said the Prior, 'I have nevertheless succeeded in arranging something to make up for the inconvenience. Let us proceed to the cellars.'

Winterman raised his hand and everyone hesitated by his chair. He held up the cylinder between his fingertips. The black-framed eyes looked away one by one. 'I must insist,' he said as he began to screw it back firmly into the lid of the box, 'that no-one touches this until I have finished work on the Imp. Do I have that assurance from all of you?'

The Prior nodded curtly. 'And I must insist,' he said, his voice slightly muffled by the black silk, 'that the sprite and its box remain here until you start work. Now, follow me, please. My knights and esquires are becoming eager for their sport.'

They descended the spiral staircase to the ground floor. On their way down a flight of stone steps the Prior turned expansively to Winterman who was picking his way down on his crutch. 'We always endeavour to ensure that our victims on these occasions are subjected to a mode of enforced possession that they personally find particularly repellent. I feel especially pleased with my choice for tonight. We have been observing her for some time with this in mind. She is very active in feminist circles in Lincoln and district and even spreads her poison in the school in which she works.'

He paused before a huge oak door. 'Her, therefore, we shall subject to what she must regard as the ultimate degradation: multiple rape. By men, that is,' he added with a chortle. 'I understand that her sorority believes that women are capable of rape. I've a feeling that after tonight's practice she may modify her idiotic theory. Four men will hold her down, one to each feeble limb, while a fifth convinces her that it is men who do things and that it is women who have things done to them. We are going to give her a practical grammar lesson in the difference between the active and passive voices of the verb "to ravish" that she will never forget.'

He opened the door and they passed through. 'Though unfortunately not what you'd call pretty, she does have a little body shapely enough to excite even my waning appetite. On this occasion, as I've explained, you must only watch while all twelve of us violate her in turn. I'm assuming, Doctor, that you wish to join us?'

'Let's have a good look at her!' suggested the Welshman.

The Prior switched on the lights. Fluorescent tubes began flickering to reveal a long, low, vaulted room. A Turkish carpet was spread near the centre. On it, knees drawn up to her chest, gagged and hog-tied, lay a woman in her mid-twenties. She began to squirm and moan as the thirteen hooded men approached her and arranged themselves around the four edges of the carpet. The swell of her naked hip held Winterman's eyes before he looked at her face.

He flinched, glad despite his altered appearance of the further anonymity of the mask he was now wearing. Even without her pink-tinted glasses and her fashionable clothes he recognised his colleague Ms Patterson. As four men stooped to untie her, he remembered as though through the haze of a fever how her knee had thudded into his groin in the chaos of that last crazy assembly that seemed now so long ago. He noticed the faint bruise beneath her eye which his elbow had caused. A mixture of emotions assailed him as one of the esquires slapped her on the other cheek as she struggled with them. They squatted, knelt or reclined on the carpet around her, each wrestling almost playfully with an arm or a leg.

'I'll most certainly join you!' panted Cadwallader-Price, tugging off his shoes and piling his clothes in a heap at the corner of the carpet as though he was preparing to take a bath. He knelt carefully between her knees and began loosening the gag. 'Now I'm doing this, *cariad*,' he explained in an exaggerated Welsh sing-song, 'so that you can tell me what it is exactly you've got against men, you see.'

Winterman half turned away towards the Prior whose glittering eyes continued to watch Cadwallader-Price's unathletic but purposeful movements. 'What will happen to her afterwards?' he asked casually, trying to keep out of his voice any hint of concern.

The Prior leaned across and shouted in Winterman's ear above the woman's yells of protest, 'You could drop her off for what's left of your Careers Evening.' He stood away from him again, laughing at his own joke and watching him to see how he was reacting to the implications of his remark.

Winterman forced himself to grin. 'But seriously?' he persisted, ignoring the reference to his connection with the school.

'Oh, she'll be injected with a disorienting drug and dumped in a ditch to sleep it off. We'll put her navy-blue suit back on, of course, as neat and as tidy and as fashionable,' he sneered with swelling venom, 'as when we took it off her. No-one's going to believe the story she's going to have to tell.' He nodded down at Cadwallader-Price, whose grunts of effort were beginning to modulate into longer snarls of triumph as the unlovely stirrings of his pale buttocks settled into a pattern of insistent lunges. He looked at his wristwatch. 'I'd better fetch you a chair. With twelve of us, this could take the best part of an hour.'

Winterman felt light-headed. He leaned heavily onto his crutch and wiped his forehead. Through his parted fingers he looked at Ms Patterson's shapely legs spread wide to enable Cadwallader-Price to ride her and winced, not at what he was seeing so much as at the sudden thought of Angharad's thighs being forced apart only by her own eagerness for Gareth Burden to be this energetic between them.

CHAPTER SIXTY-THREE

GARETH LOWERED HIS HAND AFTER WAVING FOR THE LAST TIME. ANGHARAD'S COPPER HAIR BECAME INDISTINGUISHABLE FROM THE COLOUR OF HER dress in the gathering dusk as the ferry pulled further away from the Craignure pier. He had said everything that he had been able to say during their private parting in Murdoch's study. She had been resolute, had even promised that she would pray for his safe return, admitting that it would be the first time since childhood that she had seriously prayed for anything. The knowledge of the risks he faced had quelled their physical desire for each other. To have gone up to her room then would not only have meant a breach of their promise to Murdoch but almost a trivialising of their need for each other at the very moment when they felt it to be most precious – like insisting, he had thought, on scratching an itch on one's neck while shaking hands with Royalty. He had nevertheless felt relieved that she had seemed to feel the same. He knew that he could not have resisted her if she had added anguish to her loveliness.

'I can wait,' she had said as they walked down to join Murdoch and Temple by the cars. 'Just make sure that you come back to make me glad that I did wait!' The silent tears had come as she sat beside him in Sidney's old Peugeot. He had caught glimpses of her face in the headlights of the Volvo in which Murdoch and Temple followed them to the ferry.

He rested both arms on the taffrail and pulled in deep lungfuls of the salty wind. He thought he could see the headlights of the Peugeot turning back towards Dervaig. Sighing, he turned to look for Temple and saw him coming up the companionway from the car-deck.

'My God!' muttered Temple, nodding towards the receding shoreline. 'I intend to come back here. I don't think I've ever known such peace.'

'I know,' said Gareth. 'I even managed to find time to finish editing the next issue of *Jejune Incest*. I'm going to try to deliver it to the printer, when we have the chance. Almost a futile gesture, perhaps, in the face of what's coming.' He laughed. 'But, as Murdoch keeps saying, it won't be the first time that a light came from these islands to a darkened mainland.'

They both stood in silence for a while beside each other, watching Mull merge into the twilight. When they could see it no longer they went below for a drink and to plan the safest route south. After docking in Oban, they drove to the Falls of Lora hotel and booked two single rooms for the night. In a fit of whimsy Gareth amused himself by signing his name C A Stor. Temple grinned as he took the pen from him and filled in his own name as P. Ollux.

Gareth nodded in approval. 'I'm glad to see you're in the right frame of mind for this venture. I can't tell you how brave I think you're being. Let's discuss disguises over dinner.'

Since their flight from Lincoln, Temple had not shaved his moustache. Its four days' growth was already subtly modifying his features. At Murdoch's suggestion he had cropped his long hair after his baptism. Murdoch had also provided them with brown shirts and black trousers and a pair of old trilbies. They agreed that they could both manage to pass as either Front supporters or slightly disreputable members of the racing fraternity.

'Sidney Winterman assured me,' said Gareth, smearing mustard onto his very well done steak, 'that the essence of successful disguise is slight variation from the familiar allied with change of context. Have you ever owned a B series Volvo?'

Temple shook his head, his mouth full of mushrooms.

'Good. The car, in fact, will be our best cover.'

'It's not exactly a get-away vehicle, is it?' said Temple through his chewing.

'Murdoch told me she's done a hundred and fifty-thousand and never had the cylinder-head off. But when she picks up her skirts, the old lady can run.'

'Do you think we'll have to run?' Temple's face became suddenly graver.

Gareth shrugged. 'Well have a better idea of what we must do after I've phoned Murdoch at midnight. More claret?'

CHAPTER SIXTY-FOUR

'ANOTHER GLASS OF WINE?' ASKED THE PRIOR, BRANDISHING A BOTTLE. HE DABBED AT HIS CHEEK WITH A BLOODSTAINED HANDKERCHIEF AND laughed deprecatingly. 'Who'd have thought the little bitch would have had enough strength left to bite, after eleven of us? Are you sure you've sedated her adequately?' he asked one of the esquires over his shoulder.

'No, thank you,' said Winterman. 'If Dr Cadwallader-Price is ready, I'd like to grab some sleep.'

'So would I, mun!' laughed Cadwallader-Price harshly. 'After my exertions. I reckon it needed four to hold her down, small as she was.'

'Nine-thirty tomorrow night, then,' said the Prior, raising his glass in a farewell gesture. 'Excuse us, but we always unwind with a case of wine after one of our ceremonies. Yet another strand in the rope of male bonding.'

'I'd better drive,' said Winterman as Cadwallader-Price stumbled against him in the darkness of the yard.

The Welshman sat in silence during the short journey to Lincoln, breathing heavily through his mouth, his thoughts, guessed Winterman, probably still in the cellar. 'Jiw!' he exclaimed as the floodlit magnificence of the cathedral came into sight.

Winterman thought he was about to make some comment upon the beauty of the building that was eerily poised on its cliff like a stone galleon on the edge of a waterfall.

'I'd forgotten,' wheezed Cadwallader-Price, 'how bloody good it can be with a tight young woman. How old do you reckon she was?'

'She's twenty-six,' sighed Winterman. 'Unmarried. An only child.'

Cadwallader-Price giggled uncertainly. 'Good God! You seem to know a lot about her.'

'Lacks sparkle,' continued Winterman, half to himself. 'Little rapport with younger pupils.'

'Prefers the company of older men!' sniggered Cadwallader-Price.

He was still breaking into little fits of laughter as they pulled into the car-park of the Eastgate Hotel.

Though irritated by his mirth as they entered the foyer, Winterman was more concerned about noting the location of the payphone.

CHAPTER SIXTY-FIVE

'NOW THEN,' MURMURED GARETH. 'A17 AS FAR AS LEADENHAM.'

AS TEMPLE TURNED THE OLD VOLVO OFF THE A1, down which they had steadily cruised since Edinburgh, Gareth again looked across at his face, as he had been doing periodically throughout the day. In the glow of oncoming headlights he saw the anxiety tightening in the muscles around his jawline.

'I seem to remember promising not to ask you to come back here,' he said.

'You didn't ask. It was Murdoch.'

'What do you make of him? Honestly?'

'A great deal. A prophet, I suspect.'

Gareth grunted. 'Well, I hope his predictions to you about tonight's activities prove accurate.'

'Either way,' said Temple, 'our future depends on Winterman and him. Long term, I mean. Britain's future. The Front, Murdoch was telling me, has its tentacles firmly in place: Parliament, Judiciary, Civil Service, Press, Police, Media, even the Church. How did they do it?'

'Perhaps Winterman's latest book will tell us, if it's ever published.'

'There's not much going to be published in the line of revelation, if they get their way,' snorted Temple. 'What happened to the manuscript of his book? Did he take it with him?'

'No, Angharad has it. We must read it, if we make it back to Mull.'

'When we get back to Mull,' said Temple. 'Keep saying when.' He sighed and they fell silent until the junction with the Lincoln to Grantham road.

'Left here,' said Gareth. 'And then first right. There's a back road that runs parallel to the one we want. Here it is coming up. Now, about five miles along this until we hit the Sleaford road. I want to come at it from the east. Good God! Slow down! Stop!'

'What the hell is it?' shouted Temple, braking firmly.

'There was somebody back there trying to crawl out of the dyke!'

Temple pulled off the road onto the verge. He switched off his lights while Gareth pulled a torch out of the glove-compartment.

'You stay with the car,' said Gareth. He strode back down the road, shining his torch along the verge and ditch. He was about to turn back again when he heard a groan and saw in the yellow beam an arm and then a head raised from the long grass. He ran towards what he could now see was a woman in a navy-blue suit crawling towards the tarmac. Reaching her, he shone the torch quickly over her legs to see whether, as her awkward crawling suggested, she had broken one. He found no obvious injury and shone it next on her face.

'Penelope!' he gasped. 'What's happened to you?'

Ms Patterson stared at him as though she had just persuaded herself that she was having a religious experience. Then with a shriek she began to scramble on all fours back towards the ditch.

'It's all right – ' he began. 'It's me – ' He checked himself, baffled. 'Has someone hurt you?' he asked her.

'I lost count,' she mumbled, trying to stand up. She looked hard at him as though seeing him for the first time. 'I've missed the Careers Evening!' she wailed.

He put an arm around her shoulders. At first she shrank away but then stood rigid, staring at the torch bulb. Gareth heard the Volvo reversing towards them. He led her gently out into the road towards a rear door. Temple stuck his head out of the window.

'Back to the village,' muttered Gareth out of the corner of his mouth. 'I know this girl. She teaches at my school. Something dreadful's happened to her. We can't just leave her here. What time is it?'

'Gone nine o'clock,' said Temple. 'We mustn't delay very long.'

'They twisted my arms and legs,' moaned Ms. Patterson. 'They wore black hoods.' She started screaming.

'You're all right now!' coaxed Gareth. 'You're safe now. We're going to take you to friends.' He opened the back door and guided her in. To his relief she slid onto the seat without protest and he followed her in. Temple did a five-point turn with a lot of sweating and cursing and headed back for Leadenham.

'First house you come to that looks as if it has a telephone,' said Gareth. 'That one'll do!'

Temple pulled up and Gareth persuaded Penelope Patterson to step out of the car with him. He walked her up a driveway past a parked Vauxhall and ran the doorbell of a bungalow. Temple began turning the car round again. In doing so he backed into the drive. A sharp-featured middle-aged man wearing a paisley cravat, a fawn cardigan and spectacles opened the door. He scrutinised Gareth and the swaying girl suspiciously and also frowned at the Volvo whose rear bumper was now in awkward proximity to the Vauxhall's.

'Excuse me,' began Gareth. 'We've just found this young lady crawling out of a ditch back there.' He indicated the road down which Temple was now manoeuvring the Volvo. 'I think she needs medical attention. Could you telephone for an ambulance? I'm afraid we're going to have to leave her with you.'

Ms Patterson clutched the man by the elbow. 'They raped me,' she said. 'Held me down.'

He wiped off his spectacles and looked hard at Gareth. 'Now wait a minute!' he started. 'Where do you think you're off to? Mabel!' he yelled over his shoulder at a very short woman who had appeared in the doorway. '999, Police! Quick!' He ran down the drive after Gareth but did not pursue him into the road.

'Damn!' shouted Gareth as he watched through the rear window the man standing in his gateway staring after them accelerating into the darkness. 'Sorry! Damn it! Mistake! That bloke back there thinks we've raped her. Now he'll have the police looking for us.'

'Surely not!' said Temple, changing up into top, still accelerating hard. 'Do you think he got our number?'

'He was just the sort who would. Cravat and cardigan brigade. Good solid citizen. On our side, I suppose. Salt of the earth, etc. About to lose its savour permanently, if we don't manage to do what we've come here for.' He paused for breath for a few moments. 'Do you know, it's strange. It must have been subconsciously – but I think I recognised her face in our headlights as we passed her.'

'Did she recognise you?'

'Don't think so. She was in shock. Drugged too, I'd say. I think she had been raped.'

'By men in black hoods, didn't she say?'

Gareth fell silent again.

'Are you thinking what I am?' he asked eventually.

'Yes.'

'Damn! I've risked everything.'

'Don't reproach yourself. You acted instinctively. That can't be bad. One of the reasons we're here is that we want to strike a blow for people who believe in acting according to their better instincts, isn't it? If it had been Angharad back there, wouldn't you have wanted someone to stop and do what we did?'

Gareth sighed. 'I just hope it won't mean we're going to . . .'

'. . . Fail? Don't think of it! Do you know – the reason I hardly spoke coming down the A1 was that I was scaring myself dumb the closer we were getting. But now I can't wait. What was it old Burke said? "For evil to triumph . . ." '

' " . . . it is necessary only for the good man to do nothing." Sorry to keep introducing a note of doubt, but I believe no-one's been able to find the place where he's supposed to have said that. But we go left at the junction here and left again.'

CHAPTER SIXTY-SIX

══════

'IT IS ONLY NECESSARY,' SAID THE PRIOR, GLANCING UP CROSSLY AT AN ESQUIRE WHO WAS SLIPPING INTO HIS SEAT LATE, 'NOW THAT WE ARE ALL GATHERED, FOR me to introduce you, Mr, er, Emsvir, to Ms Millington – the member of the Albion Front with whom I have conducted longstanding negotiations – '

Winterman inclined forward in his seat and smiled tightly, thinking to himself that he had never seen a more repulsive woman. In response she bared at him some lipstick-etched teeth.

' – and though, I'm sure, no introduction is really necessary,' he continued, looking around the table, where the Esquires were packed more closely than usual, and inviting a response, 'you now have the privilege of sitting around the same table as Professor Hilary Desforges – ' He smiled at the growl of approval that rippled from chair to chair. ' - whom we are all honoured to have with us tonight for what is to be a meeting none of us will forget.'

Winterman nodded at the white-bearded but moustacheless and also neckless organism that filled the chair at the bottom end of the table. The politician was internationally

renowned for his poisonously racist speeches and inflamma-
tory articles. He looked back at Winterman as though he had
at just that moment become aware of the source of a foetid
smell but was too polite to draw attention to his discovery.
Winterman continued to smile. This was a bonus, a development he had not foreseen, the answer to the prayer he should
have prayed.

'Professor Desforges,' explained the Prior, clearly grati-
fied to be able to demonstrate that he was party to the great
man's plans, 'is on a lecture tour of the East Midlands, preparing the ground for the General Election that must soon be
upon us. And Mr Fingerwight here,' he added in an almost
insultingly parenthetical tone, 'is also experienced in liaison
work between our two organisations.'

'We've met,' said Winterman, with a dismissive grin.

Fingerwight looked at him sharply and flushed, as
though embarrassed at having misheard something important but lacking the confidence to admit it. Winterman
noticed that he was watching him carefully as the Prior continued his opening remarks.

To his surprise, Winterman was starting to enjoy himself.
His heart, he knew, was beating faster than his doctor would
consider desirable but he was experiencing the exhilarating
sensation of time itself becoming expanded and elastic. By
concentrating he could slow down the rush of events and see
them as if in a slow-motion film but all in the sharpest focus.
He gazed around him, savouring what could well be the last
thirty minutes of his earthly life.

There were sixteen faces around the table, all intent on
the Prior except his own and Fingerwight's, who was still
glancing at him surreptitiously every time Winterman turned

his head away slightly. Each face was alight with admiration, envy or appetite. The presence of the celebrated politician, Winterman realised, had heightened their sense of occasion and their perception of their own importance. An agreement struck tonight would mean the eventual certainty of power, influence, greater wealth, easier access to disposable ciphers to hang from beams in cellars or to stretch out on the floor to abuse and outrage. It promised the rapid alteration of society into a system in which their values and attitudes would become permanently dominant.

' . . . and so it is with every justification of optimism that we turn now to the business of the evening,' the Prior was concluding. 'I therefore ask Mr Hamish Emsvir to outline and, if required, detail the developments which he proposes in the techniques of entity-depetrification. I am confident, Madam, Professor, that you will find them of more than interest.'

Winterman looked away from Fingerwight's stoatlike eyes to sense everyone's attention on him. He nodded at the Prior, who had sat down to his left, and stood, leaning heavily on the arm of his chair. This emphasis on his disability did not, he noticed, deflect or diminish the intensity of Fingerwight's continuing scrutiny of his face.

'I'm sure that Mr Emsvir,' broke in Desforges's voice, courteous though still abrasive as it lingered over Winterman's false name, 'would be more comfortable, and therefore almost certainly more persuasive, if he addressed us all seated.'

Winterman bowed briefly in acknowledgement and sat down. He stretched out both hands until his right touched the boxed gargoyle-sprite and his left the linen-wrapped Imp which lay now on its side on the table beside the larger, unfinished receptacle on which he had been working most of the day. He picked it up and started unwinding its cloth binding.

'Lady and gentlemen,' he began, 'when this – ' He set the Imp on its base on the table in front of him. ' - is encased like this – ' He drew the sprite's box alongside it. ' - you will be able, with our assistance, to begin the process by which you take and keep control of Britain.'

CHAPTER SIXTY-SEVEN

'PULL OFF HERE,' SAID GARETH. HE INDICATED WHAT SEEMED IN THE CAR'S HEADLIGHTS TO BE A BROAD UNMETALLED ROAD AT RIGHT ANGLES TO THE ONE on which they had just driven past the Commandery. 'We're on old Ermine Street. Turn her around and back up out of sight of the road against that hedge there.'

'There's certainly a meeting going on,' said Temple, 'so everything's as Winterman has told Murdoch it would be. So far. They're up in the Conference Room. High enough not to need curtains drawn. You'd need to be up a tree with binoculars to see in.

'We daren't park any closer. They'll have guards in the grounds, presumably.'

'A few, near the main entrance. And the Front'll have brought their own.'

'So that's what we're going to be. We walk into the grounds – no stealth – as a pair, shining torches as if we're patrolling, making no attempt to look like anything other than men who've every right to be there. If we're challenged by Tophetim, we're Front; if by Front, we're Tophetim. And let's hope, if it comes to it, it's the latter – you can bluff them with your knowledge of the place. To explain the hammers we're carrying – we're straightening a dented wheel-rim on one of our cars, aren't we? If they come too close and look for a dent, we give them one – right?'

'But we keep out of sight, if possible, in the courtyard among the cars. Until it happens. Agreed.'

'I don't think I'll wear a brown shirt and black trousers like this ever again.'

'And once we've got the Imp, straight back here. How long to go?

'Just over five minutes. It's totally dark, I should say, on the driveway. I don't know how much light there'll be from the Conference Room.'

'I suppose we have to trust Winterman is correct in his estimate of what will happen.' Temple rubbed his palms together in a spasm of excitement.

'Have you been practising the psalm?'

'All the way down here, on and off.'

'Me too, even though I've had longer to learn it than you have. Too late to worry now. Just tell me when there's only a minute to go. I need a short while to see if I can communicate with Winterman.' Gareth sat back in his seat and burrowed his neck into the headrest. He tried to relax. As he expected, he was unable to do but was relieved to find that his determined practice now enabled him to shift rapidly into the required state of mind despite the tension in his body. Closing his eyes, and concentrating first on the movement of his diaphragm and then on the sensation of light on the inside of his forehead he received almost at once the feeling that it was Winterman, not Temple, beside him in the car. Then he heard his voice. He was projecting it, as at a school assembly, speaking confidently and fluently. Next he saw him as if he were standing at his shoulder. He was sitting – despite the fact that he was obviously giving an address – at a large table. In front of him on it and slightly to his left was the stone replica of the Lincoln Imp. Then he felt pressure on his shoulder, the picture blacked out and he opened his eyes to see Temple shaking his shoulder.

'Time to go. Did you get through?'

'I did. This is it. Ready?'

Temple hesitated. 'Of course not!' Then he laughed. 'And in a sense, never more ready. Let's go.'

They stepped out of the car and felt the cool, moist air on their skin. The old Roman road ran straight towards the loom of Lincoln as they followed it for a few yards. In the cloudy, moonless dark its ancient presence was little more than a faint lightening of the gloom that pressed in on them from the fields and hedges around.

CHAPTER SIXTY-EIGHT

'WOULD YOU LIKE TO TELL ME WHAT HAPPENED, MADAM?' ASKED THE POLICEMAN GENTLY, MOVING TO STAND NEARER TO PENELOPE Patterson.

She was sitting on the edge of the sofa, staring at the glow of the electric fire, her hands cupped around the mug of hot sweet tea. She had not even looked up when he came in, removing his cap. The man of the house and his wife stood either side of him, looking uncertainly from him to her. The radio clipped inside the lapel of his jacket bleeped with a subdued, throttled sound and a distant voice crackled.

She looked up then from her drink, wide-eyed. The sight of his dark uniform seemed to uncoil a spring. 'They raped me,' she said, without indignation or surprise. 'A dozen or so of them. One after the other. On a carpet in a cellar. They held me down by my arms and legs. Always four of them – never the same four – holding me down and another one . . . They took turns on top of me.'

The middle-aged woman of the house tutted and looked away, half backing out of the room yet too fascinated to leave altogether.

279

'Who were they?' asked the policeman. 'Did you know them?'

'They all had masks on. Hoods. Black hoods with holes for the eyes. Such eyes . . . But they had nothing else on, when they . . . They took their time stripping off in front of me when it was their turn. They were laughing . . . '

She began to sob for the first time. 'They all raped me, do you understand? However long it took them, they all got what they wanted!' Her voice rose to a yell and then sagged to a whine. 'The last one went on and on. He was very tall. A very big man. He hurt me the most. It was after he'd . . . finished with me that one of the others injected me . . . with a needle.' Her face brightened as though she had remembered an important detail. 'But there was one who did nothing. He just watched the others. He sat on a chair. He had a crutch . . . '

'And I understand two young men brought you here in their car.'

'Yes. I woke up in a ditch. I tried to crawl towards the road. They stopped. One of them helped me into the car. He recognised me, you see.'

'So these two young men didn't put you into the ditch?'

'Oh no!' She looked up at him, bewildered. He had seen that look many times before on the faces of people trying to make a statement – shock at the realisation that there could be a different way of seeing what had happened. 'No! They came later. Much later, I think.'

'And you say they recognised you?'

'One of them did. He teaches at my school.'

'What's his name, please?'

'Burden. Gary, I think. No, Gareth. He's not been there

very long. Only since the start of this term.' She paused and bit her knuckles. 'And I must have missed the Careers Evening!'

The policeman paused in his note-taking, trying to suppress a smile. 'And I should have asked for your name, Madam.'

'Penelope Patterson. Ms.' She frowned at him. 'Don't you want my address too? Don't you always ask for an address?'

'Er, yes, please.' He looked at his wristwatch.

She gave her address. As he wrote it down, he asked the man beside him if he had noticed the make of the car.

'I can do better than that,' he replied, looking over the top of his spectacles and widening his eyes at his wife. 'I can give you its registration number.'

He gave it, importantly, as though reciting a poem learned at school to his parents. 'It was an old, white Volvo. You know, the sort you sometimes see in their advertisements to show how long they last.'

The policeman smiled again and nodded as he wrote down the number. 'You've been most helpful, sir. And you, Madam.' He twisted to nod at the woman who was still looking at Ms Patterson as if she might at any moment attempt to jump head first through the window. 'If you'll excuse me, I'll radio from my car for an ambulance, I think, and ask for a w p c to meet it at the hospital.'

He let himself out and watched the owner of the bungalow hovering in the doorway. He slammed his car door and reached under the dashboard for a transceiver.

'Charlie?' he said. 'Sergeant Perkins here. Our runaways are back. You're looking for a white Volvo, probably B series. It must be within a five mile radius of Leadenham at the moment. I'm going on now to check out the place where Desforges has gone. I suggest you put yourself between that place and the A 1. This is the registration number you'll want. I'll have it checked out and let you know who owns it. Don't let them give you the slip this time!'

CHAPTER SIXTY-NINE

THROUGHOUT HIS SPEECH WINTERMAN KEPT GLANCING AT MS MILLINGTON AND DESFORGES. EACH TIME HE LOOKED THEY SEEMED TO BE LEANING closer to him over the edge of the table, their faces becoming more intent and absorbed as the implications of what he was saying seeped into their consciousness. They occasionally exchanged glances. The fixed smug smile on Fingerwight's face suggested to him that he had at last realised who he was. He smiled to himself at the thought that it did not matter any longer.

'And if I may add,' he continued, 'a possible strategy of my own, could I suggest that, since the encased demon may be used on several occasions – with expert use of the revocation formula – I can think of no better time to demonstrate its powers than during the Queen's Speech. Now that such an event is televised across the nation, I need hardly itemise for you the advantages to be derived from the humiliation one could inflict upon either the Government or the Opposition – depending on where we find ourselves after the next election. As the primary energy of the Imp-demon is murderous hatred, you would have here a weapon compared with which a thermo-nuclear bomb is laughably expensive and crudely indiscriminate.'

He sat back and watched the faces of the Front representatives. Millington raised her eyebrows at Desforges, inviting him to be the first to comment. Winterman glanced at his wristwatch. It was enough past ten o'clock for Gareth to be in position. He had thought of the young man just then. It had been almost as if he had suddenly sat beside him and whispered in his ear. He waited until he saw Desforges draw breath to speak and broke in again, relishing the look of pompous annoyance on the fat, pink face at the obviously unaccustomed experience of being interrupted and relishing even more the thought that this expression was very soon now going to change into one of a terror that would be as new to him as it would be brief.

'There is, however,' he said in the suddenly bright, energetic tone of voice that a lecturer often adopts near the middle of a talk when he senses attention starting to flag, 'one problem with encased sprites and demons. It occurred to me during my work on this one.' He lifted the smaller, completed box in both hands. 'When the formula of release is uttered – ' He held its top edge level with his eyes, pointing it at Desforges. ' - in whatever language – ' He paused and increased the volume of his voice until it vibrated with conviction.

' – *O immundissimum numen, daemon occidionis iraeque, in nomine Iesus Nazareni impero tibi ut ad locum commodissimum tibi ex hac imagine lapidea statim effugias!** – one has to be very sure that the entity can, in fact, obey one's instructions.'

---

* O most unclean spirit, demon of murder and rage, in the name of Jesus of Nazareth I order you to flee at once from this stone image to the place most convenient for you!

Bewildered, as he had anticipated, by his switch to Latin, they could only watch as he put the box down again on the table in front of the Prior and stood up, leaning on his crutch.

'Indeed,' he continued, 'it occurred to me to wonder what would happen if instead of a perforated host, acting as a sort of condenser, one were to insert an intact one, acting as a barrier.' He paused and looked around the table, smiling at them all. 'That, lady and gentlemen, is in fact what I have done.'

While the others gasped and began to rise from their chairs, all staring at the box, he moved a step or two away from the Prior. The room suddenly became very still. The fluorescent lights, at first falteringly but then steadily, began to dim. The polished wood of the box, however, started to increase in brightness. Something like smoke was seeping from its seams.

'But before you witness the result of my experiment,' said Winterman, 'I want you also to watch an act for which I have been preparing for some time now.' He heard the clicking sound, like that of a stiff latch lifting, but their eyes were still on the now incandescent box. He shifted his weight onto the balls of his feet. The crutch swung in a low arc over the table, skimming the top of the smoking box. The Prior was the first to see the blade, bright in the glow from off the tabletop. He staggered up and back, his long legs catching against the edge of his chair. Winterman lunged swiftly, hard and with exultation. He connected just below the breastbone and drove on up and into the heart.

There was a scream – not from the Prior who stood as if paralysed by some gigantic sedative injection, hands clenched around the shaft of the crutch which Winterman had released

– but from Ms Millington who was turning to run for the door into the room below the lantern. As he saw some of the others start to rise also, Winterman threw himself to the floor and as his shoulder hit it rolled under the oak table.

CHAPTER SEVENTY

C ROUCHED BETWEEN TWO PARKED CARS AND PEERING
AT THE FARMHOUSE THROUGH THE WINDOWS OF THE
ONE NEAREST TO IT, GARETH AND TEMPLE WERE NOT
blown over by the blast that rocked the car on its suspension.
It was from the light rather than the hot air and the crack of
its expansion that they toppled backwards. While the sound
resembled the violent ripping of a gigantic wet canvas sail
followed by the shattering of hundreds of glass bottles on a
concrete floor, the blue-magenta light, though shining only
for seconds, blinded them for almost a minute.

Recovering himself, Gareth began at once reciting the
psalm and ran, with Temple just in front of him, towards
the front door which was hanging from one hinge by a single
screw. As he heard Temple's feet ringing on the spiral staircase above him, he switched on his torch. He paused in the
almost total darkness to try again. In whatever position he put
the switch he could produce no light at all. He cursed for a
fraction of a second before remembering to keep reciting the
psalm and followed blindly, clutching the handrail and relying on the regular intervals of the metal steps.

The floor began to wobble alarmingly under his feet. He

realised he was treading on the door of the large room into which they had burst. He collided with Temple who had pulled up short. The walls and every upright surface in the room were glowing with a faint violet bloom like the iridescence on rotten bacon. In this ghastly light they could make out charred smudges against the backs of chairs. Here and there on the tabletop were what looked like smouldering masses of rubber in the vague shapes of arms or heads. There was a stench of rancid fat mixed with the pungency of a chimney just before a fall of soot.

At the far end of the table, opposite a chair that had been hurled on to its back, he saw – and sensed that Temple had seen it at the same moment – the stone replica of the Lincoln Imp. Its surface was the colour and texture of the rind of a Brie cheese. While they both stood momentarily still, holding their breath against the stink, Gareth thought he could hear throbbing off it a faint, sibilant resonance like the noise of a disconnected telephone. They heard next shouting from down in the courtyard and feet pounding on the paving-stones.

Temple started forward and gathered up the Imp as he passed it. Gareth followed but at the corner of the table he tripped over something that rattled against his ankle. From the glow that enveloped it he recognised the shape of a crutch. Its base was stuck into something that looked and reeked like an overboiled cauliflower.

'Through here!' he heard Temple hiss. The door into the room beyond was also shattered. Passing through, Temple moved more hesitantly towards another, carpeted, flight of stairs. They descended it as they heard footsteps coming cautiously up the spiral staircase. The door at the bottom opened onto a lawn on the far side of the building away from the courtyard. Sam ran to the corner of the farmhouse and peered around it.

'We'll make less noise if we walk,' he said and set off at an angle across the short grass to where a stone wall ran to join the fence parallel to the road.

'There's a car coming towards the main gate,' said Gareth through his teeth. As he spoke they both saw the headlights dim and then go out as the noise of the engine cut off. 'They shall bear thee up in their hands,' said Gareth as he vaulted into the road after Temple at the junction of the fence and the wall, 'lest thou dash thy foot against a stone.'

CHAPTER SEVENTY-ONE

SERGEANT PERKINS WAS ABOUT TO TURN INTO THE FARM ENTRANCE WHEN, SIMULTANEOUSLY, HIS LIGHTS AND HIS ENGINE FAILED. HE WAS THROWN FORWARD abruptly and caught the brim of his cap against the sun-visor. Cursing, he fiddled with the ignition key. A derisory two-toned click answered his efforts. He had seen the flash through the treetops as he approached the farm and assumed that there must have been an electrical short-circuit as all the lights of the buildings dimmed together. Searching in his mind, however, for an explanation which would help him more readily understand the deep uneasiness he was starting to experience in the pit of his stomach, he groped under the dashboard for his transceiver.

He switched it on and spoke into it briefly and paused in mid-phrase as he realised it was as dead as his engine. Releasing his seatbelt, he stepped out into the cool air and stared around him, trying to accustom his eyes to the darkness. He thought he heard the scuff of shoes on the metal road a hundred yards or so away but the wind was freshening. Noticing the strange purplish glow from the upper storey of the farmhouse, he started to walk towards it at regulation pace but then more briskly as he heard shouts for help. As he approached the main door he saw the burly shape of a man staggering out. It bent over without warning at the waist and he heard the grunt of retching and the splash of vomit on the paving-stones.

CHAPTER SEVENTY-TWO

‘THE TORCH WORKS NOW,’ SAID GARETH AS THEY DREW NEAR THEIR CAR.

‘WE MUST BE OUT OF RANGE OF WHATEVER happened back there,’ panted Temple. ‘It seems to have drained the power out of everything electrical within a certain radius.’

‘Not only electrical! For a moment back there I thought we'd never get out. This is it, down here! I'll drive.’

They collapsed into their seats, strangely sucked dry of energy, not daring yet to relax in the knowledge that they had succeeded. Gareth turned the ignition key. The starter-motor churned and then to his numbing despair wailed into silence like a protesting tomcat. He tried again with the same result. Temple sat rigid in his seat, holding the Imp across his knees like a baby, staring at the key between Gareth's trembling fingers.

‘Murdoch boasts this car has never failed to start,’ said Gareth, speaking slowly and with deliberate irony to hide his panic.

‘Try again!’

Gareth paused and shut his eyes. ‘Surely he shall deliver

thee from the snare of the fowler . . . ,' he said, turning the key as if it were made of brittle glass. He held the ignition on as the starter whined. The engine cleared its throat, shook and died. He twisted the key back.

'Give her more petrol this time,' said Temple. 'Pump it.'

Gareth wound down his window to listen to the engine better. He took a deep breath and turned the key again. Churning, coughing, a snarl. A throttled seizure. Then the pounding on the metalled road of men running on the balls of their feet. Out of the corner of his eyes he saw Temple lift his head to listen and then duck his chin to his chest and say aloud: 'and from the noisome pestilence.' He turned the key. A whine, a cough, a snarl, a roar. He squeezed the accelerator to the floor. Another snarl. He revved until the engine note climbed to a wail, engaged first gear and slipped the clutch home as the first pursuer came skidding into the beam of the headlights that he switched on as they lurched forward.

The car was shrugging as it gathered speed over the uneven surface of the track. Gareth saw the man straighten both his arms and point them at him and saw the handgun fractionally before he spun the wheel towards it. The Volvo clipped the gunman's hip and bounced him into the hedge. Gareth swung hard left as his front tyres gripped the tarmac and accelerated west.

CHAPTER SEVENTY-THREE

A NGHARAD KNOCKED SOFTLY AGAIN ON THE STUDY
DOOR. HER RELUCTANCE TO RAP MORE LOUDLY, SHE
REALISED, PROBABLY CAME FROM A SUBCONSCIOUS
desire that Dr Murdoch would not hear her. Since Gareth's
and Sam's departure she had had several lengthy conversations with him at meal times and although she was always
engrossed by whatever he said she never left his company
without a vague sense of relief. She turned to move off down
the corridor towards her own room but on an impulse swayed
back and stealthily turned the doorknob. Opening the door
an inch or two, she peeped inside. She saw first a candle
burning in a holder and then, as she pushed the door further
open, another candle on his desk and a third in a bracket on
the wall beneath a crucifix. She then noticed Murdoch himself apparently kneeling at a prie-dieu facing the window
whose curtains were drawn back to reveal a western sky
perforated by stars. Realising that she might disturb him at
his devotions, she was about to shut the door and leave when
she noticed something else about him that made her hold her
breath as her eyes widened in disbelief.

Around his head was a faint luminescence, as if his body

was silhouetted against another candle between him and the
wall. But there was something else that she had not taken in
when she first saw him. She had assumed that he was kneeling on the cushion of the prayer-desk but when she looked
more closely she saw that his knees were about a foot above
its padded leather. In the same way his elbows were not
resting on the ledge designed for them. Doctor Murdoch was
suspended without visible means of support at least eighteen
inches above the floor.

She felt the whorled hairs in the hollow at the base of her
skull lift off her skin and a thin trickle, as of thawing snow,
spurt down her neck to the small of her back. She stared at
him for at least a minute to confirm to herself that she was
not imagining what she was seeing. His position did not alter
but the light around his head slightly increased in intensity.
Noiselessly she eased his door shut and stumbled to her room.
She sat on her bed and crushed her palms into her face.

CHAPTER SEVENTY-FOUR

═══

GARETH REMOVED HIS HAND FROM THE STEERING-WHEEL TO MASSAGE HIS FACE BRIEFLY. HE SLACKENED SPEED FOR THE JUNCTION WITH THE A 607 at Welbourn, going straight on for the village of Brant Broughton.

'We'll avoid Leadenham,' he said, speaking for the first time since they had turned off Ermine Street. He had been trying to explain to himself, and trying to forget, what he had seen in the upper room.

Temple sighed, as if coming awake, and leaned over into the back of the car. He pulled a tartan rug off the back seat and began to wrap the Imp in it. 'I don't want to be seen nursing this,' he mumbled, twisting round and laying it on the back seat. 'What do you think actually happened back there?'

'From what Murdoch told me on the phone, Winterman was researching some sort of technique for encasing charged images and controlling their release. Either something went wrong, or went just as he'd planned.'

'Which do you think?'

'The latter, knowing Sidney. I reckon he intended to take

the whole festering crew with him.' He shook his head as he recalled the crutch and the stench of burning.

'He was spectacularly successful then! But has he stopped the Albion Front?'

'He must have delayed them. Without the Imp they'll not be able to proceed as fast as they've planned.'

'They must have heard us making for the car once we'd climbed the wall. Do you think they'll be able to follow us? I mean, are we clear away?'

'We'll have to keep a sharp lookout for anyone on our tail but I'm virtually an expert at that by now.'

'And if they do get on to us again?'

'We lose them again.'

'In this?'

'Also charmed.'

'Do you really believe that?'

Gareth threw him a sharp look as he turned into Brant Broughton. 'In the past few days my belief system has been permanently reshaped. We'll rejoin the A 17 just south of this village.'

'Then what?'

'Into Newark, on to Nottingham, Derby, Uttoxeter. After that . . .' Gareth lapsed into a sudden silence as he glanced in his mirror.

Temple jerked around to look back.

'It's all right,' said Gareth. 'There's no-one after us.'

'I thought you'd seen something.'

'I did actually.' Gareth smiled. 'For a split second. In my mind's eye. As I was saying, after that I'm not sure of our route.' Out of the corner of his eye he saw Temple give him a puzzled look.

'Don't you think the main roads – A38 and A5 – would be safer?'

'Probably, as we felt they were last time when we were going north, but I'm very familiar with the way I've mentioned. I feel happier not having to think too much about which turn to take. I'm also learning fast to do things by acting on hunches.'

'Or, as the Spirit moves you, as Murdoch would say. He's quite a character, isn't he? I suppose he's in control now.'

Gareth smiled again. 'By "he" do you mean the Spirit, or Murdoch?'

'Now you're starting to sound like him yourself!' Temple laughed but his voice almost at once softened into a reflective sadness. 'As you said, Winterman seems to have lost his life in destroying the Lincoln Commandery.'

Gareth chuckled in reply and, without looking across at him, sensed his surprise. 'It's strange,' he said. 'It certainly looks that way, but I can't think of him as dead. I got through to him, using the techniques he taught me, just before we went in . . . ' He paused in his explanation as they turned right onto the main road. ' . . . but back there, when you thought someone was after us . . . '

'Yes?'

Gareth could sense Temple's agitation. 'I'm sorry to sound so . . . imprecise. But I had the distinct sensation that he got through to me.'

'Mightn't it be easier for him to do that, if he were . . . ' Temple cleared his throat, 'disembodied? What are those lines of Eliot's?

And what the dead had no speech for, when living,
They can tell you, being dead . . . '

'Oh, I know what you mean,' said Gareth.

' *. . . the communication*
Of the dead is tongued with fire beyond the
language of the living.

But dead or alive, he'll want us to finish this job.'

He sniffed and shivered himself alert in his seat. 'If we get a free run, we should reach the cottage on Lleyn about four o' clock in the morning.'

'Feel up to it?'

'No, but do you fancy stopping off somewhere with that to keep safe?' He jerked his head towards the bundle on the back seat.

'Not a hotel, certainly, but a friend's perhaps. Someone they couldn't know about. Not that I've any in the Midlands.'

'There's a possibility of someone in Wrexham.'

'Who? A relative?'

'I have relatives there but, no, that'd be too risky. If they're looking for us – and we have to assume they must be – they've probably got all our relatives on their computers. No, this is an old university mate of mine who's going to print the next issue of my poetry magazine. He'd put us up; though, if we're going to be able to use him, we'd better phone soon rather than just turn up at about two in the morning.'

Temple lapsed into a thoughtful silence until about five minutes later they were approaching the junction with the A1 at about eighty miles an hour. 'Did you have many belongings apart from what Angharad and I managed to bring out of that caravan for you?'

'A few things stored at my mother's. I tend to travel light.'

'Just as well! I suppose I've not really apologised yet to you for burning your home down.' He chuckled. 'We had to leave a lot of books behind.'

'They can be bought again.' He paused, realising what he had said. 'One day, when things are back to normal. What have you had to leave behind?'

'Virtually everything that I'd spent about thirty years accumulating.'

'That must be hard.'

'Do you know, that's what I thought. But it's strange: what I feel is, actually, the most monumental sense of relief. I had a friend who was in Uganda during the Amin business. He had to get out quick with just a stuffed briefcase. I remember him telling me the same. I didn't believe him at the time. Now I know exactly what – Slow down!'

His change of tone and volume startled Gareth and the car skidded slightly as he braked down to about sixty on a road surface that was slick after a local shower.

'What is it?'

'Keep going! Backed up off the road,' he twisted in his seat to look back. 'An x J6.'

'Birch green?'

'Hard to tell under these lights but it could be.'

'You know what it means if they follow us?'

'That worthy citizen back in Leadenham must have taken down and passed on our number.'

'But only to the Police,' Gareth said with significant emphasis, expecting Temple to comment.

'Sorry, I'm tired!'

'It was soon after a chat with a policeman that we sprouted a tail last time.'

'The Front must have infiltrated the Police some time ago.'

'I think we can be sure of that,' murmured Gareth, glancing in his mirror and sighing. 'They're onto us. He that dwelleth in the secret place of the Most High . . . '

' . . . shall abide under the shadow of the Almighty,' said Temple. 'What are you going to do?'

'Think for a minute, if you'll let me.'

Apparently smarting from Gareth's unexpected rebuke, Temple sat still and hugged himself. Gareth slowed down at a roundabout and coasted through Newark at a sedate thirty with the Jaguar now two cars behind. As they took the A46 for Nottingham and Leicester, Gareth apologised for a sharpness that had astonished himself as well and his voice took on the breeziness of someone who has decided what he must do and intends to do it.

'Just under two miles before the big roundabout where the Fosseway joins the A 52,' he said, 'there's another one with a road going north. I'm banking on the fact that they will be expecting us to run for Scotland – they must have connected us with Murdoch by now. They must also be puzzled why we didn't turn north on the A1, unless they think we saw them waiting. So, if we can lose them for long enough to turn off down a minor road, they'll play the percentages and turn north at this roundabout I'm talking about. By the time they realise what's happened, we can have slipped under the south of Nottingham on back roads. In about ten or twelve minutes,' he glanced at his speedometer, 'pray, and I do mean

pray, for a long stream of traffic coming towards us and one
slow vehicle ahead of us with nothing in front of it. If I can
squeeze by at the last moment, they won't find this road easy
to overtake on. Failing that, I'll take whatever chance I'm
given, later.'

'I think you've got it coming now!' Temple had leaned
further to his left and was craning his neck. 'There are temporary traffic-lights ahead. Just changed to green.'

Gareth looked in his mirror. The Jaguar was now hovering behind the Passat that was twenty yards behind them,
well out towards the middle of the carriageway, cruising, as
they all were, at about sixty. In front of them was a slower-
moving Citroen 2cv, green just like his own. He suddenly
remembered – for the first time since abandoning it – that it
must still be outside the school. Concentrating again, he
slowed to about forty. In his mirror he saw the Passat move
out, think about overtaking, see the lights and slide back. He
let his speed drop to about thirty. The lights changed to
amber. The 2cv was safely through and pulling ahead, its
lights illuminating the row of cones down the middle of the
road. When he was about twenty yards away from the sign
telling him where to wait whenever the lights were red, he
changed down into second. As the red light came on
he waited a few seconds but then accelerated harshly.

He heard the squeal of tyres as the xj6 swung out around
the Passat and came after them. Resisting the temptation to
look in his mirror again, he changed up to third and hurtled
down the short stretch of road towards the headlights of the
queue facing them. A van had started to move out. He saw it
check as its driver saw that he was coming on. He heard the
blare of horn and flinched as the van's lights flashed to high

beam in warning and protest. He responded by putting on his own high beam and maintaining his pressure on the accelerator pedal.

Forgetting about what might be on his left, he concentrated on missing the corner of the van. For a split second he closed his eyes. Sam's groan of relief was the first indication that they were safely through. A glance in his mirror told him that the broader Jaguar had tried the same but its nearside front wheel clipped a kerbstone and the car's body swayed enough to hit the van as it scraped past, shattering a headlight. Temple twisted round in his seat at the blaring of horns.

'They don't intend to lose us this time,' he shouted over the roaring of the Volvo's engine still accelerating in third.

'Keep praying for what I wanted,' said Gareth, changing at last into top. 'Those traffic-lights have caused a lovely steady queue coming towards us.'

They caught up with the Citroen again which was cruising at about fifty. Gareth coaxed the Volvo as near to the centre lines as he dared, ignoring the warning flashes of oncoming cars. The Jaguar was only twenty yards behind them. The road ahead dipped steadily before rising again up a long incline. He waited for a slight break in the oncoming traffic. He prayed for it aloud, tapping the rim of the steering-wheel. It came – a hundred yards gap and then another chain of lights. He changed down to third and waited until he knew he had allowed only just enough time to overtake the Citroen. He waited a little longer and went.

It was a manoeuvre contrary to all the instincts he had acquired in eight years of driving. It was the first time he had ever deliberately risked a head-on crash by overtaking.

During the next few seconds time became elastic. The most unexpected thoughts – thoughts he knew with another part of him he ought not to be having in this situation – frothed through his mind. He seemed suddenly to be living on several levels at once.

Out of the corner of his eye he saw Temple begin to turn away from him and wrap his arms around the back of his seat, burrowing his cheek into the padded top of it. In the same peripheral vision he saw too the curved bonnet of the Citroen slipping away backwards. He concentrated on the dark stretch of road ahead and to the left beyond the range of his headlights into which he intended to slot. He thought of Angharad sleeping alone in darkness. He thought with incredible accuracy of recall the weight of her legs on the small of his back. He remembered Murdoch's stern face at the quayside in Craignure. He wondered what Sidney Winterman had been thinking as that terrible magenta light flashed once in that upper room. He knew Winterman was also thinking about him. He became more sharply aware of light in front of him. It was burning the roots of his eyeballs. It was filling his skull with broken slivers of glass. There were harsh, brassy blarings like a Sibelius symphony out of synch. It was all passing to his right. It had gone.

He looked in his mirror. The driver of the Jaguar had lost his nerve and was back behind the Citroen which, no doubt in an attempt to let Gareth through, had slowed almost to a halt. Temple was peeping over the top of his seat through the back window. Gareth's sense of time meshed again with his body-clock. He changed into top and kept the Volvo flat out until they were almost at the roundabout, overtaking a few more cars whenever the opportunity presented itself. After taking the B road for the village of Bingham, he pulled up outside a telephone kiosk. There was no sign of the Jaguar.

'What would you do,' he asked Temple as he opened his door, 'if they arrived while I was phoning?'

'Reverse into them, hard.'

Gareth nodded and stepped out. Then he leant back in. 'Knew I could trust you,' he said with a wink.

CHAPTER SEVENTY-FIVE

TEMPLE STRETCHED HIMSELF IN HIS SEAT AND ROLLED HIS HEAD SLOWLY THROUGH ONE HUNDRED AND EIGHTY DEGREES, RELAXING HIS TAUT NECK muscles. For a moment, as they were overtaking the Citroen, he had thought they must crash into the oncoming car. He had known he was not ready to die. To be alive, even stiff and tired, was pleasant. He reached his hand back between the seats and squeezed the bulk of the swathed Imp on the back seat. He allowed his hand to rest there and idly tried to feel the shape of the replica under the wool of the blanket, his mind something of a blank, his eyes focused on nothing in particular, until he saw that Gareth had left the key in the ignition.

Temptation reared up in front of him like a spitting-cobra out of unmown grass. He shook his head as if to clear his eyes after venom had been jetted into them. He looked through the windscreen at Gareth speaking into the telephone. It would be so easy to slide across behind the wheel, switch on and drive off, leaving Gareth to chase after him down the deserted street. He had enough contacts in other Commanderies. He could persuade them, especially as there was now no-one left alive in Lincoln to dispute it, that the Prior had planned his defection in order to penetrate Winterman's Company. He could hide the Imp, on which his hand was still resting, and use it to bargain his way back into a position of considerable authority . . .

He let his fingers slide off the blanket, edged across into the driver's seat and reached for the ignition key.

CHAPTER SEVENTY-SIX

A NGHARAD KEPT HER EYES SHUT AS SHE SAT ON THE EDGE OF HER BED. SHE HAD NOT PRAYED SINCE ADOLESCENCE. SHE WANTED TO PRAY NOW. SHE thought of kneeling but decided to stay as she was. She knew that Gareth was in danger the whole of the time he was away from Calman House, even though Murdoch was evasive when she asked him what Gareth and Sam's chances of success were. Earlier that evening she had sensed his life was being threatened. It was during one of the worst of these spells of foreboding that she had attempted to speak to Murdoch in his study. She had also felt that Sidney's life was in danger, though this had not troubled her so acutely. That was the source of her confusion: for which of her two men should she pray harder?

Although she was fond of Sidney, she knew that she had married him for convenience. After Trevor had died she had been unable to face a return to teaching for a living and had welcomed the security that Sidney had so suddenly offered. He had charmed and fascinated her with his wit and learning. His lovemaking had been astonishing, uncovering layers of sensuality in her of which she had been unaware.

But they coupled, almost nightly, sometimes several times a night, without ever falling in love. She realised now that, incredibly, while she had accepted him for comfort, he had all along chosen her for someone else.

She cupped her hands over her womb and prayed silently that Gareth would hurry back safe to guard both his child and Sidney's. If prayer worked for Murdoch, she thought, if it was not after all just verbalised make-believe, if it really did alter events in the physical world, then she would make it work for her.

'Dear God, please!' she heard herself to her surprise saying aloud. Her voice broke in the intensity of her anxiety and she punched her fist into her open palm.

CHAPTER SEVENTY-SEVEN

═══════

SAM LET THE PRESSURE OF HIS FINGERS ON THE KEY SLACKEN. HE SAT BACK WITH A GROAN AND PUNCHED HIS FIST INTO HIS PALM. HE OPENED THE CAR DOOR and stepped out onto the pavement, sucking in lungfuls of sweet moist night air. Where would he go? How long could he live, in hiding, in hotels? How could he get access to his savings? He swung his arms about in frustration. Then he saw Gareth coming out of the kiosk, smiling at him, his thumb up. A sudden flush of affection warmed his throat. He felt ashamed.

'You drive,' suggested Gareth. As he passed he thumped Temple on the shoulder-blade with the flat of his hand. The relief of having apparently shaken off the Jaguar loosened their tongues. They talked about each other's backgrounds like students who have recognised in each other the certainty of a lifelong friendship. As they drove on through Tithby, Cropwell Bishop, Cotgrave and Tollerton, Gareth learned about Temple's time in Kenya. Through the suburbs of Nottingham he spoke of North Wales. Until Derby, Temple related his experiences at Leicester University, where he read physics. Uttoxeter found Gareth explaining how he had drifted into teaching in Lincoln.

They kept up a steady sixty across Staffordshire and had exhausted stories about their family eccentrics by the time they reached Whitchurch, where they changed seats again. Gareth drove into Wrexham at about three o'clock in the morning. He parked between a rusting Cortina and a Transit van in the safety of a quiet street of red-bricked terraced houses and rang a doorbell. A light came on in a narrow hallway behind the frosted-glass door. A sleepy head appeared around its edge and they were welcomed in, Gareth with an A4 manilla envelope stuffed with sheets of paper under his arm and Temple hugging in its tartan blanket the stone replica of the Lincoln Imp.

CHAPTER SEVENTY-EIGHT

═══

MURDOCH DABBED AT HIS MOUTH WITH A TARTAN NAPKIN AND REACHED FOR AN APPLE OUT OF THE BOWL OF POLISHED ELM. 'I USED TO BE A TEACHER too,' he said. 'A lifetime ago, it seems now. But, yes, of course it's possible to change course.'

'Would you let me help in the hospice?' asked Angharad. 'I feel so useless at the moment.'

'Your help would be most welcome. But don't allow yourself to become too attached to the patients, or let them become too attached to you. After all, we're helping them to loosen their bonds!' He quartered the apple neatly with a silver knife and turned his piercing eyes on her.

She looked down from their gaze at the remains of her evening meal. She had intended to ask him at some point why he had never married but had somehow not been able to find the moment to put the question casually. She felt certain it would not have been because of a refusal on the woman's part; he was an extremely persuasive man.

'And try not to become overfond of this place either. I am constantly having to correct myself over that.'

'What will happen to it?'

'I'm negotiating for the nuns to take it over when we leave.'

'Do you still not know for sure where we'll be going?'

He shook his head. 'I was praying about that last night – when I wasn't praying for Gareth and Sam. And for Sidney, of course.'

'I know,' she said shyly. 'I saw you. I'm sorry, I didn't mean to disturb you. I wanted to talk.'

'You didn't disturb me.'

'No, I don't suppose anyone would have.' She wanted to tell him what she had seen but could not bring herself to say anything about it, though again his eyes were searching her face.

'What makes you say that?'

She fiddled with her napkin and shrugged. 'You seemed,' she cleared her throat, 'rapt.'

He looked hard at her and nodded. 'I was. I am often. I believe – no, I know – that I was given the answers to several questions. Though not all the ones I was asking. When Gareth and Sam return and have rested – ' He raised his thick eyebrows as she drew breath to interrupt.

'You're certain, then, that they'll return?'

'Oh, yes! Later than I thought. But they'll be back. And later again they must go to Ireland to look for the place where we can all settle.'

'Will we be safe there?'

He smiled. 'Total security is never given, I'm afraid. But it makes sense to go there – I should have seen that earlier. We shall have delayed our enemies' plans. But only delayed. Gareth and Sam, but especially Sidney, have performed an act of daring surgery but the Albion Front is an infiltrating cancer and the Tophetim a virus that has infected this country – and I do mean Britain not Ireland – for centuries.' He looked out over the lawn, olive green now in the dusk. There was a sudden commotion among the doves and pigeons.

'What was that?' she asked, rising as he rose.

He did not answer but walked out briskly through the french windows, across the terrace and down the steps. She caught up with him as he knelt to take up a slate-grey pigeon, darker than all the others. He removed a ring from its ankle and gave her the bird to hold. She caressed its fragile warmth as he unscrewed the ring and drew out a thin strip of paper. He read it swiftly, his eyes skittering. Giving a little cry of triumph, he looked up at the raincloud which was starting to spatter them.

'Bring her inside,' he said. 'We must reward the bringer of good news!'

They ran in from the suddenly heavy rain. He led the way to the kitchen and finding some grain in a jar, set a handful of it on the tabletop. She put the bird down beside it. As it pecked into the pile, he motioned to her to pull up a chair.

'They've done it!' he said through his teeth, brandishing the strip of paper like a tiny banner. 'And they're on their way to us. They released this bird off the boat once they'd put off from Bardsey Island, where Gareth has hidden the Imp. They were about two days' sailing from us then. Sidney's plan succeeded.' He looked closely at her, his jaw muscles tightening a little. 'But, I'm sorry to have to tell you, my dear, that in destroying our enemies, he may have destroyed himself.'

She sucked in her breath through her lips and looked

314

down at the still feeding pigeon. 'I see,' she said after a long pause. 'I'd already come to terms with probably never seeing him again. I've prepared myself for something like this. Of course, it's never the same, when it comes.'

'Would you like me to leave you alone?'

She looked up from the bird and shook her head.

'Will you,' she asked, 'marry Gareth and me, now?'

He nodded. 'I can see no impediment.'

'Strange,' she said softly. 'Even as you were saying that, I had a sort of sudden picture of Sidney in my head. I just cannot think of him as dead.'

CHAPTER SEVENTY-NINE

===

'GEE-JAW WHAT?' ASKED PATRICIA EAMES. SHE LOOKED UP AT THE HEAVILY-BUILT MAN WHO HAD ASKED HER IF THEY HAD A COPY OF A MAGAZINE HE wanted. Noticing his face for the first time under the brim of his hat, she blanched and looked away. 'Mandy!' she called.

'*Jejune Incest*,' repeated the man patiently. 'It's a poetry magazine.'

She was surprised that anyone with a face as severely burned as that could see very well to read anything. 'We don't stock *Gee-jew Interest*, do we?'

'Nah!' said Mandy. She was chewing gum but stopped after she too had looked at the man on the other side of the counter. 'Never heard of it, have you, Trish?'

'Did you want us to order it?'

The man shook his partly bandaged head. 'Thank you, no. I don't live in Lincoln any more. I'll try elsewhere.'

Although what could be seen of his raw, expressionless face could not easily have conveyed disappointment, she sensed it in his voice.

'There's a shop on Steep Hill might have it,' suggested Mandy. 'On the way up to the cathedral.'

'Thank you, I'll try there.'

'Did you see his face?' muttered Patricia, wincing, when the man had stepped out on to the pavement.

'Couldn't bloody miss it, could you?' said Mandy. 'God! Imagine waking up of a morning and seeing that on the pillow next to you!'

'Mind you, it's amazing what the medical people can do nowadays,' averred Patricia. 'Look what they did for my Jason and Darren. As good as dead they were. Amazing!'

CHAPTER EIGHTY

HALF AN HOUR LATER, CARRYING A COPY OF JEJUNE INCEST, THE DISFIGURED MAN STROLLED INTO THE ANGEL CHOIR OF THE CATHEDRAL. HE SAT ON A wooden chair and watched the tourists amble past. One old man in a safari-suit, Stewart tartan shirt, and horn-rimmed spectacles, who looked distinctly Canadian, paused before the device that, on the insertion of a coin, threw a beam of light to pick out and illuminate the Lincoln Imp high up in the stonework on the other side of the Choir. He dug into his pocket for a coin and slotted it into the machine. When the light came on he stood blinking uncertainly at the metal box and peering at the stonework of the pillar against which the machine was positioned. Smiling to himself, the onlooker stood up and, hat in hand, came to stand beside the old man.

'Excuse me,' he said gently. 'You have to follow the light.' He pointed along the beam up at the stonework above them.

'Why, thank you, sir!' drawled the old man. 'I guess the older I get, the dumber I get!' He stood, gazing along the beam of light, his mouth slightly open, breathing through it, smelling of a peppermint mouthwash. 'It don't look as big as I'd imagined,' he said with an air of complaint, still squinting up at the top of the pillar. Looks different from the photographs, somehow.' His tone of voice invited agreement.

The bandaged head tilted stiffly towards the image high above them and nodded.

' "Not only does it look different, sir," said Winterman with authority, "I can personally assure you that it is different," ' said Winterman with authority.